Silver's Threads

Book 2

Other Titles by Penny Reilly

Silver's Threads Series

Book 1, Spinning Colours Darkly
© 2012 First Edition
© 2013 Second Edition

Book 2, Grey Weavings
© First Edition 2012
©Second Edition 2013

Book 3, Warp and Weft
© First Edition 2012
©Second Edition 2013

Book 4, Silken Web
© First Edition 2014
©Second Edition 2014

Book 5, Skeins of Tyme
© First Edition 2014

Silver's Threads

Book 2

Grey Weavings

Penny Reilly

ISBN 13: 978-0-9924759-3-2

Silver's Threads Book 2
Grey Weavings
© 2014 by Penny Reilly

Cover and interior design by Penny
Cover Art "Spirit of the Forest" by Josephine Wall

Self-Published by Penny Reilly
Project & Series Editor Penny Reilly

Printed in Australia

First Published 2012

Revised 13/06 /2014

Dedication

I dedicate this book to my beloved, for encouraging me to let my creative spirit fly.

Acknowledgements

Gratitude and thanks go to my patiently waiting friends who purchased my first book in the Silver's Threads series, Spinning Colours Darkly and who still clamoured for more. Thanks go yet again to my wonderful friends at "The Reading/Writing Coven" for continued support and mutual brainstorming …Kim, Carol, Aynia, Stacey, Joanne and Luke …good luck to you all in your own writing endeavours. Special thanks to the quiet and not so quiet, followers of my author, "earthly rites" and Daylesford TarotReaders Facebook and blog pages…and to Susan Chambers and Kat Lakie for their constant encouragement on the journey.

Special Acknowledgement

The extraordinary artwork on the cover of this book, "Spirit of the Forest" is by the very talented Josephine Wall …her work has inspired me and thanks to this, I feel I could write a story for each of her paintings. Perhaps one day I will…

Please visit Josephine Wall on …her face book page…
www.facebook.com/TheOfficialJosephineWall
Support the artist, visit her Gallery and buy her beautiful art at… www.josephinewall.co.uk

Foreword by Penny Reilly

When I first began to work with the processes of story-telling, I was aware of the potency that stories hold in the human psyche. Governed by our personal store of images and symbols, these allow us to connect the dots whenever triggered.

"Once upon a time," for instance, everyone immediately recognises as a commencement to a story and shifts perhaps in their mind, to a rainy day by the fire with a good tale or a favourite yarn, told as a bed-time treat.

Even as adults we have certain fantasy stories that kindle, memories or inspiration within ...Lord of the Rings ...Harry Potter ...worlds apart in their time of creation and yet they hold sway in our image bank equally.

My characters wrote themselves with the help of the most predominant voice and image in my head, namely Silver. I call her my true self, my wiser self and it is through her that these books came about. To wake with a song line ready to write down or a twist in the plot unfathomable before sleep, is a gift indeed. As a Hedgewitch, a Pagan, I respect the otherworldly influences that can make a somewhat complex process a little simpler.

My aim has been to give readers an opportunity to search their own psyche for the triggers in the books, hidden within the plot and story line …an opportunity to see the planet through different eyes and to hear the cries for help, not from her for she can look after herself, but from deep within ourselves.

We do all know that without Her we cannot survive and if we continue on the current path of, "having" over being, of consumerism rather than "how much is enough," …then indeed we may not…

Contents

Grey Weavings

...the story so far

Sybille, wise and enigmatic teacher of the Wytchways has disappeared into the 'Between'. The Skeins of Thyme, damaged possibly beyond repair, caused a Maker to fall. In falling, it tore the gossamer cocoon from its moorings on the Birthing Tree, where Sybille was renewing with her Trueshaper Silver.

Silver is battling to remain conscious as her Littleshape Sybille becomes lost in other aspects of multiple lives and the little Makers; beings of pure light, become corrupted by the pollution of human thoughts and deeds.

Three of her students and her niece, together with the group that has formed around them, wait to discover whether the Samhain Rite has been successful in tracing Sybille's whereabouts...

...manke sinta handasse kel belass'a sira
...where your mind goes energy flows

...the story continues

Grey Weavings

Grey the threads once coloured weave,
As all souls this realm must leave,
That man himself could so deceive
…the failing Skeins of Tyme

Each mortal a thread that woven must,
In perfect love and perfect trust,
To rise above the cut and thrust
…that snaps the Skeins of Tyme

Where to mend and where to sew,
Loose threads fly no colours glow,
As all beyond this realm must go
…into the Skeins of Tyme

Through the gateway once, star bright,
Its edge now tainted by the blight,
Into shadow's darkest night
…beyond the Skeins of Tyme

…Arianwen Isil'Lindir & Aithlin Farandir
…from the Skeins of Tyme

Grey Weavings
Prologue

Slender Birches whisper secrets to a flock of noisy sparrows, arrowing like darts into the depths of ancient twisted limbs; their last leaves clinging stubbornly, shaken loose to circle, drifting down to join their siblings on the earth to begin their journey to mulch-hood.

It was cold, but the sounds of nature were undiminished; a Raven's caw, a kookaburra's contagious chuckle and the sweet sound of a thrush, echoed across the garden to the silent group sitting beneath the canopy of branches, soaking up the sun's last warmth, before winter's final grip held the earth in stasis.

After the Samhain rite, the group, tired and confused, did not know if the outcome of their ritual had been successful in locating Sybille, but aware that much was riding on it.

They had witnessed things they could not name and so much more, to their frustration, hidden from sight as they had stood backs turned, to the events unfolding.

Claire had disappeared unnoticed, as had Tara, shortly after the rite. At the time, the remaining eight were more concerned for the welfare of their friend Beth as she disappeared, then as suddenly reappeared, unconscious but apparently unharmed.

As they had closed the circle down around Beth, several Fae stepped forward. Led by the Fae Lord, Aithlin Farandir and, ignoring all the rules of entry into human dwellings without permission, had carried her effortlessly into the house. Laying her on the couch in Sybille's old study, Aithlin had gently covered her with a wrap of silken thread and sung her the song of rest.

Now, while Samantha, Maeve, Flora, Susan, Alex, Morgan, Max and Cal waited, Beth slept on.

She walked the other realms …finding her way through the folds and twists of the Skeins of Tyme; through the forest circle of her one-time sisters, to a lichen and moss covered jetty where an inky-black Raven sat and an Otter waited.

Chapter 1
Silver

Silver felt her very essence tearing apart as if all her composite Littleshapes were separating …like cells in an amoeba. How long had it been since she had experienced such a physical sensation? She had expanded her consciousness, no longer a part of the mortal and sensate lives of her Littleshapes, merely an observer.

She could feel a density …a solidifying of her etheric form as if the whole process of becoming was in reversal. All that she had aimed for originally was diminishing as she became more and more human-like.

So this is what it is she sang distractedly the dark and light Makers pulled at her alternately …this is why the humankin die when pain and suffering become too extreme to bear?

Once I was singular too she remembered, one small Maker and yet not separate but then through knowledge gained I became many, to make one greater than the first, more than the sum of its parts.

Each life known on the wheel, a spark of the first light, a Wytchlight but it is not so for all humankin. For many, the Onceborn, know only one aspect consciously, believing that is all there is to them, seeking the other missing parts of themselves that float forever unheard, so many miscellaneous items on the etheric tides. They become unrecognisable as Maker Souls so far have they fallen.

I have a myriad of Makers creating my form in an image of the Lady but with several sparks missing, I cannot be whole. I need the Eldrytch to complete me …one life, one pure spark is all that I need and I shall be whole.

Her memories of Sybille and all the other Littleshapes that combined to give her existence meaning and growth were fading. Her thoughts focussed on Sybille, clinging to an identity almost lost to the world, …with Nina, who had agreed to host a second consciousness within her own frame of existence and with Bethan, …or was it Leah who held so many of the Threads of Tyme in her slender hands.

Silver faltered as the dark makers slowly encroached deeper within. She watched with horror as the blight leaked from her wounds.

Where was the Mother she grieved before drifting away, struggling for reason and then rallied to help the Makers heal the darkness growing inside her? Why did She not step in?

With effort, she accepted the energy the Makers gave her, drifting through the Mysts 'Between', she approached the circle that glowed brightly in the grove of familiar sycamore trees.

She floated sedately through the group standing protectively around Bethan. Silver saw her falter a little, as she strained to reach out to Sybille and to hear her song on the ethers. Bethan almost followed her own song line until Silver, reaching over placed a drop of pungent oil between her brows. She whispered to her to focus, to follow Sybille's song not her own. The familiar and trusted fragrance allowed Bethan to relax enough for the Lord and Lady to take her hands, guiding her from her body into the 'Between.'

For the humans watching it was only a moment but in the other realms it was a lifetime.

Chapter 2
Walking the 'Between'

Dare you walk the between, in the places unseen
...will you dare to engage with your shade?
Will you walk, will you stray ...senses lost on the way
...with the mists calling home ...will you wander alone
...dare you walk the between, unafraid?
Walking the 'Between'...Bethan Fenner

A small, sleek head broke the surface of the lake soundlessly; her fierce face shed droplets of bright water as Oonagh the Otter slid effortlessly onto the jetty and spat the small, black polished stone at Beth's feet. As it dried rapidly in the sunlight, she could see a marking, a Sigel of some sort etched on its surface. Squinting in the glare from the bright dappled water, she looked more closely. What was it, a nut, a bud? Picking it up, Beth slipped the stone into a small pouch she wore at her waist and, with a puzzled sigh, stepped into the waiting coracle. She tossed the rope's looped end and the small Otter grasped it in her sharp teeth. Diving under, she pulled the little craft out to the centre of the lake where she paused, waiting for the next signal from Beth before she could complete the distance to the island, still shrouded by mists; the large Raven took flight in pursuit.

She could smell smoke drifting on the breeze; it had the aroma of apple wood but no trace of a dwelling was in view as the fine mist closed in around her. She felt slightly panicky, hoping she could remember the 'words of changing' to speak and just in that moment of pausing to consider, found the words were there in her mind…

'*Part the mists of Tyme;*' she lifted her hands palm upwards. '*Let fall the woods of nine,*' reaching into the pouch she pulled out a small pinch of woodsy fragrant ash, letting it fall over the water. '*Together air and water blessed,*' she dipped her hands in the lake and after kissing the water droplets on her fingers, blew them away, '*dispels the veil into the West,*' with a banishing pentacle to the mists, '*and hear the sacred chime,*' and a bell sounded from afar. '*Mother, may you guide this seeker home,*'…she sang.

The veil parted and she could just make out a figure standing cloaked in mist, on the shore. The smiling face of The Cybil immerged, a white Owl on her shoulder. One strong, lean hand reached down to take the rope from Oonagh's jaws, while the other fluidly tossed her a fish head as reward, then grasping Beth's hand, The Cybil pulled her ashore.

In that moment, Beth could not recall whether she was Bethan or Leah but then the words came, unbidden, into her mind,

'You are both, all and more, child,' said The Cybil, 'Come, the journey has been long and there is but a small window open between this realm and yours.'

They walked together through an orchard and Beth realised it could easily be the one at the farm transported to here …or was it the reverse? The ancient boughs were bursting with pale green leaves; pinkish white buds adorned each double leafed stem as spring blossoms began to open, filling the air with fragrance. Soft voices, muffled by the sound of the winds, heard as the tree Dryads settled into a cool evening's gathering; Beltane, the time of fertility …already anticipation for the Great Rite was felt on the breeze. Soon, the Bel Fires would flare.

Pausing to transfer the Owl from her shoulder to a low hanging bough, The Cybil led the way up the slope to the Hearth. Heat and the sounds of young girl's voices raised in laughter, bursts of song drifted out as the doors opened. It was so loud; on entering, Beth was tempted to put her hands over her ears.

The Cybil led her to the fire pit, a young girl of no more than 10 bowed, smiling and nodding shyly; she offered an earthenware bowl of water, smelling of wildflowers, to wash hands and feet. Another youngling brought a wooden trencher of vegetable stew and a chunk of soda bread to dip into the succulent, aromatic depths. Bethan and The Cybil shared the meal and a cup of hot, apple and honey mead to warm their inner.

As the rest of the women returned, on completion of their chores and devotionals, the noise level increased again as they welcomed each new arrival home as if they had been gone for weeks rather than just that morning. They glanced sidelong at Bethan occasionally, but made no comment, respectfully lowering their gaze as they served the food then leaving them to speak together.

Again, Beth felt bewildered as the pull of being Beth and the lure of being Leah tugged at her memory. There was so much that she needed to ask, to know and was confused where to begin. Turning, she looked at The Cybil and saw a rippling change flit across her face. For a split second, she saw her dear friend Sybille, then a young dark haired girl with olive skin. A myriad of other faces came and went quickly, creatures unknown and then The Cybil again. All else gone before Beth had a chance to blink.

The Cybil clapped her hands once and the younger girls dispersed to their sleeping chambers, the older priestesses to their devotionals to tend the Bel Fires in preparation for the great fertility rite of the year. Turning to Bethan and taking her hands, The Cybil drew her forehead to forehead in a tired gesture of fondness, before taking her deeper into the silent ritual of mind melding.

She showed Beth the journey, from her return to the cocoon on the Birthing Tree to the loss of awareness that had overcome her and the subsequent events thereafter.

There was no memory remaining of her life as Sybille and this was the crux of the dilemma, for without those memories she could not continue on to renew. Silver would be missing all the information she needed to glean from that life aspect.

Her work with Beth and the others was lost. She knew only that Beth was Leah, gone before her; returning now like a shade. The rest was only subtle glimpses when she scried at the sacred well of the Lady of a perceived, 'future life.' All other twists and turns on the web obscured the very life that would allow her to go home to the Summerlands.

Beth showed The Cybil what she knew of her life as Sybille, from her own perspective of student and friend, in an attempt to jog her memory. She spoke of the events since Lammas, the fall of the Maker and the poor, twisted creature it had become, when captured by Aerandir Sensarrius; the blighting of the trees and the sticky black web that captured and mutated, both Makers and birds alike.

She sent mind picture links of her own concerns about the dreadful changes in Annie Savage and the posturing farce the Mabon Rite had become. Shyly, she skirted around her own fragile joy amidst all the pain, regarding her shared experiences with the Greenlord Hercurin.

Then she told The Cybil as much as she could about the new Centre, the farm at Covenstead, her niece

Sam, Flora, Maeve and all the other people who had appeared as helpers on the journey to bring Sybille home. Finally, Beth showed her images of the Samhain Rite and her journey to the lake; at this The Cybil abruptly closed the mind-link, causing Beth to reel with shock at the tearing feeling this invoked. Pulling her fragmented thoughts together, she opened her eyes to find The Cybil watching her with a look of absolute awe on her face.

'But this means you're renewed in the Lady Herself' she whispered. 'Nobody else could make that connection with the Greenlord but Her and tonight is Beltane!'

Bethan having no idea how to respond to this, stuttered, 'No! That's not possible. I'm a Halfling Fae and the rest I'm not sure of, but the Lady! Never …that's too much to even consider'…trailing off at a loss, 'and it's Samhain!'

'We all carry The Lady's spark,' The Cybil replied, recovering her calm composure, 'it's just that some are more conscious in Her than others. Here in this space on the tapestry of Arianrhod's weaving it is Beltane. I am very aware of Her spark of life within; the thread that binds me to the Silver Wheel she spins and to all my priestesses and acolytes here on the Seer's Isle.'

At that moment, the Owl flew in the window to alight on her shoulder, ruffling feathers in consternation at The Cybil's apparent distress, clicking her beak in her Owl

speech. Flying to sit on the mantle, she looked down to watch the stirrings of a small child curled on the hearth, ostensibly sleeping. She was awake however, observing Beth and The Cybil silently through huge green moon-eyes that mirrored those of the Owl who watched un-blinking.

'Ah little one, how long have you been awake? Come here to me daughter,' which the child did with alacrity, not taking her huge eyes from Beth's face the while as she climbed, unhesitatingly, on to The Cybil's lap.

'I know your face,' said Beth, 'where have I seen your face before little one?'

The child made no reply, merely yawned, stretched and with a sweet knowing smile at Beth, curled into The Cybil's embrace trustingly and slept.

Suddenly the air around The Cybil and the small girl shimmered, the walls of the Hearth on the Seer's Isle crumbled; dissolving like a mirage, disappeared into the mists. She heard The Cybil's voice cry out, 'NO …not yet, no!'

Beth found herself standing in a time that was not a time in a space that was no-space …no shape or form existed, only shadows changing shape to become light …energy becoming matter; becoming life as the Goddess Arianrhod spun the silver web of Ungwe. All else faded away into a peace beyond mortal dreaming

…she heard a great horn sounding …summoning and she had to follow…

 Bethan woke drenched in sweat, gasping for air; she fought for her identity in what felt like a split reality. Confused at the abrupt interruption of her journeying, she had to pull all of herself back into the moment before she could gather one clear, rational thought.

A loud caw from outside the window and a sharp tap on the glass had her quickly centred in the now. She found herself on the soft, familiar, couch in the room once Sybille's study. A large silver-grey cat watched with alarmingly human-like interest, then feigning her usual feline distain, Morgana began washing behind her ears thoroughly.

Bethan lay gathering her wits, wondering how long she had been gone, the whole experience played itself out behind her eyes as her awareness centred back into the day.

Gingerly she stretched, flexing her tingling hands and feet and scrubbing her hands over sticky eyes. On a small table next to her was a thoughtfully placed jug of lemon water still warm, fresh with the aroma of tangy fruit. Some of Tara's wonderful nut and honey cakes lay on a pretty plate and a wild rose in an earthenware pot graced the space between. Breathing in the scent the little wild rose exuded; its natural sweetness had an underlying aroma of musky oak moss that was undeniably familiar. Bethan closed her eyes for a moment to thank the unseen bringers, blessing their offerings. Sitting up cautiously, she poured some lemon water and sipped slowly to allow the underlying restorative drops she could taste, despite the sharp fruit tang, do their work. Gently they aided her to reassemble her energies into the person known as Bethan.

Her eye opened wide again; she remembered that today was her birthday, her 29th.

Chapter 3
Samhain Morning

Sitting quietly with the group Morgan appeared to be dozing. He was in truth linked in, via his familiar Ruark, to Tara Saark as she sat in her Raven shape on the mooring post of a small wooden jetty.

Tara watched intently as Bethan stepped into a coracle and a small pretty Otter began to tow her out across the lake. She took flight in pursuit, relaying information as she flew, back to Ruark nd thus, to Morgan as he sat in a light trance.

Tara could not enter the Hearth on the isle uninvited so she sat on the roof; all senses charged she listened to the Owl, perched within on the mantlepiece.

Morgan's communications ceased abruptly as Maeve stood up to begin pacing around the group in obvious frustration. His sensitivities to the slightest change in energy snapped him back to awareness, the link broken with Tara, before he could translate the information.

With a muttered curse, he watched Maeve's pacing with some irritation but his compassionate nature recognised quickly that she was deeply distressed. Anger caused two bright red spots to flame on her cheeks and was the recourse she used to hold her pain in check.

He reached out gently with his mind, not to invade but to sooth, only to have her shake her head. Turning, she scowled at him before continuing her pacing.

He realised that Flora had been quietly observing the interplay. She sent him her sweet sunny smile before closing her eyes again, lifting her face to a watery ray of sunshine as it broke through the veil of cloud.

What a group of amazing people, he thought quietly to himself? What an extraordinary set of circumstances had led them together on this day! He never ceased to feel baffled by the workings of his inner self and his patron The Lady Morrigan, although he still questioned what his roll would be in the continuing search for Sybille. Had Bethan been successful in finding her he wondered or had the whole rite been for nothing? He sighed wearily, closing his eyes as he too sought consolation in the weak ray of the sun, warm on his face.

He found he could not rest, so decided to risk life and limb and attempt to speak with Maeve, to see if he could coax her to share what appeared to be a constant burden. He stood, stretching and flexing his muscles as if readying himself for battle. Once again, Morgan noticed Flora watching him with that same cheeky glimmer of amusement they seemed to share, particularly where Maeve was concerned.

How simple it would be he thought, not for the first time, if it were Flora, he felt drawn to for more than friendship. How much less complicated she was to Maeve with all her hidden agendas and complexities. Flora's smile widened as if reading his thoughts. Her gaze shifted to Cal who appeared to slumber peacefully, his unruly mass of hair flopped forward over his eyes. She sent Morgan the silent message of where her heart was taking her. He smiled back in acknowledgment, rolling his eyes in sympathy. Friends, his eyes queried; friends, came her reply.

No, he had felt something for Maeve from the first sight of her in a photo with Sybille, Flora and Bethan a few years ago. Meeting her had not lessened the attraction and he knew it was mutual. He knew Maeve was scared by her own emotions and unable to sort them amidst the upheaval of Sybille's disappearance and her own self-doubts. She continued to keep him at arm's length although, on the odd occasion, he would feel her warming to him in spite of herself.

Sensing their shared amusement at her irritability, Maeve bit back her need to vent; they were not the cause after all for her feelings of impatience at the wait for Bethy to wake up. With a deep breath to steady her, she exclaimed, 'So happy to be the source of such entertainment for you both. I'm just off to fetch my clown hat before I check on Bethy,' and with that stalked off with her accustomed long stride, a gale of friendly laughter followed her and in answer, they heard the door slam.

'Well that's likely to have woken Beth anyway,' said Flora sobering. 'Ooh; sometimes Maeve!'

Morgan's deep, rumbling chuckle was the only response.

Maeve did not understand the emotions she felt when she watched Morgan's relaxed ease with everyone, male and female alike. She only knew that her response to him went beyond anything comparable.
Strange feelings, a combination of irritation and dare she think it, jealousy arose as she saw all her friends respond to his natural, relaxed warmth. Instead of relaxing herself around him, she became like a shrew in his company. Sighing, she took a detour through the kitchen grabbing an apple on the way; she shoved it into her jacket. She went out the back door, pausing to stroke Jess the goat as she gently butted and nuzzled at her pocket. 'Yes. I have it Jess,' said Maeve, carefully cutting her offering in half with her pocket knife as Dolly, Jess' sister came hurtling towards her at full trot, 'Here you are girls,' holding the apple halves for each of them to take, Jess in

her usual gentle manner and Dolly with her accustomed grab and nip at Maeve's fingers, 'Ouch! Don't bite the hand that feeds you Dolly! I don't know how Flora puts up with you,' she exclaimed.

She wandered out the gate, heading through the orchard to the pond where she always found solace from her ceaseless, mental entanglements. She sat to lean wearily against a tree; an old twisted willow overhanging the water, its leaves made a soft carpet beneath its shade of autumn gold.

It was the cold and damp saturating her jeans at the seat that woke her from what she thought must have been a catnap …somewhere a voice had been calling to her …a child's voice, but then as she came to her senses groggily, she heard Samantha calling, 'Maeve, MAEVE …where are you, lunch is ready!'

Gathering her wits, she attempted to get up, feeling stiff and cold in her joints, 'I'm coming Sam,' she yelled in reply as Sam approached. A flock of marauding Corella took flight rapidly and vocally, from the canopy above, causing a shower of leaves.

'Are you alright?' Sam asked Maeve, 'you've been gone a while and we were worried. It's freezing out here,' raising her voice to be heard over the resounding cries of the departing flock.

'Tell me about it,' said Maeve, 'now I know what freezing your arse off means,' she laughed, good humour returning, in spite of the chill that bit into her bones.

Sam laughed, giving Maeve a quick squeeze of affection before proffering a hand to pull her to her feet.

'I'm fine,' said Maeve, 'I must have dozed off from sheer exhaustion. I'm frozen to the core.'

'Perhaps you should get in a hot bath Maeve? None of us can afford to be sick right now.'

'I'll get into some dry clothes and have one later Sam …I'm starving and you know what I'm like when I get hungry.'

'OOH NO! Not the low-blood-sugar-monster …NOOOO,' laughed Sam, making a fork-fingered, warding sign at Maeve, 'save me, save me,' she shrieked.

Maeve made a teeth-gnashing face at her as Sam broke into a sprint; she could only hobble after her. As she followed Sam, she heard childish laughter and a splash of water as if someone had just dive-bombed into the dam; then all was still. The dank odour of stagnant water drifted to her causing her to wrinkle up her nose in disgust, 'Hmm,' she said quietly to herself as she followed Sam back to the house, 'that dam's not stagnant.'

Warmth and laughter drifted from the kitchen as Maeve went in; the old table was set for a splendid lunch. Bethan sat quietly relaxed while the others all spoke at once. She merely blinked and smiled gently at their enthusiasm and impatience, waiting for them to quieten, 'Afternoon Maeve …Sam,' she said, as if nothing odd had occurred at all.

As one Maeve and Sam hugged their friend, with a sense of relief that she was all right. They felt trepidation at what may have occurred and fear, battled excitement at what she might reveal.

She hugged them, but withdrew gently as if their touch caused her physical pain; they could not know the amount of information they transferred to her through all their rapidly questing senses. They may just as well have been shouting at her, such was the impact her journey in the 'Between' had had on her own heightened awareness. She smiled at them however, in her usual sweet way, allaying the fears she saw in their eyes at her withdrawal.

'It's okay you two, it will pass; at least I hope it will, the amount of input is phenomenal and I need to learn to temper it I guess,' she finished, trailing off in astonishment at their faces, '…What is it?' Beth said, 'You both look as if you've seen a ghost'

'What,' said Maeve? Max and Morgan both stood rapidly, moving as one in their concern.

'You're all scaring me …what is it?' Beth repeated.

'You're speaking in the Gaelic,' said Morgan with a laugh, they can't understand you,' he translated for the shocked group.

'I can a little,' said Max looking around at the others questioningly.

'Not me,' said Cal, ''least, only a smattering.'

'What's happened to her Morgan,' said Flora, 'has she some sort of memory loss do you think?'

There came a clattering on the roof and then a loud, resounding thump. The kitchen door burst open and an unusually harried Tara flew in, still in the midst of her shapechange; forgetting to wait for an invitation in her rush to get to Bethan.

'Fuck, shit, SHIT!' Tara exclaimed, racing over to Bethan, feathers changing to velvet and lace, flying indiscriminately, 'Arianwen!' she soothed, 'here let me help you,' she reached out to gently taking Bethan into her arms, 'shhh, melyanna …suula lindor, suula,' she whispered. 'Shhh, dear one …breathe, little songbird, breathe.' Tara stroked her between the brows, helping Bethan to rearrange her thought patterns into the language of her friends.

'I didn't realise I wasn't speaking English,' she laughed, smiling at the concerned faces around her, hearing their sighs of relief.

'This can happen in the beginning,' said Tara, 'you can become confused after such a long journey into the 'Between,' some never regain their wits and roam the lands of the Fae forever...' she trailed off as she saw the look of horror on Maeve's face.

'What! You knew this and didn't warn her or us for that matter?'

'It's okay Maeve,' Beth said,' I did know the risks involved; the Lady warned me that I may be disorientated on returning to earth's vibration.' She grabbed Maeve's hand to soothe her, squeezing Tara's with her other in thanks.

'Yes,' said Tara, 'this is all normal but I had planned to be here for your return Arianwen. I'm sorry,' she said with a grin, 'I was waylaid by a spectacular fight between a sisterkin and a humankin for a fallen biscuit in the park; surely a fallen morsel is anyone's for the taking. Thing is, it hadn't yet fallen and the humankin was about to take a bite...' she trailed off as she heard the laughter from Morgan and the answering chuckle from Ruark perched outside. Laughing at the bemused faces of the others, 'Never mind,' she gurgled with glee, 'you had to be there I guess!'

'Okay,' said Max, 'can we eat? The excitement has brought on a huge appetite and I personally would like to hear what's happened in the...er... 'Between'?' he finished, 'I'm bursting to know, actually!'

'Will you stay Tara,' said Flora, 'there's plenty and I know your appetite by now?'

'Well if you insist,' grinned Tara, 'I can't stand waste!'

They gathered around the old honeyed oak table, chatting to each other about nothing much. Waiting, between mouthfuls of vegetable terrine and Flora's home baked bread …some more patiently than others, to hear what Bethan had to report and to share their own experiences of the night before.

Chapter 4
Morgan Trethaway

Morgan, from his vantage point beyond the circle, saw the Fae and the Greenlord walking toward the edge of the grove accompanied by creatures and nature spirits he had never seen before. Some were so ugly in human eyes and yet so beautiful in their differentness. He watched entranced as they wove their way through the trees to the edge of the circle; the Fae standing between the other men lending strength and protection for what was at best, a dangerous eve to be out working in ritual.

He could not see what the women were doing, but the smell of the incense and fragrant candle wax filled his nostrils. He recognised the voices of the four women as they cast, Bethan's sweet, ringing tones bringing the circle to completion as the Greenlord stepped from the trees to walk among them.

A radiant light shone through as if someone had lit a beacon and Silver, accompanied by the most exquisite woman, who walked ...no wafted into the grove; the scent of roses and other exotic fragrances followed her, along with a tribe of small winged beings.

It all seemed to happen so fast as she stepped into the circle; there was a pause as all sound stopped, even the soughing wind in the branches above him ceased, then the horn sounded and he saw the Hunt ride out of the side of the hill.

Was he the only one who could see them he thought with some alarm, knowing their notoriety; none of the others seemed to be reacting at the sight of them.

Wild Fae, male and female alike, rode shaggy horses of every colour, sleek white hounds ran, ears tipped with a rusty red not unlike the colour of dried blood. Pink tongues lolling, they ran barking and baying, apparently chasing something across the glade. One, the lead female he could only think of as Mabh, Queen of the Fae realms, paused next to him, looking him up and down as if he were a morsel of food on display. She felt his discomfort and grinned, baring white, sharply pointed teeth at him. He remembered distinctly thinking …no vegetarian here then …one of the Unsidhe no less, before she had moved on to join the others waiting in deference for her.

He could see that the beings were rounding up spirit creatures and humans alike, to bring them to the gateway that they may pass finally from the 'Between,' into the Summerlands. Here they may review their lives and hopefully find peace.

Then once again, silence had fallen in the grove and the brilliant light had faded. Only then had the tall Fae Aithlin stepped forward from between himself and Alex. With a gesture, he had called the other Elven kin to turn toward the centre of the circle, where they had scooped up the unconscious Bethan, carrying her gently and ceremoniously down to the house. Morgan had realised then that Aithlin was not simply another Fae amongst his kin, but a respected leader.

Chapter 5
Flora Jenkins

Flora was feeling strangely calm, almost removed, as she waited for things too unfold. Beth sat behind her; she could feel her friend's energy as warmth against her back and could hear the rustling of her robes as she settled herself to the task she had undertaken.

From above in the trees an Owl hooted as if in celebration of the rite; she glanced up in wonder.

She hoped that their choice of herbs, resins and bark had been the right ones, as she heard Airmhid's voice again in her head, when the Lady had told her that there would be no room for error this night.

They had performed the circle casting in what she could only describe as a trance state; she had little recall until they were standing facing outward, Beth protected in the centre. She had heard the Fae singing, seen the Makers fighting the dark, encroaching blight and briefly, had seen Silver as she stepped from the edge of the forest into the circle where Beth sat.

Then the Greenlord strode through the grove into their circle; the light and music had swelled and then ...silence.

She had seen the Fae, led by Aithlin approach and had responded immediately by opening the circle, Maeve moving forward rapidly to help.
Turning briefly, as she pulled the energy back into the Athame, she had glimpsed Bethan reappearing from the ethers, lying limply on the ground. Then the Fae had carried Bethan away and they were all rushing to follow.

Back at the farm, Beth was sleeping soundly in Sybille's old study, her silvery hair wildly curling around her, a hoard of Makers singing her dreams. Morgana and Teddy sat on the back of the couch their wide-eyed gazes watchful.

Where was Bethan, Flora thought as she quietly waited? Where was her friend, what was she seeing and experiencing? She knew Bethan was safe, the Lady and Lord would have her safely home again; she could not imagine anything else.

These last weeks and months had been full of tension mixed with hope, discovery mixed with awe and a sense of unreality at the tasks they had all been entrusted. She often wondered why them, why this little group of friends, when so much depended on their work and discoveries?

At times Flora felt like a raw recruit in spite of all Sybille had taught. It just did not seem as if they had enough experience to be the hope for the world they were supposed to be.

There again, Sybille had told her often enough not to …what was it? Ah yes…'not to hide her light under a bushel,' an interesting statement. Sybille had been, no was …full of those wonderful old-world wisdoms. Where was her friend and mentor Sybille, she cried, weary and spent she buried her face in her hands.

Chapter 6
Samantha Cartwright

They bathe in her light as they cling to her skin
They dance and cavort up her arms, down her shin
...through her hair, when they dare ...over here, over
there ...her song ...yet unheard ...except by these kin
From Sprite Song by Silver

Sam felt as if she was running around inside her body looking for a way out, she was so restless and agitated. What she had seen the night before on the Mount went beyond anything she had experienced in her life, even since Sybille had vanished.

Although comfortable with the ever-present leaf creatures that were a part of everyday reality now, she could find no words to describe the entities that had come to watch and join them in the Rite of Samhain. It was evident that there was more at stake than anyone could possibly envision, as the presence of the Greenlord and the Lady had proven.

She had seen beings surrounding their circle in the grove, previously only glimpsed as mental images or pictures in books and dreams; she knew now that the dreams she had had in her life were in fact real. These extraordinary beings existed side by side in the next di-

mension, the next realm, just a breath away. Sam realised then just how much her Aunt's niece she was.

As she stood with her back turned to where Beth
stood in the centre of the circle she could see the energy
raised by the shared casting. The barrier of light visible,
her own energy azure blue, Bethy's silver, with splashes
of green from Flora, fire red from Maeve and golden yellow from Susan, all blended as a huge bubble of protection around them; as above, so below.

The outer rim beyond had been pitch black except for the now familiar radiance of Morgan's blue-
silver and the clean bright energies of Max, Cal and
Alex; the surrounding Fae a beacon of light as they came
to stand guard with their humankin. She had sensed that
further out the Dark Fae had stood waiting for just a
small weakness in the circle to step in and she knew that
their target was Bethan. What did Tara call her? Arian
…no Arianwen, Silver. How strange that Bethy shared
in part the Trueshaper's name she thought.

She had wondered when Silver would appear to
assist, or was there danger of contaminating energy from
the blight that the Makers were fighting. She had seen
them, even in the darkness, their small firefly lights,
working hard to cleanse the land.

All up her arms she could feel the little leaf creatures stirring, waking. Their energy was nothing short of
ferocious and, although Sam knew, they never meant to
hurt her; their little sharp hands and feet were as needles

on her skin. Only recently, she had woken to find that the tattoo-like images were growing, spreading further up her arms and neck and down over her chest.

Sam didn't mind though; strangely, it felt almost normal to see her skin covered in the very lovely images they were creating. It felt as if she were becoming a human tree, her leaves the colours of the season, but Sam couldn't help but wonder what would happen when winter came or when spring and summer took over on the Wheel, whether they too would change to match.

On turning her back in the circle with the others, every fibre of her being had cried out, 'let me watch, let me see,' as her fears for Beth and the processes she was undergoing became an urgent prompting, making her heart thud and flutter with concern for her beautiful, gentle friend.

Sam had seen the encroaching darkness of the fallen Maker's blight, fueled by the tall, dark Fae. Aerandir had bared his teeth at her when he realised that she could see him amongst the dark veil of his mother's magicks. Sam had snarled an answering grimace, shocking herself and had felt the little tree sprites respond to her anger and fear as they linked with the huge ancient trees around the grove and turned toward the dark Fae as one, in her defense.

More gathered on the peripheral of her vision, even in the darkness she could see them; feel them entangling themselves in her cap of dark hair, hanging on with their little claw like hands, waving sharp thorns from the trees from which they came. Hawthorn sprites she had realised were now present among the original Oak.

As tiny as these beings were, Sam could feel their fierceness and for reasons unfathomable, they were there in her defense as much as Bethan's. This link with them was a mystery to her but she was glad they were there, that they felt her every emotion, responding without hesitation as their bond became stronger.

Suddenly a light, blindingly bright had shone through the Grove and again there had been an overwhelming temptation to turn, to look from where it came; she had to clench her fists and bite her lip to stop. The light had grown and with it music swelled as the Fae gathered, heads bowed in reverence to what, she could only imagine.

Then the Greenlord arrived, entering the circle he brushed past her as he made his way to Beth, releasing an aroma that was so intoxicating Sam thought she would faint. Woodlands, moss, wet leaves and loamy soil, earthy and male; the scent filled her and the wee leaf folk clambered over her to get closer to Him as He passed.

He gently stroked their excitement with His song and they replied with notes of the sweetest melody; her friends Maeve and Flora, Beth's mother Susan and Flora's mother Claire, had responded with a sharp intake of breath that matched her own. He had passed between them, some of the braver leaf sprites leaping, clinging in His hair and on His broad shoulders, riding with glee, flourishing their tiny thorn-swords in triumph.

Then all had become still, an empty silence falling; Bethan, Hercurin and the Lady, gone, vanished.

It had only been a heartbeat before Beth had reappeared, lying like a small, fragile doll on the ground. They had rapidly opened the circle; Flora knew immediately what needed doing. Her mother Claire had appeared again from out of nowhere, together with Susan and Maeve, she tended to Beth while the men had stood their impatience palpable, waiting to come in from beyond the circles strictures.

Before they could even take a step, Aithlin Farandir and several other tall Fae had gathered Bethan up in a fine cloak of silken threads and without even a glance at the waiting humans, had taken her away.
Aithlin had remained at the cottage to reassure them that all was well and Bethan merely sleeping. He left, obviously uncomfortable in human surroundings, instructing them sternly to let her wake naturally.

Now sitting with the group, quietly reviewing her experiences of the night before, Sam jolted back to the moment at Maeve's rapid departure. Sam realised how similar she had once been to Maeve, ever ready to become extremely angry when things were not happening as expected or planned and how much she had changed in the course of the last few months. She was however, the one most able to understand Maeve; how her mind worked and thus, was the one who might possibly help her too.

Morgan had stood as Maeve left and so Sam rose quickly too, she knew how Maeve would react if he followed her,

'I'll start some lunch and then I'll go after her, I know exactly where she'll be,' said Sam.

'I'll come with you,' said Max with a quick grin.

'Yes, someone mentioned food,' said Alex and Susan together, laughing.

'It's funny how it appeared everyone was asleep until I said I was going to make lunch,' said Sam, giving Max's ear a friendly tweak as she passed.

Cal stirred, 'Mm food?' he said, opening one eye to smile at Flora as she too rose to her feet.

'All right then gang,' said Sam, 'let's explore the leftovers.'

'There's a vegetable terrine in the fridge Sam,' said Flora.

'Of course there would be Flo,' she laughed, 'you're always prepared. I don't know how you found the time to make it though, with all that's been happening.'

'Well it's my form of meditation really. I just seem to find my centre when I'm in the kitchen or the garden,' replied Flora.

'Let's see if Beth's awake after Maeve slammed the door,' said Susan with motherly concern. 'She was so pale last night and we haven't even thought about her birthday, although I don't suppose she has either come to that.'

Alex held her close to soothe her, 'she'll be fine Suzie. You know how resilient she is. She's become so much more purposeful and strong since having this load dumped on her. I wonder if Sybille knew what she was really leaving these girls as a legacy,' he questioned to the group.

'I personally don't think she could possibly have known what was going to happen,' said Flora, 'I wonder if anyone knew, the Fae, the Makers,' …she trailed off as Cal said,

'Has anyone seen Claire?'

'She disappeared last night,' replied Flora, 'after the Fae brought Bethy here, but she came in later looking drawn and tired so she could still be sleeping.'

With that, they walked together to the house, the peace of the morning broken by disturbing thoughts of the night before.

Chapter 7
Maeve Hedinger

Maeve felt like a warrior readying for battle; every nerve tense, waiting for an attack that never came thanks to the presence of the Fae and the Greenlord, who had stepped through their cast circle as if it had been nothing but a flimsy veil of light.

On the one hand, she had wondered at this, on the other she had been shocked that it was possible in spite of all their training and effort to make it an impenetrable fortress of protection for Beth.

Her rational mind argued, 'well he is the Horned God after all,' while her little self, pouted and said, 'that's just not right after all the work we've put in,' then there had been no more time for thought as she saw a figure standing on the edge of the forest watching, in fact watching her. It appeared to be female, small as a child, with wild red hair. She was dressed in layers of ragged clothing and wearing a cap of some sort that glinted in the torch light and the Wytchlight she exuded. Staring directly at Maeve, she had a serious knowing gaze of recognition that chilled to the bone; it had been less than friendly she recalled. Then the light in the grove had intensified to such a degree there had been no time to think of anything but the Greenlord as he passed through, his entourage of sprites trailing in his wake. Still she schooled herself not to turn, not to look when after his passing, the music of the moment faded, the light dimmed and utter silence fell.

Without a sound, the tall Fae Aithlin pushed gently past her; Maeve, finally unable to contain herself any longer, spun around to see him kneel next to Beth where she lay unconscious on the ground.

More Fae followed and as Flora came to her senses, Maeve helped her open the circle for the others. Claire and Susan had broken ranks first in their hurry to reach Beth. After that, everything blurred around the edges. They had followed the Fae down to the house where they laid Beth on the couch in Sybille's old study; a fine throw over her, Maeve assumed by the Fae.

Sheer exhaustion had overcome her as she heard the Fae singing outside; the next thing she knew she was waking, feeling hung-over, on the rug where she had fallen.

Chapter 8
Claire Jenkins

Owl flies at night . . . eyes huge in moon's light
Hear her soft calling; quiet as leaves falling
Then comes the scream . . . a mouse floats into dream
Not right or wrong, yet all part of the song
Not good nor bad, happy or sad
Just simply life that unfolds as She gives and withholds
. . . from . . . Owl Dreams

Claire sat in her Owl form high above the circle as her daughter and friends cast. She could see the swirling energies building as she observed them with her strange Owl detachment. It was literally a bird's eye view as she watched the Fae arrive, one moment invisible, then simply there.

Other creatures from the 'Between,' walked the Ways and, as she heard the horn sound, the Sidhe emerged from beneath the hill, riding their shaggy horses as fierce as the Sidhe. Unsidhe rode too, their battles and disagreements forgotten on this the most sacred night on the Wheel of the Year.

Claire watched in wonder as the Greenlord strode from the 'Between' and walked the human realms with The Lady. She flew down to a lower branch to be closer, The Lady smiled at her need. For a moment,

Goddess and Owl eyes met, energy passed between them arcing like a rainbow, encompassing Claire as she sat, fully conscious of being two in one ...human and Owl.

'Naboo,' Claire as Owl heard her name spoken, forgotten until now, 'Naboo,' whispered Arianrhod, 'watch and listen, be their eyes and ears in the dark.'

Naboo bobbed on her perch in answer, Claire and her Owl form one in consciousness. Naboo held all the secret wisdom of the ancient ways and Claire could now completely embrace her ancestry. With a celebratory hoot of sheer pleasure, she saw her daughter look up briefly, wonder in her eyes.

With a feeling of exhilaration, she flew to another tree across the Grove with a better vantage point. She could see the Lord and Lady bending over Bethan; Arianwen she thought, before finding her attention caught by a strange little being that stood on the fringe, held back by the circle of Fae and humans. Small and 'other,' the entity had an air of innocence that hid a darker self, a darker need. Red capped and tiny in stature, like a human child of 7 or 8 years, she appeared to be dressed in bits and pieces from nature's own compost bin. Shells, seaweed, driftwood, starfish skeletons and tiny fish bones hung in her wildly tangled hair and the phosphorescence of the ocean's deep waters, shone from her skin and cap.

Claire felt she should know this being, cloaked in her own Wytchlight, but a name escaped her, her attention taken by the Fae. They were moving in to pick up the physical Littleshape Bethan from the ground, whilst the Lord and Lady took her etheric Trueshape with them, through the open gateway to the 'Between.'

 Claire had slept until she heard the group returning in from outside. She had flown back to the house in her Owl form the night before, chasing the fast moving Fae through the grove and down to the old converted barn that Sybille loved so much.

She felt numb with exhaustion, her body not used to making the change so suddenly or so often, after the long break from shapeshifting, she had taken to placate Harry. Now Harry, ensnared to all intent and purpose by Annie Savage, would no longer be a part of her life. Although she thought, he had probably not been for quite some time, after rejecting his own daughter when she had disagreed with him on her choice of career.

This was all just water under the bridge after what had occurred that night there being more important issues to concentrate on, for the sake of many lives.

Finding Bethan safe and sleeping, Claire crashed into a dreamless sleep to wake, if not refreshed for her joints were aching, at least alert to the sounds of the house waking and the gentle distant laughter of the group.

The sound of a door slamming brought her thoroughly awake and aware as she heard and felt the anger and frustration, that so often accompanied Maeve.

Yawning and stretching, Claire realised her life was now her own, she had reclaimed herself and her ancestry in a matter of weeks …free …and in that freedom all her Owl senses heightened. Anything she had felt for Harry was gone after his final act of betrayal. Whatever had been amiss between them, they had still always had the ability to converse, but that too was gone. Claire had expected sadness, instead there was an element of relief she need no longer participate in Harry's game of pretence; in fact, Annie's betrayal saddened her more than anything else did.

Hearing a door close as the group came in and Sam's voice calling Maeve from outside, she realised she must have dozed again. Stretching, she rolled off the couch she had made her bed for the night in Flora's room; Flora must have snuck out like a mouse she thought, not to have woken her from her usually light sleep.

This time Claire felt refreshed and ready to face the day. She showered quickly and dressed in fresh jeans and sweater before turning to the mirror to brush her hair. Chestnut brown, wavy and still as thick as her daughter's, it fell to her shoulder the silvery streaks, usually artfully concealed with a natural colour, were showing.

She smiled at her reflection, enjoying the evidence of cronehood, really only ever concealed for Harry's benefit; he had called them her 'hag hairs,' said it showed her age. Enjoying too the little laughter lines that appeared at the corner of her eyes when she smiled, she realised that the other lines of care and stress that had started to form across her brow were gone. Just like Harry, she thought with a grin of something akin to relief before, with a final stroke of the brush, she went to join the gathering below.

Chapter 9

Saturn Return...

Teeth sharp and pointy ...their bite venomous the dark Fae ride out. They only have anything to do with humans if it is to their own advantage.

Fairy and Folklore of the British Isles, Max Fenner

Silence fell as the friends, finishing their meal, turned as one to Bethan. She had not eaten much but had a glow about her, an ethereal quality that grew a little each day. The Gods, thought Morgan as he watched, had indeed touched her.

Bethan cleared her throat nervously, not sure where to start, then with a deep breath she began to describe the events of the night and the journey into the 'Between.'

When she was finished, the group remained quiet to process what she had shared. Only Maeve, with her classic restlessness stood rapidly, clearing away plates as if to keep her hands busy while her head ran amok.

'It's okay Maeve,' Beth said gently, 'this isn't just about you; you're not alone now,' she finished.

About to reply, Maeve simply sat down, mouth open at the affect Beth had on her. It was as if she could see into her mind; no her soul. She blushed, looking down at her hands, wringing her napkin and shredding it into strips. She didn't even know why she was feeling the way she was and she wasn't ready to share it either, at least not until she worked it out for herself first.

Max broke into her thoughts with his usual candour, 'Maeve? You have something to share?' he questioned.

'Er …no, I'm not ready,' she exclaimed, close to tears and not knowing why.

'Leave her be Max,' said Alex, who had always had a soft spot for Maeve; seeing through her bravado easily, 'she'll share when she's ready, won't you Maeve?'

She answered with a watery grin, her churning thoughts quietening a little at his kindness, 'Yes,' she stammered, 's-soon. Let someone else start,' …she trailed off as she caught Morgan's eye. He was looking at her with concern and there was something else …yes, she thought, there was deep caring. She broke the connection, blushing. What in the world was happening to her? She was behaving like a total dork! What must they all be thinking of her?

A touch on her hand brought her back to the moment and she felt a pressure in her head as a voice spoke in her mind this time, very much like Sam's, 'Snap out of it Maeve, this is much bigger than you and your personal ego.' She started in surprise glancing at Sam, quickly recovering herself but not before Morgan and Beth had both risen to stand with her.

'What is it Maeve, what just happened?' said Bethan.

'I heard that too! Someone is projecting thoughts to Maeve,' said Morgan, 'does anyone here have something they need to get off their chests?'

'It's not necessarily anyone here,' interjected Bethan, 'there's another influence at play.' Turning to Maeve she said, 'Have you been protecting yourself Maeve? What happened last night and since then, come to that?'

'Well it looks like it's going to be you to go first after all Red,' Max said, grinning fondly.

'No, enough!' broke in Susan this time, 'give Maeve some space. I'll go first if need be but first there's something else, in spite of all that's been happening I have to say this,' she turned to Bethan, smiling broadly, 'Happy Birthday Bethy.'

Silence fell for a moment then the tension in the room eased.

'Thanks Mum,' said Bethan, 'but this is more important than my presumed, earthly birthday. In truth, we don't know if it actually is! No, we need to deal with what just happened and to protect Maeve.'

'I don't need protecting! I'm not a child,' exclaimed Maeve.

'Ah that's more like the Maeve we know and love,' laughed Flora stepping in as always in support of her friend, 'I have something for you Bethy; we need a break and then we can address all that needs to be dealt with.

I know so much has changed for you but give us this …let us give you this' …she trailed off.

Bethan sighed, 'Okay,' she said, 'but then we need to get to the bottom of what just happened.'…so just for a while to ease their stress the friends broke open some bubbles. Flora brought out a luscious lemon cake she had hidden at the back of the huge pantry; no one had known she had baked it in secret the night before Samhain.

They each gave Bethan their gifts; Flora, Sam and Morgan had collaborated in the making of a Book of Shadows for her. Morgan had worked stretching and tooling the leather, embossing it with Celtic symbols on the cover. He'd helped Flora bind the handmade paper that she'd made, pressed with flowers and herbs, fragrant from the garden.

Sam had taken all Beth's songs and poems and hand written then bound them into the book. She had illustrated the first page with a drawing of Beth's favourite lap harp and each verse with a small delicately painted design that enhanced the words.

Morgan had written her a song that he said he would sing for her later, Sam had written this into the book too.

Callum, showing his creative side, had handcrafted a delicate wand for Bethan from a piece of matured silver birch. He had worked with Morgan and Maeve to get the balance right and to find just the right crystal for the end. Maeve had made the final additions, using delicate silver filigree-work round the top to hold the crystal in place, showing Cal how to work with silver and her soldering iron.

Susan and Alex had given their daughter a voucher for a season of massage and spa visits at one of Springsmeet's best Spa venues and an album of photos of her mother, taken as a young woman at college. She had been Susan's best friend, much as Beth and Flora were now.

Max had found a statue in an antique shop of an Otter playing with a stick, lifelike in its detail the colours muted and natural, as if the sculptor had sat on the edge of a pond shaded by trees to create it.

Claire had made Bethan a smudging fan with feathers she had kept from her own Owl moults years ago and Tara an iridescent, Raku-fired incense bowl, that shimmered in the now fading afternoon sunlight, the colour of Raven feathers.

Maeve was the last to give her gift, shyly bringing out her package, unusual for her, her confidence normally high where her art was concerned. A seemingly fragile, mesh-like net, fell out of the wrapping as if alive; glowing like a silvery web, encrusted where the threads adjoined, with tiny crystal beads …moonstone, citrine, merlinite and calcites in various aqua colours; deep within the silver strands, a glint of red fire.

At first, Beth could only stare at what had fallen into her lap, softly and supplely; she could not work out what it actually was. Maeve knelt at her friend's feet taking the slinky object from Beth's fingers, 'This is what it's for Bethy,' Maeve said as she gently gathered up Bethan's silvery cascade of hair, slipping the mesh over it like a snood she had seen in old artworks. 'It's to hold your hair back when you weave or play the harp. I've made it from the finest gauge silver wire I could find and its sterling, so it won't discolour your hair,' she paused for breath, 'Anyway I hope you like it.'

'Like it!' exclaimed Beth, 'it's a master piece Maeve!' although feeling a little hampered, even by its fragile weight …and something else that made her ears buzz, subtle but …recovering, she continued without noticeable pause, except to the ever watchful Morgan, 'When did you have the time to make it, it's beautiful?' she asked Maeve.

Embarrassed by the praise, Maeve fiddled with the net adjusting a few stray curls that insisted on escaping from the confines of the fine mesh, 'Well that's alright then, as long as it fits and isn't uncomfortable,' she muttered.

At that, Beth simply grabbed Maeve's busy hands and pulling her to her in a gentle hug whispered, 'It's okay Maeve; I love it, thank you so much. Now,

when you're ready, you need to tell me what's been going on with you.'

Maeve recoiled and then recovering herself said, 'Yeah,
alright.'

Generous acclaim came from everyone for the
gift, which made Maeve squirm as all the attention focused on her. She felt Morgan's gaze and seeing the ad-
miration for her work in his eyes, coloured up in response.

Max, always the jester said, 'Well that takes the
old hair net to the designer level then,' causing even
Maeve to collapse, giggling at his silliness.

With that, Bethan stood calling immediate quiet
simply with her bearing, 'Okay, it's time gang. Let's get
down to it.'

'No one last thing Beth,' said Morgan as he
pulled his Dulcimer from behind the couch, 'this is for
you lovely.'

This time only Max sitting next to Maeve saw
her reaction to Morgan's tenderness toward Beth. He
felt her rage as it threatened to rise to the surface, held in
check by sheer will as she clenched her fists, jaw jutting.
Making an excuse to leave the table, she walked casually
to the window, in pretence of watching the birds in the
tree outside.

Morgan and Bethan exchanged glances as they
heard the voice again plaguing Maeve, childlike and
peevish, 'See, told ya e's not intra'sted in ya ...s'er e's

afta,' the voice then quickly faded at the realisation they could hear it. Maeve shifted again uncomfortably before returning to her seat.

Clearing his throat, Morgan strummed the first chords of a lilting melody and to everyone's surprise; Sam came to sit with him, bringing out a flute from her jacket pocket.

'Ha-ha,' she grinned, 'be afraid, I've not had nearly enough time to practice for this, but Morgan can be very persuasive when he wants.'

'See,' said the voice in Maeve's head tauntingly, 'told ya, any piece of skirt'll do im!'

'Shut UP,' hissed Maeve.

Bethan heard the voice again clearly, even over the music as Sam and Morgan played the first bars. Morgan broke into song; the others gathering behind him to hum in harmony enriched by the surprisingly sultry, husky voice of Tara…

'When she awakened from earth's deepest sleep, …the Wildhunt came riding her company to keep, …the horn that then sounded came from the deep, …and the Greenlord came striding, his lover to meet.

At this Bethan broke into peals of laughter, 'You ham!' she exclaimed to Morgan, 'That's not what you wrote for me you're just having a laugh.'

To which Morgan, pretending to be hurt, hammed it up, as with a flourish he put the back of his hand to his forehead, closing his eyes in a mock portrayal of the wounded 'artiste.'

'Alright,' said Beth, 'Let's have it then.'

With a smile, Sam raised her flute to her lips and played a haunting air, Morgan joined in on the Dulcimer…

'Moonbeams are caught in the web of her hair, tree spirits gather to sing of their care; winged ones descend, their energy to share …the light will return to the earth.

Who can imagine the life that in-dwells as subtle melodies ebb and then swell; all who know her, caught in her spell …the light will return to the earth.

The light of her truth shines bright from her skin, for all nature's beings are surely her kin; though deep shadows fall you can still hear her   sing …the light will return to the earth.

The silence of darkness will not stand her light; the song that she sings will outsmart the blight, as deep shadow fall and the day becomes night …the light will return to the earth.

As each day renews and the Makers sing true, the sky may grow grey before it turns blue, we gather in close and we trust only you …for Her light has returned to the earth.'

As their music stilled, through the applause that ensued, a rather embarrassed Beth said her thanks to Morgan and Sam.

'There's more to it but that gives you an idea,' said Morgan, giving Beth a quick hug before putting his instrument away carefully.

'I'm honoured,' she replied, 'thank you, all of you.'

'So, where to from here?' said Tara in her candid way, 'There's much that needs sharing, things to work out for the next steps on the journey.'

'I feel and with no disrespect for Beth's need to recover or that it's her birthday, we've really wasted most of today,' said an otherwise quiet Cal. 'We haven't even had a chance to look more deeply at the inferences of everything Beth has shared with us and what it actually means in giving us the answers to Sybille's whereabouts. If I have it right, Beth and Sybille are linked by their soul being of the same Trueshaper, Silver. Beth is now receiving Sybille's memories from the time when she was The Cybil; together with her own memories of that same time as Leah; the two lives have linked again through Silver's need to find the required memories. Thing is,' Cal paused briefly to take breath, 'which memories are actually the ones she needs?'

All eyes swivelled to Cal, who only spoke out in the group when he had something valuable to share and, as always this was the case; putting into words all that the others had not been able to.

Tara, did a high five motion to him, 'Ah, a man after my own heart,' she said, grinning to the room in general, 'There's nothing like a mystery to unravel is there?' she grinned.

'Yes, I have to agree with Cal,' Sam said, 'so, who wants to go first? Then we can see what we can do to help Beth sort out the memories of her experiences, because there's a piece missing.'

'What do you mean Sam?' said Beth, 'I've told you as much as I remember, for now at least.'

'Well,' replied Sam, 'what about when you first disappeared?' You physically vanished, even if only for a few seconds you were gone and, as we now know from before, time means nothing in the other realms.'

'That's true I guess,' said Beth, 'I'll have to think about this carefully; see if I can capture the moment somehow.'

'I might be able to help with that,' said Claire, 'years ago Harry and I did a course in hypnotherapy perhaps that would work?'

'No need,' said Tara, wriggling her fingers at Beth, 'I can fish out the memory for her ...give it a nudge so to speak,' she grinned.

'Errrm, not too sure Tara,' said Beth, pulling away rapidly, 'I'd prefer it came naturally.'

'Yes, of course Beth, but we need to hurry this whole process along now. It's gone beyond everyone's personal needs,' interjected Morgan, to where he was looking outside.

They stood in unison, to see a host of dark Makers coaxing Silver, less than gently as she struggled, bowed down with the weight of sticky threads that were beginning to grow from her. The gap within her light, before shadowed and clouded, was now like a dark vortex of swirling energy, full of tiny mutated Makers.

'Shit,' said Tara aloud, 'if the dark Makers are within Silver's energy centres, they will soon start changing everything that Sybille is and has been,' she trailed off, 'and therefore you too Bethy. You said yourself, Sybille is starting to lose huge fragments of who she is, in this aspect and in others.'

'I feel sick,' said Beth tearing her eyes away from the scene outside the window,' her eyes filled with tears and she ran from the room to be violently ill.

Susan stood quickly, making to follow her but Max grabbed her hand, saying,

'Let her be Mum! She'll be alright in a minute; you've seen how strong she's become.'

'I know,' replied Susan, 'but how much more of this can her body take?'

'That's just it,' said Tara, 'you'll be surprised Susan, there's nothing she can't take,' she finished enigmatically, before following Beth from the room.

'But she's only human!' cried Susan.

'Is she?' came the enigmatic reply from Tara.

Quiet voices hid their concerns for their friend; the group cleared away the dishes trying to imagine a normal, mundane world for a while at least.

Tara and Beth sequestered themselves in the

study, voices muted but all were relieved to hear Beth's laughter, along with Tara's husky chuckles.

Taking a large tray with mugs and a huge flask of hot, honey mead, Flora wandered outside to the table under the trees, the others followed, voices muted.

A black and white Willie wagtail and a flock of little Wrens, thronged the grass and surrounding Silver Birch trees, fighting and squabbling to see if there was any food forthcoming from the quiet group of human-kin. Small leaf creatures sat silently observing, as the group found seats and settled once more in the after-noon sunshine.

'What a strange Samhain,' said Flora to no one in particular, 'I think I might wander into town to work this evening, I have a few tinctures to make up for clients and I'm sure there will be other things to do. I don't think I can stay still much longer.'

I'll come in with you,' said Sam, 'I can catch up on my writing and some more study into the plant his-tory for the Grimoire, although I feel like something a bit more physical; perhaps a clean and tidy of the dis-plays. First though I think a walk might be a good idea; apparently we have a wet spell coming so I'll have cabin fever soon enough,' she laughed.

What about a walk now?' said Maeve, who had been abnormally quiet, occasionally casting about her as if she expected something, or someone to turn up? She didn't dare to tell anyone about the voice in her head.

She couldn't speak of the strange Fae looking child she'd seen the night before who constantly interrupted her thoughts with nasty, spiteful chatter. Everyone would think she was going mad and in truth, with the constant peripheral vision images of a child, her clothes dripping wet and a strange shiny cap on her curls, she probably was.

'I'm up for that,' said Morgan, stretching his large frame.

'Yeah, me too,' said Cal, 'You Flora, Max?'

'Sure,' said Flora, 'let's make the most of this sunshine. What about you Mum …Alex, Susan …any takers?'

'We have to be getting back to Melbourne,' said Susan worriedly. 'But we'll try to get back late tomorrow afternoon,' finished Alex for her with a grin. 'We're both worried about Beth, but at least she's safe with you lot.'

'I'll come,' said Claire.

'Alright, we'll go collect our things at Bethy's,' said Susan, 'I'll just call in to say goodbye to her first.'

'I'd leave her be for now, Susan,' said Flora tentatively, 'It may not be good to interrupt the process with Tara right now. I'm sure she'll understand.'

'You're probably right,' Susan sighed, 'Okay, we'll be off then.'

They all hugged the obviously concerned parents, Max giving his Mum an extra-long hug of commiseration before seeing them to their car.

The remaining group set off for a stroll in the late afternoon sunshine …a strange Samhain indeed, for all of them.

They walked, picking wild blackberries from the hedge-rows, eating as many as they collected, laughing like children at their blue-black fingers and lips.

Sam strolled along lost in her own thoughts, listening to and watching, the little swarming leaf creatures that followed her everywhere. She thought she could almost understand some of their piping song-like communication, but it still fell short of her grasp.

She came back down to earth suddenly, when a hand reached out and grabbed her, pulling her firmly behind the sheltering trunk of a tree. An offering of blackberries were proffered, held in slightly grubby male hands. Max grinned at her before pulling her to him.

'I've wanted to do this since I first set eyes on you!' he exclaimed and without further ado pulled her into a passionate lip-lock that took him by surprise, as Sam responded without reserve.

'Well,' she said laughing, after regaining her breath, 'that makes two of us,' before she angled her head and dove in again for a second round.

This time Max pulled away first, looking her deep in the eyes. Then again, holding her gaze with his, he gently kissed her lips, running his tongue gently between them, kissed her eyes, stroking her cap of thick, silky hair with hands that were less than steady, before pulling her to him body to body, his response evident against her belly.

They sank to the ground hands linked, eyes searching before leaning breathlessly, against the trunk of the tree. At this, the little leaf-sprites became active, their anxiety reaching a fever pitch as they attacked Max as he held Sam.

He yelped, unable to see them but feeling their little thorn swords as they pricked and bit any exposed skin they could find, pulling at his clothes.

'Oi,' yelled Sam, 'that's enough, he's not hurting me!'

'What's going on?' yelled Max, 'that hurts. I can't see them; only feel their anger at me.'

Sam stood trying not to laugh at the little being's attack on Max. She held her hand out to him to help him to his feet. He went to hold her but once again, they attacked, as ferociously as wasps.

'Alright, enough we're going,' said Max in frustration and taking her hand, drew Sam back onto the path to follow the others.

'We'll have to continue our discussion in a more private place,' gurgled Sam to him before they caught up with the group.

'Where have you two been?' said Maeve, wiggling her eyebrows suggestively at them.

'Oh,' said Sam innocently, grinning back at her, 'we found some very fat juicy, blackberries and we're sated now.' Max coloured red and laughed aloud with her as he saw the tell-tale trace of berry juice around Sam's mouth.

'Goddess, I want you!' he murmured to her quietly, before taking her hand and possessively pulled her along with him, laughing at the expression on Maeve's face.

Maeve straggled along behind the group; Morgan, Claire, Cal and Flora, were already heading back to the farm.

'Ee could 'a wait'd,' came the mocking voice of the strange child spirit.

'Oh shut up!' grumbled Maeve.

'What' replied Sam?

'Nothing,' muttered Maeve before breaking into a sprint, overtaking them in her hurry to get away from the cruel laughter that followed her, no matter how hard or how fast she ran.

Sam and Max strolled hand in hand back to the farm where Beth and Tara sat waiting for them. Beth said nothing as Max asked a silent question with his eyes, shaking her head; she simply smiled at their joined hands.

'Ah, what took you so long?' she grinned, to which Sam gave her a friendly punch on the arm.

The group stayed a while longer before gathering their things to return to Wells and Springsmeet respectively, leaving Flora and Claire to spend some much-needed time together.

Claire had things to share with her daughter about her shapechanging ancestry and had been putting off the inevitable time that she must tell Flora about the ending of her relationship with Harry. She had yet to confront him, but with everything else that had been going on in her daughter's life, she really did not want her being the last to know what her father had been up to of late.

Mother and daughter so similar in size and looks and often taken for sisters at first glance, sat together with mugs of tea, a bowl of sweet ripe berries between them to chat.

Claire knew that Callum had been loath to leave, hoping to spend some time alone with her daughter and she was happy at the thought of Flora finding a little happiness with a man she knew was solid and reliable and who would appreciate Flora, simply for who she was. Her beautiful girl deserved a break where relationships were concerned, her last with Dan ending as it did, had left Flora devastated.

In turn, Flora had known all along that things were not as they should be between her parents. She had long forgiven and forgotten her father's behaviour towards her, being of the mind that a leopard cannot change its spots and hoping that one day, he would at least admire her for what she had achieved on her own.

So now, the time had come and in her usual direct manner, Claire told Flora all that had happened in and since, her rapid return from Yorkshire.

Flora listened silently, her face giving nothing away until, after letting her mother vent a little she interjected, 'So it *was* Dad I saw at the Mount and in Springsmeet,' she exclaimed! 'What was he doing, following you here when he has no time for the Craft and never has really?'
'Well,' said Claire, 'I wasn't going to tell you this but, it's Annie …'

'What's Annie got to do with it?' then mouth open in shock, it dawned on her, '*Nooooo*,' she spluttered, '*…dad's bonking Annie!*' she shrieked, unable to contain her laughter, then sobering at the thought of the pain it must be causing her mother.

Claire was unable to keep a straight face at her daughter's outburst and the two collapsed in fits, laughing and crying at once.

Flora was both relieved and shocked at Claire's apparent acceptance of the situation but nonetheless, glad that she was moving on strongly, evident by her relief at not having to hide whom she was any longer.

'So what will you do now Mum,' said Flora when they had recovered slightly.

'For me as you know, my work is important and even more so now with recent events and Sybille's disappearance. I have my own money saved and with the sale of the house split fifty-fifty …or he can buy me out, there's really nothing I want from him. I'll build myself a studio somewhere and write those books I always said I would and now I can join with my kin on a regular basis for all the meets and earth rites …I'm free.' Claire grabbed her daughter and pulling her to her feet, whirled her around the room in a silly dance.

'What about here Mum, what about the old dairy on the hill near the grove …would that do? It's had a new roof just recently, has solar panels and a huge stove. It would be easy to divide the space for a loft bedroom and studio. I'd love to have you living out here with me, when you're in Oz anyway and that way we wouldn't be living in each other's space either,' she trailed off as she saw Claire's face. 'What is it Mum! I didn't mean to upset you …it was just a thought.'

'No it's just perfect Flora; I can't think of a more perfect plan. I'm not even going to hesitate in saying yes …ah all that space, privacy …I can come and go in whatever shape I choose,' she finished gurgling with youthful giggles, hugging Flora to her.

'Wow!' said Flora, 'Who are you and what have you done with my mother?' she chuckled.

'Come on said Claire, 'let's grab a lamp; it's getting dark but let's take a look now, yes right now …come on Flo!'

Arm in arm they strolled together in the fading Samhain light. They took the time in rediscovering their mother-daughter relationship and, more importantly as equals, as women and as friends, all else forgotten just for a while.

In the shelter of the huge sycamore trees Aithlin watched and smiled at their fragile happiness and in the forest beyond, Aelish and Aerandir sneered at the women, somewhat disappointed at the resilience these strange creatures possessed.

'Your little witch won't be happy with her moving here, now that she has her puppet moving in with her,' whispered Aerandir to his mother.

A slap was her reply as she flounced away and disappeared from sight.

'This will be the last time you do that to me,' Aerandir spat on the ground in contempt, rubbing his reddened cheek.

Chapter 10
Morning

With the sunlight streaming
…we stir from our dreaming
All senses waking
…as dawn's light is breaking
But where have we been
…what things have we seen?
…when we wander alone in the Green
Into the Mysts of Tyme by Morgan Trethaway

 Dawn crept over the horizon and over the window ledge, into Bethan's little loft bedroom. The light, gentling now as summer passed into autumn, filtered through the giant elder tree that stood, boughs still heavy with late fruit, to shine dappled rays on her face.

She slumbered on, her dreams intensifying as the little Makers swarmed around her, forming and reforming patterns, energy maelstrom swirling with colour and the essence of life itself.

Beth stirred as the light wove its way through her eyelids, intruding itself into her consciousness.

She woke, moving from sleep to full awareness in a few seconds, all recall momentarily gone about where she had been. Bird song, the late call of Magpies before winters semi-silence and the sounds of what appeared to be squabbling Raven on the roof.

Sighing, Beth stretched before rolling out of bed to wander to the window. The early morning sun was slowly dissolving the ground mist and frost that had come in late the night before. She stood watching the watery rays move slowly across the ground, before they hit the corrugated iron walls of the old groom's quarters above the stable and flashed off the side mirror of Sam's car.

Ah, she chuckled to herself; I thought that might be where they were heading. As if on cue, the window thrust noisily open and the tussled blond head of her brother immerged. He spotted her and waved, grinning broadly, obviously in fine good humour.

He mimed drinking from a cup and pointed down to the kitchen. She waved, nodding in agreement, pulling a fine wrap of silvery thread around her, which had an intricate pattern of skeletal leaves; it was a rare gift from the Fae after they had carried her in after the Rite. She could see it mirrored her own work; as light as it was it was warm and very soft, sometimes appearing alive, the leafy shapes moving and stirring, changing pattern.

Opening the window a little Bethan was surprised to see the large Raven Ruark, who followed Morgan everywhere, sitting on the ledge outside. Craning her neck, she leaned out and spotted Claire's car. Heavy dew droplets covered the windows but she could make out the large sleeping form of Morgan and wondered what he could be doing there and why he had not asked to come in.

Hurrying downstairs and out the back door, she tapped on the car window gently; Morgan stirred. He grinned somewhat sheepishly before opening the window.

'Morning Beth,' he said, 'I'm sorry too have lobbed up here unannounced.'

'How long have you been out here Mor and why aren't you back in Springsmeet with Cal?' replied Bethan.

'It's a long story,' he chuckled.

'Anyway, come in. I was about to put a pot of coffee on. Max is awake and he has a visitor,' she grinned, indicating Sam's car parked discreetly behind Max'.

Morgan smiled in response, 'That's great,' he said, 'Max needs a partner who can understand his mind …He …never mind, that's another story,' he trailed off.

'Come on in,' said Bethan, 'you must be frozen.' Morgan extricated himself from the car, groaning a little as he unfolded his length from the cramped space within and followed Bethan indoors.

Max appeared at the same moment, raising his eyebrows and smiling as he saw Beth in her nightwear and Morgan just about to sit at the kitchen table.

'Whoa,' said Morgan, 'I've been sleeping outside in the car; not what you're thinking!'

Max put up his hands in a mock warding gesture, 'Okay it's cool …would have been good to see though!'

'Max!' exclaimed Bethan as she came in from the pantry, 'it would be none of your business anyway.'

Morgan and Max exchanged a look and did what was the most sensible thing to do in the circumstances; shut up.

'What are you doing here Morgan?' said a broadly grinning Sam from the door.

'Morning Sam,' said Bethan giving her friend an affectionate hug and a smile.

'Yeah,' said Max, 'morning S'mantha,' hugging her too him possessively.

Morgan simply smiled.

Completely unembarrassed, Sam took mugs from the cupboard and put them on the table. Relaxed and familiar now with Bethan's kitchen, she fetched fresh goat's milk brought from the farm and sugar, for Max's sweet tooth.

'What brings you here this early in the morning Morgan?' she questioned in her direct way.

'Well,' said Morgan, 'Maeve threw another hissy-fit after you left and took off, leaving me stranded at Flora's. Cal had already left so Claire loaned me her car. I didn't feel like driving back to Springsmeet alone, so I wandered out here in the hopes that one of you would still be up and around but, you were all in bed,' he finished quirking an eyebrow at Max and Sam.

'I would have been up Mor,' said Bethan, 'I didn't go to bed 'til well after 11.00, I was in the studio. Did you think to look there for me?' she finished with a gentle smile.

'Actually no, you seemed so tired after Samhain, I didn't want to disturb,' Morgan replied.

'Oh well,' said Sam, 'I think we all need to keep a serious eye on Maeve, she's been behaving very oddly since the rite and I can't for the life of me work out what's going on. Any ideas anyone?' she finished.

'I distinctly heard a voice muttering something a couple of times yesterday,' said Bethan, 'The first time it sounded like you Sam and then the second time, like a petulant child. I think we need to talk to Tara or perhaps my father about this.'

'Do you think she could be possessed?' asked Max nervously.

'I've seen possession Max,' said Morgan, 'it's not feeling the same but she could have something attached to her energy field. What are your thoughts Bethy,' he said turning to her.

'Sybille taught us that possession is very rare and that it's usually auto-suggestion anyway. She said it's a little like curses, they only work if the person believes they do. That said however, Maeve had a raw deal though her childhood. Recently I thought she was making good inroads in coming to terms with what she can't change, only integrate, but it seems I was wrong. She's always been a dark horse and I don't think she's ever really allowed herself to open up fully to anyone except Sybille and now she's gone,' she broke off her voice catching slightly.

'So what's her history then?' queried Morgan.

'I don't really like to be the one to tell it second hand Mor,' answered Bethan, 'but…'

'But I can blondie,' interrupted Max, 'I don't have the same scruples you do,' he grinned. 'Maeve was raised by a woman with a very addictive personality Mor. She conceived Maeve by a man she never really knew, having turned to prostitution to pay for her substance abuse. Maeve was raised by the neighbours, or other 'ladies of the night,' in the 'Cross' in Sydney until she was able to heat up baked beans or make toast for herself. She ended up looking after her mother more than she was ever looked after herself, as any child should be,' he paused, disgust evident in his voice.

'So how did she end up in Melbourne?' Morgan asked.

'She ran I'd say,' said Sam sniffling.

'Yes she did,' said Max, reaching over to wipe the tears coursing down Sam's cheeks, she hadn't realised were flowing. 'She finished school and ran, literally, living on the little she'd saved from doing jobs around the place; fixing trinkets, cleaning for people and generally making herself useful in any way that would earn her a dollar, except the way of her mother that is.

She told me she'd found a stash of money her Mum had hidden with an ounce or two of cocaine and bit by bit she would take a few dollars here and there. Judy her mother had never even known it was gone; she was out of it most of the time. When she finally ran, she dobbed her mum in and the police put her into rehab but for some reason dropped the charges, perhaps because she was a user herself and, as she was little more than a skeleton from what Maeve told me, needed real help by then.

By the time we met Maeve,' continued Max, 'she'd worked her way through the last years of high school living where she could in cheap digs and then qualified for a scholarship after her talents at creative arts manifested. She was lucky enough to be encouraged and understood by her art teacher who saw her potential and put in a good word for her; her abilities did the rest,' he finished.

'When we met,' continued Bethan, 'she was a prickly, talented and impossible girl with a chip on her shoulder the size of a bus but her quirky humour and sheer enthusiasm for everything she did was irresistible. Flora and I had known each other longer but when Maeve turned up in answer to the ad for sharing our space, it was obvious not only did she really need a break but also that we would get on because we were all so different.

Then we met Sybille and we all blossomed. I thought Maeve had finally put her ghosts to rest. She plucked up the courage to let Judy know she was alive, but ever since Judy has hounded her for money and has tried every trick in the book to get her to move back to Sydney to look after her. She has a totally different idea about how Maeve owes her for giving her birth, when she could've had an abortion and how she'd looked after her when she was little, sacrificing her stage career…'

'…she was a lap dancer,' snorted Max

'…exactly but of course, she's delusional about the truth of her own behaviour, which is common in addicts apparently…'

'… or in denial!' exclaimed Sam

'…yes of course,' replied Bethan, 'but under that tough veneer Maeve has a heart of solid gold. Even now she says she feels there should be something she could be doing to help her mother heal,' she trailed off, her compassion responding to the helplessness and frustration she'd witnessed in her friend in the years they'd know each other.

'Shit,' said Morgan finally, 'I knew it was bad but…'

'Oh there's more,' said Max harshly, 'her mother tried to sell her into sexual slavery as soon as she reached puberty and it was only through sheer cunning and courage she survived, by making sure she was never around when her mother's 'friends' visited and that she never looked attractive to them, if she was. She'd pretend a constant cold and cough, even used flour to make her face look white and sick.'

'How do you know all this Max?' asked Morgan.

'Well, for some reason Maeve trusts me because my, 'serious nerdy look,' as she calls it, makes her feel safer. Our father has the same effect on her.'

'Yes I noticed he always comes into bat for her,' said Morgan, 'makes her feel protected, which is exactly what she was missing growing up I would imagine?' he said, before falling silently contemplative.

'There's so much more,' said Bethan, 'but the rest is for her to tell when she's ready.'

'Wow,' sighed Sam, 'I understand a lot more now, especially when she revealed to us she was still a vir...'

'SAM!' exclaimed Bethan, 'that was only between us.'

'Oh sorry Beth, my mouth's running away with me.'

Max and Morgan exchanged glances, they had the drift and were both astounded at the idea of a young woman of today being sexually inexperienced; their glances said 'later,' to continue that topic.

With a sigh of relief Bethan said, 'Well I guess it's time to start readying for work then. Breakfast everyone?' She filled the kettle to keep her nervous hands busy with the simple and familiar tasks.

'Sure,' said Morgan, 'thanks Beth, I'll help you.'

'I'll go shower if that's all right with you Bethy?' said Sam.

'Sure,' said Max, mimicking Morgan, 'I'll help you,' he grinned wickedly, following her.

Chapter 11
Earthly Rites

Life has it twists and turns on the wheel
Fate is not kind to those who cannot feel
When we ignore the truths of our soul
...we miss all the beauty ...we never become whole

Life must go on and so the friends met later at work that day. All except for Maeve, who was conspicuous by her absence, holing herself away in her studio with the excuse that she really needed to do something with the Lemurian shard that had fractured into several pieces.

Goggles on, her mane of red curls knotted up and thrust haphazardly under a cap, she worked on a piece of the shard for the end of a wand. It was surprising how laid back the customer who had brought the crystal to her had been. Insisting Maeve make one piece from it for them and the others, she could do with, as she will. There had been something a little odd about that person; now, nothing seemed to be working for her. Everything she tried just seemed to fall apart in her hands and she was becoming angrier than ever at the constant rumblings from the water tank, which at times, sounded like laughter.

It was as if she were no longer in charge of her carefully controlled emotions. She had long realised that her feelings for Mor were more than a passing attraction; there had been a few attractions before but none she had ever considered following through on. Now here he was obviously mutually attracted and all she could do was behave like a petulant teenager, she didn't even understand why.

As she worked, she became more charged up and her anger fuelled, she was ready to ignite. Turning off her soldering iron, she walked over to fetch a cool drink from the fridge. There came a rap on the door and once again, the water tank rumbled ominously, vibrating the whole floor with the quaking. 'Who is it?' she grumbled and then grudgingly before a reply, called out, 'come in!'

'It's me Maeve,' said Morgan, 'I brought you a mug of soup. It's getting cold again,' as he came in carefully carrying a plate of fresh bread and a steaming mug.

'You shouldn't have,' muttered Maeve ungraciously.

'But I did so get over it,' he replied grinning.

Maeve could only laugh, 'Thank you Morgan.' My pleasure, can't have you fading away can we?' he chuckled

'No chance,' she laughed turning to find him closer than she had realised, 'Oh, sorry,' she said as she bumped into him, causing him to spill some of the hot broth down his white shirtsleeve. 'Did it burn you?' she said with concern.

'It's okay, no damage done.'

'But your shirt,' she said, 'I can get that out quickly, while it's still wet; here,' she grabbed a clean towel.

Morgan simply took off his shirt and handed it to her and she thought her heart might just stop. She had seen and drawn male bodies many times in her art school days, but nothing had prepared her for the pure electricity that coursed through her at the sight of Morgan's well-made, naked torso as he handed her his shirt.

To cover her discomfort, she turned to the sink next to the water tank, to rinse out the sleeve of the beautiful Irish linen shirt, but before she could finish there came a belching sound from the tank, a geyser spurted into the air, once more shaking the stand. A gush of muddy green, stinking water spurted all over the clean sleeve and over Maeve's hands, spattering her own shirtfront. She screamed as the water touched her skin and she could see it blistering before her eyes.

'Maeve,' cried Morgan, 'your hands,' as he watched the blisters appearing. Lifting her off the floor, he carried her down to the bathroom on the next and did the only thing he could think to do. He shoved Maeve under the cold spray in the shower. She screamed at the cold, but quietened as the water soothed the skin of her hands and a few blisters that had erupted on her neck from the spray. She stank of rotten eggs. 'Pond weed,' she stammered, shivering now.

'Pardon' Morgan replied?'

'We both stink of it now.' Pond weed, stagnant water …Ugh!' she retched.

'Are you alright? Let me look at your hands Maeve,' turning off the taps he gently took her hands in his.' To his surprise, they were unblemished. 'What the …?' was all he could say.

'What,' said Maeve 'Is it bad?'

'Their gone, the blisters are gone,' he replied.

Maeve looked at her hands and went to the mirror to look at her neck. Blotches of red still covered her skin, but the blisters had vanished.

'What just happened then anyway?' said Maeve recovering herself.

'I don't have the least idea but I'm going to find out,' he said, handing Maeve a towel and her robe that hung behind the door. 'Dry off. I need to take a look at what just happened.'

Maeve reached into a draw and pulled out an old baggy T-shirt, ragged but clean. 'Here,' she said, 'put this on in case it happens again,' as an answering rumble came from the floor above.

Morgan took it and was out the door in a flash, donning it as he went, racing up the stairs two at a time, Maeve heard the door slam and the thundering rumble of the water tank ceased abruptly.

Drying off and changing into a T-shirt and jeans, she cautiously followed Morgan up the narrow spiral stairs to her studio …silence. She paused at the door listening …all was still so she walked in; and nothing could have prepared her for the sight of the small child sized being, baled up in the corner of the room by several large and extremely irate Ravens. There was no sign of Morgan and with some trepidation, Maeve realised that the largest, glossy blue-black bird was he.

Tara's white flash of feathering was unmistakable as she sat, side by side with Ruark and Morgan on the floor of Maeve's studio, speaking in the guttural Raven tongue of her kind, interspersed with the sibilant sounds of the Elven language Maeve had become accustomed to hearing recently. *'Lle au'. Mani naa lle umien alu Mirdhaucha? Onsint' amin. Mankoi naa lle sinome Peredhil?*

'You again, what are you doing here Water Merrow? Answer me …why are you here Halfling?'

The small entity, obviously not scared by any means, was smugly chewing on the sleeve button of what once must have been Morgan's beautiful shirt. The rest she had reduced to rags and tied in straggly ribbons in her dreadlocks. She spat the button onto the floor at Tara's feet and immediately the Ravens closed in. The strange creature merely grinned at Maeve revealing her sharp white teeth and disappeared into the water cauldron in one blurred movement; water cascaded over the gathered Raven and humans alike.

With a rustle of feathers and a muffled curse, Tara changed into her human form followed by Morgan a little more slowly, which gave Maeve the opportunity to witness the amazing process of shapeshifting. She saw his facial structure, bones and skin morphing from bird to human …his long limbs re-shaping and stretching into human length.

She thought to herself, 'but where do the feathers go?' somewhat inanely before the change was complete.

'Who …what is that thing?' said Maeve wide eyed. She's a wicked little child. Did you see what she did to our skin with her nasty spells? I thought, 'with harm to none,' was all of the law, but it would appear not to dark folk like her.'

'It was illusion Maeve,' said Morgan, 'Look in the mirror there's no sign that it really happened. Look at your hands, there's not a mark to be seen.'

He seemed irritated with her and she didn't understand why. What had she done and what about the beastly little creature that had ruined his shirt? Suddenly Maeve didn't feel too well, she felt tired and edgy. It was still only just lunchtime but she felt she needed to sleep.

Tara and the other Raven were observing her strangely; Morgan had withdrawn and was receiving strange images and messages from Tara and her Corvidae kin that he couldn't quite understand. Ruark was unusually raucous and appeared to be trying to communicate something to him in his head. Images of the little Merrow and of Maeve, superimposed on each other and of a shapechanger with one damaged wing, just as Ruark had been when he'd found her. The image seemed to be of long ago though, so he could make no sense of what she was trying to tell him but he knew that, somehow he was more than a little involved, then as now.

'You must practise the language Morgan,' said Tara, 'Ruark is trying to tell you of the sisterkin Cal unearthed on the Yorkshire Wolds. Perhaps you need to speak with him and to Claire about that day.'

'You were there too though Tara,' Morgan replied, 'why can't you tell me again what happened that day?'

'I can't solve all the riddles for you my friend,' Tara replied her usual cheeky humour returned, 'It's for you and your humankin to sort it all out after all.'

'What is exactly your role in all of this Tara?' interjected Maeve, 'You act as if you have all the answers but you don't appear to share much of it with us. You just smile enigmatically or make a joke of it all and frankly, I'm over it!' she finished before slamming out the room in a classic miff.

'Well that went well,' said Tara with another grin.'

'What are you doing?' said Morgan, 'She's hard enough to understand at the best of times but she appears to be in a state of intense emotional upheaval, so why do you seem to be going out of your way to stress her more?'

'I don't think anything I do would change the situation Maeve finds herself in Morgan, these events are based on another time and place. Her connection with the Merrow is a clear indication that somewhere she has not been completely honest in her dealings; the Merrow don't hang around humans for any good reason. Have you noticed the creature turns up when Maeve is already enraged and incites her to express it more than she ever did?

Somewhere Maeve has incurred a debt and I assure you even I am unaware of what that might be. Only The Morrigan or perhaps Queen Mabh can help with this one but it has to be Maeve herself who asks for that help. She's convinced that only she can do it for herself, which of course stems yet again from her present life history with her mother. She's going to have to come to terms with that or she'll never be able to move on with her life.'

'Well that's rather stating the obvious and as humans we seem to have the greatest difficulty in letting go of outworn ways,' Morgan spoke his thought aloud.

'…but what about you Morgan?' Tara countered, 'You've come to terms with much in your life and are made all the more whole by the adversity.'

'Well I've learned that it is a waste of both energy and effort to hang on to things of any nature,' he grinned at her; 'after all I've had the best teachers.'

Tara gave him a friendly punch on the arm and said, '…and that's the very reason that we can't let even Maeve hinder the journey to find Sybille and help Silver renew again on the Wheel of the Mother. This must be the primary goal and focus and no earthly sentiments or needs, may interfere with this,' she finished, eyebrow raised in question.

'Yes,' Morgan replied, 'of course you're right, but I still feel that Maeve is our unknown factor, particularly as she seems to be getting more highly strung as each day passes. I believe you're right and it is the influence of that little creature.'

'I agree and so we must keep a wary eye on both of them. We can't afford to let them hinder the search again,' finished Tara, then with a small frown, she turned back to the water tank from which strange rumblings were echoing.

'*Dina e'eller Mirdhaucha n'amin tult i' Alu'quesser yassen ron ehta a' lingwe lle n'e.*'

'Quiet in there Merrow or I'll send the Merfolk in to fish you out with their tridents!' she called and all was suddenly still.

'Right then,' she said, 'crisis passed. I'll go see what's happening in the shop and if there are any clients around for me,' then in a louder tone called out, 'we'll deal with you later Mirdhaucha,' and so saying she was gone.

Morgan took a moment to thank the still gathered Ravenkin, before he went to find Bethan to finish a song they were writing together.

Chapter 12
Sybille's Book of Shadows
Aynia/Aine

Watery depths of oceans and lake

...calling your innermost soul to awake

Float in her darkness both salty and sweet

...ride on her waves to the shores of deep sleep

Life is her gift, through the blood in your veins

...the lymph that flows gently as it pools and drains

...through every cell and under your skin

Swim in her depth s...find your tail, grow a fin

...in her dark pools seek; find your watery kin...

Aynia, known as both a Fae Queen and an ancient Celtic Goddess, is Lunar in nature. Her counterpart in the myth is Aine, who it is told, walked both the solar and the lunar paths, therefore it is possible that Aine was the solar and Aynia the lunar, aspect of one Deity.

Aynia, sometimes known as the Spirit of the Moon Herself, of death, of the ocean tides and as the keeper of treasures, such as precious stones and crystals. She may bestow psychic gifts and be called upon in fertility rituals, due to the lunar and tidal aspects of her nature.

Aynia is the master teacher of the fairy doctors, so one of her students could well have been Airmhid. The study of herbalism falls under her guidance and, in some stories, she was against the letting of blood through surgery, teaching only the art of healing herbs as the cure for all ills.

Her domain is the sea, where she is said to lure those who break the sanctity of 'harm ye none,' alternatively sending them 'moon mad,' through her connection to the lunar cycles, that rule our sanity. Beware the taking of small stones and other items from the coastal beaches, as She may ask for a sacrifice in return.

The other side to her patronage is for artists, poets, authors and playwrights as she stirs the creative brain to express itself.

Anything to do with the sea or moon, silver jewellery and moonstones are offered to her; bottles of moon infused water and plants such as Moonwort and Starflowers, may also be appropriate for this temperamental Fae Deity.

Chapter 13
Samhain Eve ...now and then

Daylight is fading ...winter draws in
Cold winds are blowing ...ice on your skin.
Slowly as leaves fell ...golden light fades
Dreams of snow falling ...in quiet loamy glades
...weaving the magic in silent moonlight
Softly He comes in the frost of dawn's light
...a blanket of cover ...as sparks on the earth
Listen carefully you'll hear Him
...with His deep-bellied mirth

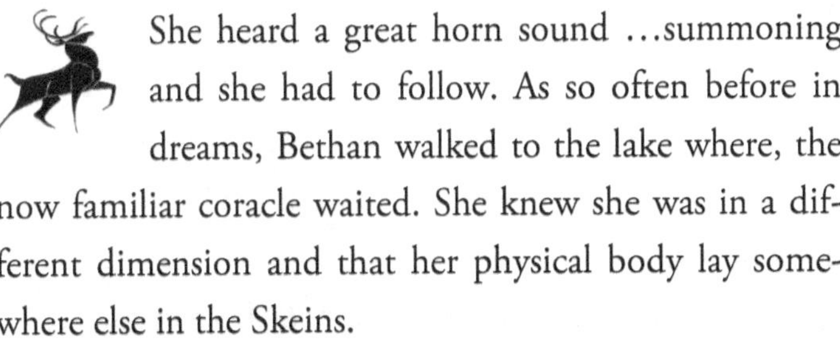

She heard a great horn sound ...summoning and she had to follow. As so often before in dreams, Bethan walked to the lake where, the now familiar coracle waited. She knew she was in a different dimension and that her physical body lay somewhere else in the Skeins.

Mists swirled around her but everything was sharper somehow, the very mist itself held sounds; music filled her. For a moment, she saw Aithlin standing ahead on the edge of the forest, smiling at her in encouragement. She could hear his song clearly.

She turned away from the lake and walked toward the forest; Aithlin disappeared again like smoke. Other beings walked the shore and the forest edge; faces from other realms, other lives.

Looking down at herself, once again she wore the blue robes of her dreaming, but the silver tracery around the edges appeared to have taken on a life of their own…she heard the words Oak, Ash and Thorn then…

'Re naa' sinome' 'She's here,' she heard the whispers of the trees in the winds that sighed through them…

'Re naa' sinome,' echoed the voices of her one-time sisters of the grove…

'Re naa' sinome,' the reply came from the small Fae folk riding their pretty steeds, their hounds baying at foot…

'Uma, re naa' sinome' 'Yes, she's here;' the voice came from the forest as the Greenlord stepped from beneath the canopy, huge wolfhounds milling around, great horns spread wide from his brow, The Lady at his side.

She realised she was no longer Bethan, but Leah and it was as if their two personalities had merged into one to share each other's memories, joy and pain alike. She felt relief at this, for she was more herself than ever before; memories flooded her mind as she remembered her Littleshape life as Leah, Priestess of the Isle of Seers.

More than that as she watched, so too was she the Greenlady …morphing in and out between physical and etheric forms …if only she could wake up …somewhere an agreement had been made, but she could not remember what that agreement had been.

Images passed before her within the tangled threads and she saw her friend Sybille curled in the hollow of a vast tree. She was as translucent as the ice that frost forms on windows, but appeared to be sleeping peacefully.

She wanted to run to her, but something prevented her, tangling the skirt of her robes to trip her. Looking down she saw a myriad of small dark Makers slashing at her feet with their sharp spikes, casting black sticky webbing over the hem of her robe, their evil smelling blight corrupting everything.

She screamed out for Hercurin but he was gone and she was simply just Leah again, standing at the entrance of a vast cave in the forest beneath a huge spreading Oak. Duir she remembered its name …Duir and it was the tree of strength, courage and endurance.

Today was her final initiation on the Isle of Seers, her 29th birthday. Samhain and she was so scared. More than anything, she was fearful that she would fail and so, disappoint her teacher The Cybil …High Priestess of the Grove.

She heard a Bodhran thumping out a heartbeat rhythm and knew that soon she would have to enter the cave to renew in the world of man. Reborn as an initiated Priestess, she would answer only to The Cybil and to the Lord and Lady of the Grove. Placing her hand on the bark of the ancient Oak, she listened to what else it might have to tell her before she made that final journey from which many had not returned... *Inner strength and endurance must reign ...free from the fear of human pain. Centre yourself and in Duir born again ...and your heart shall renew in the blue-silver flame.*

Then from Nuin shall be fashioned a spear ...or feathered and fletched for a bow, but no fear. Not made to kill, but protect all that is dear Transformed by the Hunt at the turning year.

*A crown of Huath next must you wear ...tangling deep in your silvery hair. The thorns will not harm for ...she knows that you care. Be at peace, listen ...she will share ...*the words echoed through her head and vibrated her whole body ...'ta' lu'ume' 'it is time,' the voice heard again in her ear, so close she started looking round for the source of it. She saw a wraith like form floating upward and into the massive Oak. Why that looks like The Cybil she thought momentarily distracted, then she was alone, of mortal kind anyway ...the tree sprites gathered and the Bodhran started to pick up the rhythm again; with a deep breath she entered the cave of initiation, calmer now and without fear ...where Hercurin waited ...and the veil thinned...

Chapter 14
Sybille's Book of Shadows
Duir the Oak Tree

Inner strength and endurance must reign
Free from the fear of human pain
Centre yourself and in Duir born again
…and your heart will renew in the blue-silver flame

People who have the qualities of Duir, the Oak, are strong and reliable. They will have overcome much through pure endurance and have learned how to stand their ground with strength against all adversity.

The foundations of Oak people are deeply rooted in tradition. They will be strong even if frail in appearance, a force to be reckoned with when weaker folk are threatened, for they will provide shelter.

It is dangerous to misuse energies received from Duir but applied with honourable intentions. Their power is not for self-aggrandisement but is for the defence of others. The Celts associated Oak with the concepts of connection to power, be that between sovereignty, prosperity and land, or between the realms. The Druids gather in Oak groves for their seasonal rites.

The fruit of the Oak, the acorn has many applications such as a mash for livestock and even for a coffee-like brew as a hot beverage. Seers would chew on a green acorn before trancing to make prophecies.

Chapter 15
Nina Giraldi

Nina and Magdalena sat untangling skeins of coloured embroidery silks. In a moment of insight, Nina said. 'Do you dream Magdalena ...dreams where you are other people in other times? Since I was sick I have been having the strangest experiences and right now I,' ...she trailed off embarrassed at her need to share with someone what she had experienced recently.

Sensing the young woman's hesitation Magdalena paused in her work. Looking at Nina as if trying to gauge how much she should coax her to explain, she replied, 'Yes Signorina all the time. I dream of being a young woman from a future time, at least judging by the strange apparel. I am working in a wonderful place

…one I could only dream of, where I am growing herbs and vegetables in a huge garden and the nature spirits play with me all the while. There is a large Silver Cat too but I am sad for some reason; yes that's it, someone close to me is missing and I have to find her.'

'How very strange Magdalena,' said Nina wide eyed, 'What do you think La Stregga would say about our strange dreams do you think?

'I tell her everything Signorina,' said Magdalena, about to continue but Nina broke in …

'Magdalena, we are almost of an age, please call me Nina, when we are alone together at least,' she said, touching Magdalena's hand gently.

The response was immediate, 'I would be honoured Signo…Nina,' she, finished laughing. 'Please tell me more about your dreams Nina.'

'Well it's more than dreams,' she continued, 'there is a beautiful woman, Silver she calls herself and she comes to speak with me in my dreams and meditations …sometimes, even when I am just sitting quietly I can hear her in my head,' she giggled, 'I don't really know why I am even speaking of this. Do you think me quite mad Magdalena?'

Magdalena smiled gently, replying, 'Not at all but I am puzzled as to what initiated the discussion I must say. It's not unusual to dream of someone speaking with you in sleep but I sense something else triggered your thoughts Nina.' she paused her question unasked.

'Yes you are right of course Magdalena. I was looking at the coloured threads as we were sorting them and thought that they would easily represent the frail threads of our lives. Some are more brightly coloured than others are; some frayed on the ends, whilst some appear stronger even though they are of the same thickness as the others. I was thinking that, if we were to sew or even weave with them a tapestry, a pattern would form and perhaps we would get a glimpse from a different perspective of all our lives at one time from one moment...' she trailed off, unable to find adequate words to describe the complexity of her reasoning.

'Why Nina, that is most profound! What has happened to you since your illness? Do you want to start at the beginning and follow the train of thought back to where you first began to think in this way?

'It's a long story Magdalena but yes, I would like to try. Perhaps you may have different insights into what has happened to me...'

At that moment the Nonna stuck her head round the door and called out to Magdalena,

'Come on girl,' she addressed Magdalena, 'we have some special marketing to do for the Signorina. Her nightgowns are completely outgrown and her Papa has instructed me to buy her new ones. I need a younger eye with me however, as he said I was not to buy the ugly things I would usually choose, but to buy some beautiful silks for the little Signorina,' she stopped out of breath from her ramblings.

'Oh please Nonna,' said Nina,' I really want Magdalena to stay with me and finish what we have started. I'm sure otherwise I will put it aside and go back to my books, then it will never be done,' she finished, pouting a little to make her point; winking cheekily at Magdalena, as her Nonna turned away for a moment to inspect the pretty threads of silk.

'Very well Signorina I shall do it myself, but please do not blame me if the nightgowns and under-garments are outmoded!' she huffed.

'Oh dear Nonna,' said Nina,' no one but us sees me in them anyway,' she giggled, 'Even Papa is not privy to such a sight now, unless of course,' she paused, 'I were to take a lover,' which brought a chuckle from Magdale-na that was quickly stifled by a look from the Nonna. Nina noted however, that Magdalena actually blushed at the mention of her Papa. She looked at her quizzically but said nothing. Her Nonna left rapidly in a flurry of aprons and petticoats, wringing her hands at the men-tion of her little Signorina and a lover.

Oh, she thought quietly to herself, so my friend finds Papa worthy of a blushing thought no less! She hugged the thought to her as she silently contemplated the possibility, that within the next short year she might be gone and her Papa left alone. She could think of no one else she would rather see comfort him in his inevitable grief and, who knows …she let the thought go, storing it for a later moment alone.

The two young women collapsed in giggles on Nonna's rapid exit and this is how Eduard Giraldi found them as he passed the door, their dark heads close together over a shared joke and a tangle of brightly coloured silk threads. His heart gave an unaccustomed lurch as he found himself lost in the eyes of the beautiful Magdalena when she looked up from her work, sensing him there.

Just a few years older than his own daughter, he was horrified to think that he had such thoughts and feelings about one so young, but he knew it was reciprocated. There was already a feeling of having known her somewhere in time.

He was an open minded and openhearted man, well educated in the laws of nature and the new sciences combined. He had studied and debated ancient teachings with La Stregga and was receptive to the concept of lives continuing beyond what he saw and sensed in an existing period. He believed he truly knew this young woman and decided to go to see La Stregga, to find out more about his unresolved feelings.

Chapter 16

La Stregga

The witch wheel turns ever-round
Winds blow strong o'er sacred ground
...go with the tides, love abounds
Fight and life's fire is no longer found
From Wytchway Round

The Wytch scried in her clear quartz bowl filled with pure spring water ...drifting back across and through the ages, following lifetimes, together and apart. She was tired and felt as if just recently a piece of her had gone missing.

Thank the Goddess for Magdalena her student, for she would be the one to pick up the reigns should she falter and she would watch over the younger woman Nina Giraldi as she faced her greatest test yet.

La Stregga had made a deal with Eduard Giraldi, Nina's father and the result of that would be dire, of that, she had no doubt.

How had this all come to be she wondered? So much work had gone into her future selves being ready and then finally, with all the aspects merged into one consciousness, she would go home. She would no longer have to play the game of life from an unconscious perspective ...no she would see it all as one ...as of course one it is. All the threads would untangle to create the beautiful tapestry, clear and untarnished, that multiple lives in the Skeins of Tyme reveal. Like a web, sparkling with drops of dew, each life a droplet. A drop falling from the web causes a vibration, affecting every other droplet as it travels along the strands.

As she thought and scried, moving in and out of awareness between conscious and otherworldly deliberation, she was aware that something new was occurring. She could hear music, chiming, pulsing music that swelled to a crescendo of beautiful liquid notes. The room where she sat at her worktable started to vibrate, as did the floor beneath her feet.

If she shifted her eyes from the bowl it stopped, when she looked down into the water again, it restarted.

She had difficulty remaining focussed in spite of all her years of experience, the movement making her queasy and small beads of sweat, pearled on her brow and upper lip. She swallowed hard, licking her lips, gripping the table edge with both hands.

Her eyes widened as the true sight came upon her and the Lady stepped from the shimmering mists at the edge of her vision, looking at La Stregga with an unreadable visage. In her head, she heard the words…

'Through meddlesome ways so much is bound, a young ones life is turned around …and when the hunt rides out with the hounds, once more the mists will this child surround.

*No mortal's see the hidden ways yet meddle they
have since the dawn of day. Each one from the Crooked
Path will stray and so must return again into the fray.'*

La Stregga knew her patron the Lady Aradia was
reprimanding her. She felt the guilt she had laid on herself move like bile into her mouth. Fat tears rolled down
her face and her hands, gripping the table's edge, went
into spasm.

Even as she had worked with Eduard Giraldi, she
had known that there would be a price to pay for their
working and yet, as she raised her eyes from the bowl
and met those of Aradia, she knew that something else
was afoot as she heard her voice again…

'You have let your heart overrule your head but
that may well be the saving grace for the young girl Nina
and for yourself …what it means in actuality in your
world view, is that something started long ago will take
many more turns of the wheel to play itself out. Remember this before you play with power …time is an
illusion and all Littleshapes and Trueshapes alike answer
eventually only to themselves, for you are all one in each
other and in me and all return to me at the end of days.'

A small, strange being entered the room unannounced as La Stregga was sleeping the sleep that always
came upon her after a true sight. It took a large shard of
crystal the size of a small slender dagger, choosing with
care before leaving as quickly as she had manifested,
through the well in the courtyard.

La Stregga woke hours later her head, laid on her arms on the table in front of her, pulsed with pain, her huge ancient scrying bowl, passed down through the ages had shattered into a million fragments.

La Stregga had the ability to help the bowl re-model itself as it had done many times over the centuries but this time, no matter what she did, there appeared to be a large piece missing.

'Mother, what will I do?' she exclaimed while crawling round on her hands and knees looking for the missing fragment …to no avail.

This was how Eduard found her after knocking repeatedly on her door. Finding the courtyard gate open at the rear of her cottage, he went through to her workroom unannounced.

La Stregga was on her knees in tears, her beautiful, ancient bowl, shattered in many pieces.

'Lady,' he said, 'it can be mended surely; you have told me that it has been broken before.' He gently helped La Stregga to her feet and courteously led her to a chair.

'Ah Signor Giraldi there is a shard missing and I cannot find it. How can such a piece have disappeared?'

'Here let me look,' Eduard soothed, 'I'll search under the table and the carpet too.'

'Thank you Signor, perhaps a second pair of eyes will see what these old ones cannot, but I have been looking this hour past.'

Eduard, without a thought for his costly clothes, crawled around the floor anyway, in the hope that the piece may have broken into smaller fragments and hidden in the carpet folds or the hanging drape of the tablecloth La Stregga used for her readings but nothing, not a splinter.

'I came to ask you about Magdalena and if there was a distant connection you could sense between us, but I can see this is not the time,' said Eduard, after La Stregga had settled herself a little. He poured them both a small glass of the sweet amber liqueur she kept for her clients and they sat in silence while she recovered.

'Magdalena is the best apprentice I have ever had Signor and will take my place as La Stregga when the time comes, therefore she may not marry you understand?'

'Ah yes, traditionally La Stregga remains single but that is not something I have found is written anywhere and of course I am sure most Stregga will have their share of lovers?'

La Stregga smiled at him, 'So your heart is taken again Signor Giraldi? She is very young yet; only four years your daughter's senior and yet very mature for her age of course.'

'Yes Lady, she has taken my heart in deed. I dream of other times when we didn't make it together, as a couple I mean and so I fear that this may be my only chance and I am too old to wait too much longer.'

'You are still a young man in truth Signor, 42 is nothing. Young indeed, especially when you reach my age,' she chuckled. I am sure Magdalena would be delighted to know your heart, I am aware of her feelings for you.'

With La Stregga now more herself, Eduard left with a gladdened and relieved mind. He decided he had nothing to lose in asking the lovely Magdalena to dine with him; Nina could be their chaperone he laughed to himself. He didn't know what his peers would think but then, they thought him somewhat strange anyway. These thoughts filled him as he walked the familiar streets of his beautiful city. City of lovers, he said to himself with a smile.

Chapter 17
Sybille's Book of Shadows
Nuin the Ash Tree 

Then from the Nuin shall be fashioned a spear
…or feathered and fletched for a bow, but no fear
…it's not made to kill, but to protect all that's dear
…transformed by the hunt at the turn of the year

Part of the Fae triad of Oak, Ash and Thorn. The Norsemen knows Nuin as the Tree of Yggdrasil, the Tree of Transformation through action.

Ash is utilised for musical instrument making, spears and bows. The Bard of the Druids can also be the warrior poet, as handy with the staff as the stang, the Silver Branch of ritual. Proficient in poetry and music, as much as with bow and spear, for these are the gifts attributed to Nuin. Transformation, through music or battle craft as each art must have the dedication to claim something of value …be that a song, or an inner battle won, to transform the self as spiritual warrior who can also tell the tale as the Bard.

One of the anomalies of the Ash Tree is that it switches between bearing all female and all male flowers, rarely having both at the same time. The seed pods produced are as the little winged beings that inhabit them; simply carry them in a pocket, as a powerful protection against enchantments.

Ash does not allow a person to avoid the things they need to face, rather pushes them to face adversity head on.

Chapter 18
Alma.

Side by side in the other realms
…are the Fae who left long ago
Side by side in the Otherworlds are the elves
…the nymphs and the gnomes
So if our planet was sick, was gone
…where will we be when that's done?
Floating on ether, flying the wind
…and what would happen to all our kin?
So when you imagine you go somewhere else
…where is that place …alone …by yourself?
…and do you consider the planet Herself?
So where will you be when that's done?

Sheer terror ripped Alma from sleep in her little cot in the goat byre. She knew that something big was about to happen but she had no idea what. She had always been able to sense changes afoot in the weather, when a kid goat would birth, or when the fish would run and knew she had interesting gifts that the rest of her tribe apparently had not. This was something else; her world was about to change irrevocably.

She was a small thing, even for her few years and told often enough plain, not worthy of much attention. She felt unconcerned about the latter, because it meant people left her alone for much of the time; told too that she would probably never wed; her looks and temperament were not as other girls.

Born into a family of eight, she was the runt of the litter and the only girl. Her family would joke that she was a throwback for she looked nothing like her siblings or her parents, being red haired and fair skinned, to her family's blond, almost Saxon looks.

Only just seven summers old and wise beyond her years; a look from her would have the villagers making the horned sign of warding behind their backs. They never engaged directly because often when they did, it would cause the catch to be lost, or the nets to tangle for no reason.

The last straw recently, was when one of the goats went dry, losing a kid in the process, there being no milk for it; the other goats would not suckle it. It was not hard to derive a conclusion even for these simple folk, when it was known that the child Alma had been lurking around and often slept in the goat byre. She had, had words with the goatherd that same day, when he had caught her stealing a cup of the precious milk that supplemented their fish, curd and bitter wild greens.

Superstition rife among them, they could not imagine that she had no reason for such an act of harm, even if she had been aware of the power she exuded. She loved the goats and spent many of her nights in their company; they responded to her without fear. Animals were safe from her, for she loved all creatures.

The tribe lived on the edge of a tidal river, upstream from an estuary. Sometimes the waters would race in across the salty marshes and cover the land, but the stone crofts withstood the tides and dried out quickly enough when they receded. They never thought of moving to higher ground merely took to their fishing craft. They simply lived with the hardships that the inclement conditions brought them, seeing themselves as simply a part of the elements. Today, something was majorly different and for the first time in her short life, Alma felt fear.

At the last Dark Moon, her parents had found her in her shift, standing on the edge of the river arms raised to a moon that was not visible. Chanting in a strange tongue, the river waters were responding, leaping bright droplets high into the air that formed shapes of strange beings with wild tangled hair, much as their daughter's. Alma had no recollection of how she had come to be there.

The couple were simple folk who lived their lives in the Goddess and God and this was more than they could comprehend. They sought guidance from the village Cunning Man who suggested that she be fostered somewhere, with those who would better understand Alma and her strange gifts. He had often observed her speaking with invisible beings that she called her friends; she wondered why not everyone else could see them. He was not without the sight himself given his gifts, but this was something beyond his ken.

Acting as a go between, the Cunning Man Bran sat to scry, to call on the Seers for their guidance and was surprised at the speed at which they responded.

Only a matter of hours later he received a small parchment, carried to him by the bird of his naming, Bran; Raven. He wondered how the bird had flown so far, so fast. Written in the sigels of the Seers, he translated that they would offer the child's family a purse of coins. They would collect her at the Seers Lake's edge, on the next full moon.
Rapidly calculating, Bran realised they must leave within the next day to reach the Lake by the allotted time and wished for the speed of the Raven. He hastened to the girl Alma's family to tell them his news.

They were surprised at the outcome of their query but were relieved, ashamed as they were by that feeling. They would no longer have to withstand the worst of the villager's superstitions about Alma and would be free to live a normal life, enriched now by the purse of coins the Priestesses would pay for her.

Therefore it was the very next morning at dawn, little Alma began a new journey that would take her to unforeseen places and experiences. Her father bundled up her few small belongings and sat her on a small, fat pony.

Bran arrived to guide the way, the strangely un-emotional child left for the long ride across country without a backward glance, or goodbye. Alma remained stoic on the long ride, only brief stops taken, to water the horses and hastily swallow a bite or two of journey bread.

Almost a full Moon cycle had passed when Bran, Alma and her father reached the edge of the vast lake that disappeared into moonlit mists as they approached. Dawn broke as they sat silently waiting and heard the sounds of a craft approaching from across the waters.

Alma sat her fat mount, eyes popping and mouth agape, as she watched a beautiful apparition appear from the mists, standing straight and tall in a small craft, the like of which she had never seen before. Her father too was astonished at the delicacy and buoyancy of the small vessel, the fishing boats they used appeared heavy and cumbersome in comparison.

Behind his back, he made a warding-sign, as the beautiful creature approached; he was sure she must be one of the shining ones, the Fae who must not be angered. He was not disappointed to see the haughty expression of contempt flit across the young woman's face, as if reading his thoughts.

Pulling herself to full height, she stepped from the coracle, deftly throwing the looped rope to the waiting Bran who had dismounted at her approach, he bowed in deference. Their eyes met briefly and a spark flashed between them in recognition of a previous meeting that was not of this time.

Turning away from the split second encounter before it threw her off guard, with stately measured stride she approached, tossing a purse of chinking coins to the man who, hastily dismounting, only just managed to catch his prize for the betrayal of his daughter.

For a moment, Alma's father could have sworn the coins glinted red in the bag and the words 'blood money.' echoed in his head. He started around to meet the cold, unforgiving eyes of his daughter.

The young priestess rubbed the nose of the little pony and whispered a greeting to Alma in a strange tongue; the child realised she actually, magickally understood,

'Cormamin lindua ele lle, Amin na'a Leah,' 'My heart sings to see you,' said the beautiful woman, 'My name is Leah. Come little one, we must be away before the sun hits the waters,' and without further acknowledgment to the man, the child's father she presumed, helped the little girl from her pony, slipping the fat creature a small wizened apple as a reward for its courage in making such a long journey.

The pony, never of a particularly docile disposition, took it gently and gratefully between her worn, discoloured teeth, with a small whinny of pleasure. Leah patted the poor old thing again before, with a glance at Alma's scant possessions said, 'If there are things in there you value child, take them now the rest is not needed, for the Isle will clothe you, as She does all Her peoples.'

Without hesitation Alma took a small pouch from her bundle that held a few little treasures from the place that had been home; some shells and little bits of driftwood, a few shiny pebbles, one black with a strange Sigel on it and the spiny fin of a strange fish. The rest she discarded without a backward glance at them, or to the man who was her father.

Straightening her back in unconscious imitation of Leah, Alma courageously placed her little hand in that of the pretty lady before stepping with her into the coracle. Leah wrapped her in an oiled skin to ward off the cold and damp, settling her into the prow.

Bran stepped forward to pass Leah the rope, their hands touched for a second and again an electrical recognition arced between them, not easy to ignore.

The interaction went unnoticed by Alma's father who, with a tear in his eye, realised that he would never see his daughter again. He felt another moment of shame, as he hefted the weight of the coins in the pouch the Priestess had tossed him so disdainfully. It was as if it was a mere trifle, rather than enough to feed and clothe his family for many turns on the wheel.

His greed for the coin outweighed his emotions quickly, when he thought of returning to a peaceful home. No more would he have to abide his wife's constant screaming at the child, to be better, quicker, smarter and prettier. With a last look at his daughter he turned, silently wishing her luck on her journey, before pulling the reluctant pony with him to start the journey home with as much speed as he could muster.

Bran remained, staring after the departing coracle and its precious cargo long after it had disappeared into the Mysts of Tyme.

'Later,' he heard the words drift to him on the breeze, as an Otter raised her head from the water to observe him closely, with uncannily human eyes.

Leah stood in the prow of the boat while Alma curled, a little overwhelmed, wrapped in the oilskin. She could hear Leah speaking but she couldn't see to whom or what. Every now and again water splashed over the side of the boat as if something leapt out of the water.

Oonagh the Otter was agitated. She was attempting to communicate with Leah about her strange cargo. She sensed deep within that this was no ordinary child, but how could she explain this in the limited human language or even the Fae tongue. She could only swim up and down trying to convey to her friend the danger she could see approaching.

As Leah neared the shore, Oonagh could see The Cybil standing, waiting for the cargo she was bringing and wondered, in her Otter way what was so important about this strange child. She lifted herself out of the water onto the edge of the little craft to meet the huge eyes of the child called Alma who watched, eyes widening even more, as she saw her visitor was an Otter. She smiled in delight, reaching out her hand but it didn't allay Oonagh's fear. She turned, diving back into the water and disappearing from view, rapidly swum back across the waters.

She didn't understand what drove her but she knew she must reach the Raven-man, who had been standing on the far shore. Perhaps with his shapeshifting abilities, he may understand her tongue.

Bran stood on the edge of the lake. He knew he should follow Alma's father to make sure he returned safely to the village, but he needed a few moments to understand further the connection he had felt with the Priestess Leah.

He pulled a flask from his pack, filling it from the crystal-clear lake and drinking thirstily, before filling it again for the journey home. As he did, the whiskery face appeared again from the water's depths, watching him with the same curiosity he was feeling.

He heard his horse stir restlessly as a large Raven landed within a few strides of her. Fluttering and bobbing in a curious way it hopped toward Bran, making eye contact without fear.

Well thought Bran, an Otter, a Raven, Flidais and The Morrigan's creatures, together in one place; how strange. He squatted on the edge of the lake so that he could see the creatures as they both came closer to him; the Otter into the shallow water almost at his feet and the Raven to a rotting tree stump on the edge, where she proceeded to wipe her beak vigorously. Bran didn't want to know why, knowing the eating habits of the Corvidae kin.

She hopped closer, blue-black feathers glossy in the rising sun, her eyes intelligent and seeking. He almost backed away but held himself in check, not wishing to appear either fearful or disrespectful in case the Lady herself had awareness here. The Otter came nearer, her eyes on the Raven suspiciously.

Bran took a deep breath, preparing to still his mind to be receptive but to his horror, the large Raven appeared to morph and change in front of him. Feathers turned to spider-web fine cloth, wings and legs to human limbs and the sharp, hook-beaked head, to a fine-featured female creature with dusky skin. His shock at this had him flat on his back as he toppled off balance, causing the strange creature to laugh outrageously at him. She extended a small hand toward him to help him back up. He could only stare in astonishment, while Oonagh the Otter looked on.

She spoke in a strange sibilant tongue that the Otter appeared to understand, coming closer still, until she was staring into his face. He heard her inside his head, speaking in the same strange tongue as the Raven-girl began to speak. He realised she was translating, so that he could understand what the Otter had to share.

He could only listen open-mouthed, as he heard of the Otter's fears for the Priestess Leah, the Seer's Isle and for the unknown future lives of which he would be a part. He would play a role he was told. He would learn the music of his kind and remember it forever. He would become a warrior Bard and a healer with his voice.

He could find no words to reply to this and felt humble and small when he thought of what this would entail.

He wanted to ask some questions of the Raven-girl but couldn't find the words to ask. Without the need of speech she heard and answered him, 'Rowan is my name,' she said aloud, 'and you'll remember me one day, but for now you must journey to find your teacher, to learn the shapechanger's way.

'Shapechanger, me?' he said. 'That's impossible! How could I learn that and who can teach me.'

'Well I can help,' she said, 'but your teacher will soon appear. In fact I think She's here already,' turning, she indicated to the copse of trees a little way away. A dark haired woman, pale skinned and slender stood in their shadow; a flock of Raven silently accompanied Her.

Fear stroked icy fingers up his spine and through the hair on the nape of his neck at Her approach. Her voice husky and sweet, however, soothed his nerves as he thought he would lose his bowels or his breakfast, whichever came first. She looked him directly in the eyes and without a word he heard, 'Ah there you are Bran,' before she turned and simply disappeared again.

A noise close by had his horse nearly bolting, but the Raven-girl Rowan, had the presence of mind to grab the leading rope, the Otter slipped smoothly underwater like silk over skin.

'*Go!*' she exclaimed to Bran, '*quickly flee!*' as she thrust the reign into his hand and almost lifted him onto his horse, with the strength of one many times her diminutive size, slapping the now terrified horses' rump.

'Why? What's happening,' he cried in alarm, as his horse bolted, he clung to her mane.

'*Flee!*' he heard again and then piercing screams. Looking over his shoulder, battling to pull his horse around, he saw Rowan fall, shapechanging as she fell her arm, now wing, pierced by a slender arrow; from the copse stepped tall stately beings, dark haired and wild, blue woad spirals painted on their skin. One lowered her bow, meeting Bran's eyes with a sneer as his horse bolted for home.

Chapter 19
Sybille's Book of Shadows

The Morrigan

Depths of deep blue and inky black feathers
...so much knowledge hidden within
Out in the rain and content in all weathers
...she will fly far to be with her kin
When you she chooses,
...you will know from the start
...as the bird of the Lady
...arrows straight at your heart

The Morrigan, sometimes known as the Phantom Queen and even the Queen of Death, is the ancient Celtic Queen of birth and death, fertility and destruction and is ironically, associated with well-being and sovereignty, of tribe and individual.

Historically known as a battle Goddess, she may even be the instigator of war but is also the one to call on for advice on strategy. She is the one who determines the outcome of all battles, bestowing victory on whichever warrior or army she most favours, but those favours are never, taken for granted, for her mind can change abruptly and radically.

Her battle shrieks are legendary, as she drives warriors to the battle frenzy of the 'Berserker.'

As the Goddess of fertility, she is an eager instigator of ritual sex in fertility rites and the Great Rite, the
sacred rite of transformation.

Chapter 20

Earthly Rites

...morning

We are they ...the magick; the Fae
...we are the masters in the Skeins of Tyme
...we created the realms of this world
...but we are the ones who have lost the rhyme
When we awaken ...when we remember
...not all is lost if we were to awake
When we remember ...when we awaken
...we will recall it was all for Her sake...

After the incident with the small creature, Tara had called a Merrow, everyone seemed to revert to normal except for Maeve, who was having difficulty going back to her studio to work and so was wandering around the shop like a lost child.

'How odd,' said Sam to her, to break the unusual silence, 'that we go through all these strange events and then seem to just carry on as if nothing had happened? I'm not sure if that's healthy or not,' she questioned to Maeve.

'Well I'm not the one to ask at the moment Sam,' replied Maeve, 'I'm not coping very well with this morning and I think I am close to just moving out and starting again somewhere else.'

'But you can't Maeve! We were all shown, how tough the journey could be, we all have our parts to play and it's imperative we continue through to the end. We have to find Aunty Sybille.'

'Well that says it all!' exclaimed Maeve nastily; Sam saw a small shape manifest in her peripheral vision close to Maeve, 'It's always about you isn't it Sam, not really about Sybille at all,' Maeve continued.

'Maeve that's not you talking,' look to your left there's something there; I can hear it muttering to you, invading your energy and your psyche. You need to get help moving it on, whatever it is.'

'I am Mirdhaucha,' a voice spoke from the direction of the entity; its lips didn't move except to grin at Sam wickedly.

'What do you want with Maeve ...with us?' questioned Sam directly to the strange creature, whose outline was becoming more solid as it communicated. Sam felt the leaf sprites anxiously gathering at the window, causing the glass to rattle; she soothed them with her mind.

'What are you doing Sam?' said Maeve, 'don't interfere with what you don't understand.'

'...but that's just it Maeve, I don't believe you do either and you're certainly not open to listen to anything else but this creature who's invaded your consciousness somehow...'

Sam trailed off as she saw Maeve pull herself up to her full height and approach her; fists clenched, but before she could reach Sam to actually touch her, Tara and Ruark together with several others of their kin, appeared in a great flapping of wings and Morgan came crashing down the stairs, into the shop.

'*Enough,*' roared Tara, in a voice that brooked no argument. 'Maeve you need to come with us now, there's work for you to do to help yourself …and as for *you,*' she said, her voice dropping ominously, to the small Merrow, 'the Mother will take care of you soon enough, meanwhile stay away from these people or you'll have to answer to my kin and I.'

With that, the Ravenkin drew close around Maeve and before Sam could say a word, gathered her in and were gone; a lone feather circled down to land at her feet glinting silver on the end …

 'For your ink,' Tara's voice spoke through the ethers.

Sam picked it up and turned to Morgan who stood waiting quietly, his thoughts his own. 'Are you alright Morgan?' she said.

'Me?' he said distractedly, 'I should be asking you that question Sam. If Tara hadn't heard me call out, Maeve would have broken every law of the Wytchwise and injured you. She is totally out of control under the influence of this creature, but I think there is something else in her, other than her excuse of it being her past, her childhood. There's more and it's not from this time but from somewhere else on The Way.'

'I guess I have to agree with you Mor, after what I just felt; the malice coming from Maeve, transferred through that creature was a very tangible and frightening thing. Just recently, I'm less easily frightened after everything we've witnessed together …this though. Hmmm, I don't know what to think frankly, but something obviously needed to be done and it looks as if the Lady has taken it into Her own hands.'

'I'm just glad they got here in time Sam, you're a pivotal part of all of this; you and Bethy.' With that, he crossed the floor in a few long strides to gather her into a bear hug, which is where Annie Savage saw them as she passed through to the front desk. Instead of them drawing apart rapidly, as she expected they simply remained holding each other.

'Ahem,' coughed Annie feigning politeness, 'You're wanted on the phone Sam, it's one of your suppliers.'

'Oh thank you Annie,' said Sam, unperturbed at her entry, knowing full well what it must look like when she had been seen with Max so often recently. She gave Morgan a kiss on the cheek, before stepping unhurriedly out of his embrace and as she did Max, walked in the door.

Saying nothing, he simply looked at Morgan quizzically before following Sam to reception. Annie had stood watching the whole interaction wordlessly: saving it for later to consider whether it was worth telling her patron Lady Aelish about.

Chapter 21
Sybille's Book of Shadows
Aife

The witch wheel turns ever round
...the winds blow strong over sacred ground
Go with the tides and love abounds
...fight and life's fire is no longer found

 Aife, described as a sorceress, shaman and mistress of the martial arts, may be the sister to Scathach, the Celtic Warrior Maiden who trained male and female warrior alike in the tribes of ancient Celtia or possibly, her twin sister. She is a fierce protector of women. When called on, she will train them in the arts of self-defense. Sometimes associated with Aoife, patron of shapeshifters in bird form, hers being the Crane; the spelling of her name varies naturally, between the Welsh and the Irish aspects of this Deity. Known as a being who lives between the realms, due to her shapechanging nature, she has a foot in either world, or straddles the two perhaps, but never completely present in one alone.

Aife/Aoife is occasionally associated with the ocean, in one tale, cursed to spend three hundred years on one of Ireland's famous Lochs, Darravagh, three hundred flying over the Atlantic islands and three hundred flying the seas between Ireland and Scotland.

Chapter 22
Maeve's Journey Begins

Feel her cold breath as winter draws in
Icy winds blow ...the lake freezes thin
Layers of stories lost in the Mysts
...places of mystery ...of magickal gifts.
Standing stones rooted ...sentinels to loss
What words do they whisper?
What is hid 'neath their moss?

Maeve experienced the same, 'moving sideways' feeling she had felt when she had first become aware of the strange little entity that had begun to invade her dreams and her waking reality. It made her feel quite sick, but there was no ability to reason at the speed they were travelling. Tara's hand, talons perhaps, had grown and were digging into her skin, as too did those of the others as they carried her helpless, through the Skeins of Tyme.

Buffeted by winds, her senses assaulted by fragrances unknown and strange colours not seen in the realms of humans, making her think of candy floss as the smell of caramelized sugar could be smelt on the air.

The end of the journey heralded by a loud rushing in her ears, she felt a bone crushing sense of falling back into the earth realm's gravity.

It took Maeve a moment to realise that everything had fallen silent. Her face pressed into sweet smelling soil, damp and cold with early frosts; all of this registered in a few moments as she felt a weight suddenly pushing on her back. On attempting to move, the weight became a firm pressure holding her down, face still crushed against the earth.

'Let her up,' said a harsh voice in a remembered tongue.

The Gaelic, Maeve thought to herself in amazement. I can understand it, harsher than I've heard but recognisable.

With the pressure suddenly gone from her back, she felt herself hauled to her feet unceremoniously as if she weighed nothing, to find herself in a circle of moss covered, standing stones. The voice came again and on standing Maeve, tall herself, found she had to look up to meet the curious amber eyes of a tall red haired female.

Muscles rippling, the impressive woman stepped back and indicated to what or whoever was holding Maeve's arms, to let her go. Maeve turned slowly to find Tara and a few other of her bird-kin standing behind her, together with another half-naked female warrior, painted with blue spiral symbols as if for battle, that matched the engraved images on the monoliths around them.

Tara stepped forward and, ignoring Maeve, spoke quietly to the warrior, 'This is the one spoken of, of old the tempestuous, Maeve. Her patron is Lady Aife but she has recently disclosed that her affiliation through the Skeins has been Mabh all along. In this aspect here,' Tara gestured to Maeve, 'she was innocent of knowing, but now has been too easily led through the whisperings of Mabh's folk and would have attacked one of her sisters.'

'Aife eh?' chuckled the warrior, causing Tara to barely conceal a grin in reply, then continued, 'It is her inability to forgive or forget the early days of this aspect that has left her open to invasion, as has recently been demonstrated. She must remember her true self and her Trueshaper that she may grow. We had wished for her it would be other …however …So Mote it Be!'

'Ah, I see,' said the warrior woman, 'she will learn more than just to curb her temper here. She will re-learn and remember her warrior self, for the battle of the Spiritual Warrior is always with herself.'

Tara and the warrior bowed formally to each other and, before Maeve had a chance to say a word in her own defense, Tara was gone …words trailed behind her as she left…

'…Take heed, Maeve, this is no game, you will need all your strength for the days to come…'

Maeve stood still. She pulled herself up from her somewhat defeated stance, squaring her shoulders as if for a fight. Thinking with a quiet smirk to herself, that what Morgan had taught her about self-defense, might finally be of use.

As if reading her thoughts, the giant female stepped closer, looking deep into Maeve's eyes she said, 'Don't even think it child, for t'would be like a gnat taking on a wild boar in rut.'

Laughter followed as more and more warriors stepped from the trees, blue painted as if battle ready, accompanied by a man in homespun robe, a healer perhaps she thought; he seemed oddly familiar. He looked at her long and hard as he rode past to the long house of the males where he dismounted, casting one last disconcerting look in her direction before following the others inside with his pack.

Maeve slumped helplessly, the brief adrenal rush spent as they led her away. I've stepped into a movie she thought ironically, King Arthur with Keira Knightly surely.

Light was fading as the sun, set and Maeve, given a wooden bowl found it filled with some sort of game meat in a broth. She thought she would retch as globules of fat bubbled to the surface as her shaking hands took the bowl. 'I'm vegetarian,' she said but on seeing the blank faces said, 'I don't …I mean …I can't eat meat.'

'Then you will possibly starve youngling,' said the woman who had given it to her, 'we don't waste food so make up your mind or there are many who will make it up for you,' before walking away.

A child of about ten years, fine boned and wiry, sidled up to Maeve with a gamin, gapped tooth grin, calmly taking the bowl from her still shaking hands and woofing the food down in a moment, belching and giggling delightedly. The little girl delved into her own scant clothing, bringing out a handful of acorns and some shriveled, dried mushrooms that she handed to Maeve solemnly.

Maeve could only blink at the child's audacity and good humour, before recovering asked, 'Where am I?'

The child looked at her for a long moment, gauging the validity of the question before saying, 'Why this is the warrior camp of the Lady Scathach, although don't let Her hear you calling Her Lady,' she grinned, 'she has a quick aim,' then hearing her name called, turned and ran in the opposite direction, chuckling gleefully.

'Alma,' a woman's voice called again, 'where are you, you little tike ...*ALMA*! It's time for sleep.'

'Now where do I know that name from?' muttered Maeve to herself.

Chapter 23
Earthly Rites
…afternoon

'Maeve, where are you?' called Flora, knocking on Maeve's studio door. Hearing only silence, other than the usual faint rumbling from the water tank, she stuck her head round the door. Nothing, where could Maeve be she wondered.

Flora ran back downstairs and out to the back room. Maeve's Athame and Wands, displayed in glass cabinets sparkled; still no sign of her. Morgan stood in the middle of the space wearing an old T-shirt of Maeve's that had definitely seen better days, the look on his face that had her hurrying to him.

'You look as if you're in shock Mor, can I help?' Flora said with concern.

At that moment, Sam re-entered the room looking as pale and drawn as Morgan did.

'What the hell's going on?' said Flora becoming agitated. 'Have either of you seen Maeve?'

Morgan shook his head as if to clear it, 'she's gone Flora; Maeve's gone. The Shapechangers took her after she almost attacked Sam …if I ever get my hands on that creature I'll.'

'Whoa, wait up Morgan. You're not making any sense, who took Maeve, what creature? Calm down now it isn't like you to lose it …breath.'

Sam touched Morgan on the arm and said, 'Do you want me to explain this a bit more rationally Morgan?'

'Yeah,' he grunted the reply, 'I'm all out of words right now.'

'I think we need to tell everyone though, don't you?' said Sam to Morgan.

He grunted assent.

'Where are Claire, Bethan and the other blokes, Flora?' Sam queried.

'Can you see if you can find everyone then Sam? I need to take Morgan to the apothecary for some Rescue drops I think.'

'Okay, will do. How about we meet in the seminar room in fifteen?' Sam ran out, while Flora took the shell-shocked Morgan up to her rooms.

Passing through reception again, Annie quizzed Sam about what was going on and if it was anything she should be concerned about; this said in a sickly sweet voice to over compensate for the previously snippy tone she'd used when she'd called Sam to the phone. She was curious about what was happening and had witnessed Max leave, slamming the door behind him and scaring a customer who was just arriving in the process.

'Oh not now Annie, sorry,' said Sam as she flew through.

'Well!' Annie snorted; 'the rudeness she thought, 'What would her Aunt think!'

Sam walked to Bethan's space, hearing her music and the sweet voice that had become so much stronger in the last months…

Moon tides turning …fires burning, winds blow cold across the land; inner dreams, like visions glowing, bringing warmth to cold, cold hands. Winter's darkness now approaches, creeping closer on tiptoe. Go within to seek the silence …move in the cycles that ebb and flow.

Sam could feel the cold of winter in the words and the chill of post Samhain darkness in the tone.

She stood listening and watching Bethan, lost in her music, hair held back by the extraordinary snood Maeve had made for her. It looked as if it were alive, little currents of energy ran from stone to stone along each little filigree wire. The red stones seemed sudden to glow brighter and the lovely sounds came to a cacophonous halt as Bethan yelped, ripping the snood from her head as if bitten. Sam could see a miniature Merrow holding a small snippet of Bethan's hair, reflected in the stone and laughing uproariously.

Taken aback for a second, Sam then continued in to tell Beth about the meeting they needed to have. Bethan stood, hurriedly picking up the snood; she placed it in a box out of the way, handling it as if it were something poisonous.

'So Sam,' she said, 'what's going on?'

'Well, rather than repeating myself several times, I'd rather tell everyone together if that's alright Bethy.'

'Yes, sure,' she replied a small frown marking her brow, 'but it's about Maeve isn't it? I felt the Skeins of Tyme move today. Something shifted and Maeve was involved. It was something serious too.' Turning to Sam she exclaimed, 'No! Oh Sam did she hurt you?'

'Well she would have but she was interrupted by Tara and her gang, Morgan too. He seems to have a sixth sense for danger that man,' she laughed.

'What? Oh not you too Sam, I thought you and Max were an item. I mean I can see his charm, I'm not blind to it but...'she trailed off, 'now I sound like my Mum!' she laughed. 'I've seen Max so hurt though, so my instinct is to protect him ...but that's a story for another time, or rather he should be the one to tell it.'

'Don't worry Bethy; he did ...Lily wasn't it?'

'Yes, Morgan's sister actually.'

'I didn't know that,' said Sam, 'well that makes the whole thing even stranger then.' Chattering together, they headed for the seminar room, bumping into Flora and Claire on the way.

Cal was already there, sitting amongst a pile of books as he researched the shapechanger bones he had found on the Yorkshire Wolds. He knew he would probably never be able to publish them though, particularly with the knowledge he had that they were no myth.

Max was nowhere around. Sam and Morgan exchanged glances at that.

'I'll call him,' said Cal, 'I think he went for a walk earlier.'

'We'll give him a few minutes and then start, he'll have to catch up later,' said Sam quietly.

At that moment, there was a knock on the door and Max stuck his head in

'Were you guys looking for me?' he grinned at Sam sheepishly. 'Sorry' he mouthed to her.
They sat with cups of tea as Sam and Morgan filled them in on the day's events.

Tara returned the unconventional way tapping on the window; shifting shape as she flew in. They all pounced on her talking at once. 'Where is she ...where's Maeve ...where did you take her?' There were a million questions that Tara, frustratingly, would not give a complete answer. She held up her hands for quiet,

'I can't tell you where she is, just be assured that she's safe and will be trained in other ways that, would better suit her volatile disposition.'

'What about her work, her clients Tara?' asked Bethan '...and the Mirdhaucha. Where is it?'

'She will be working on the relevant pieces from where she is. I'll take them to her when I go back. Trust me it will all be taken care of,' Tara answered. 'As for the Merrow she will have followed Maeve in some shape or form to where she is. They are inseparable at this time with her aspect as Maeve and there are things to sort out between them, between this whole group in fact,' she paused looking at all of them, 'but right now and most importantly, there is the urgent need to consider the work that is still to be done to find Sybille.'

'Well I think I have,' said Bethan, causing an echoing silence as all eyes turned to her.

'Where Bethy?' said Tara urgently, 'here or in the otherworld?'

'In the 'Between' Tara, first as Sybille and then as I merged again with Leah, she appeared to me as The Cybil.

'When was this Bethy?' asked Sam.

'I actually did what you suggested Sam. I went to the time between disappearing in the circle and reappearing. There was more, much more. The Lord and Lady took me out of my body, I felt it distinctly like a tearing, ripping sensation and then I was walking alone in the Mysts.' She then continued to relate all that she could put into words of her initiation and all that had come before.

'Morgan,' she said turning to him, 'you were there, you were a Cunning Man named Bran, I'm sure of it.

'Bran the Raven, Priest of The Morrigan? Oh, I remember that aspect! Then and now it's haunted me. I'm sure there will be much more to follow Bethan as we move through the wheel together. I believe we were all somehow involved with everything that has happened to Sybille and to Maeve too in fact,' he said sadly, 'Nothing happens in isolation after all.'

'Now we have to find the links to each other said Sam. Perhaps our rhymes left by Sybille can help with that. Perhaps it's the very reason that you and Bethy connect through your music,' she finished.

'I'm convinced you're right Sam,' said Tara. 'Each and every one of you has a role to play in the outcome and in fact the beginning of the whole scenario. Lifetimes then and now …in truth it's all the same anyway,' she grinned and on a lighter note said, 'Morgan, your fiery red head is safe and will be changed, as you all will be by the unfolding of your journeys together and apart. Now I suggest you all take time individually for yourselves, or for pursuits that may take your busy minds away from everything but a little indulgence.' So saying, she shifted and, with a chuckle was gone.

Chapter 24
Flora and Cal

Moontides turn and sunlight fades
...shadows lengthen in dappled glades
Rain showers fall in bright cascades
...another season's done.
Fast falling dark in midnight blues
...forsaken all the coloured hues
Grasses now bedecked with dew
...another season's done.
Frost and ice the grasses covered
...all warmth gone...all brightness smothered
Misty mornings ...blackbird's warning
...another season's done...

After the meeting, Flora decided to finish herbal preparations for clients to collect. On finishing, she took them down to reception, their collecting point for all services.

The atmosphere of the day seemed suddenly gloomy and Flora felt the need to be out in the fresh air. Working in the garden always counterbalanced her stress and stressed she was, about Maeve's removal from the equation.

Annie was at the desk and as usual recently, could not meet Flora's eyes. Flora had carefully given Annie no reason to think she knew about her relationship with her father; Claire had wanted to keep it quiet in order to see how things unfolded.

As Flora was leaving, Cal came out of the reading room that Tara worked in. She had given him the space on the quieter days for his research and he would hole himself away for hours. Like Flora, he was restless and needed some physical activity to curb the agitation he was feeling at the news of Maeve's leaving.

'Hi Flora,' he said smiling, as if he hadn't just spent an hour or so in the meeting with her. She returned his smile with her beautiful sunny one,

'Hi Cal, what are you up to for the rest of the afternoon?'

'I was thinking of a walk actually, you?'

'I'm heading home to work in the garden, the last of the elderberries need harvesting before they ferment on the tree,' she laughed, 'although there's no funnier sight than tipsy Ravens, euphoric on the berries at this time of year though.'

'That I must see,' he chuckled.

'Why don't you come out and join me, there's a lot I need to catch up on, I'm way behind with harvesting. Mum …Claire, will be there later to help. She's out working on the old dairy. She'll be moving in their before too long, the way she's going at it.'

'Wow that's fast,' replied Cal, 'She never was a person to waste time once she made up her mind though.'

'Ha-ha, too right Cal. Okay, if you're coming I'll be ready in five; I'll even feed you if you're good.'

'Well that's an incentive if ever I heard one,' said Sam coming in at that moment but on seeing Cal's face fall she said, 'have a lovely evening, I'll be upstairs writing if you need me Flo.'

'Come out for breakfast tomorrow Sam, I meant to tell you earlier, everyone's coming out for a brainstorming and them a working bee in the garden for harvest. I love the weekdays we don't work and everyone else does,' she grinned.

'Done, I need some physical work. I love the training with Morgan but I need something else to balance the discipline.'

'Yeah, I must be using a totally different set of muscles to usual,' giggled Flora, 'in fact I think I'm growing muscles on my muscles.'

Bethan and Morgan came down the stairs together talking about their music, Bethan's beautiful hands, gracefully expressive as she spoke of her art. Morgan carried a basket of soft wraps and shawls Beth had finished that afternoon, ready for display to sell.

'I'm off Bethy,' said Flora, 'See you in the morning Mor.'

'I'll be upstairs,' said Sam, leaving rapidly, feeling Annie's eyes, on her retreating, figure.

'Night Sam,' called out Beth and Morgan together.

'Oh Sam,' said Bethan, 'Have you seen Max?'

'Yes,' she said a little sadly, 'he went home an hour ago.'

'If you need to talk Sam,' said Morgan, 'I'll be here for a while.'

'Thanks Mor but no thanks, I'm fine truly. I'll see you all tomorrow. Oh and do you need a lift in the morning?'

'No thanks Sam I'm heading out to Beth and Max's shortly,' he replied, to which Sam's smile was just a little bleak in response to his.

Flora and Cal drove in companionable silence to Covenstead. There never seemed to be awkwardness between them or a need for mindless chatter, no matter the dynamics of the rest of the group. They were aware that somewhere in time, they knew each other but it wasn't even relevant to find out when or how ...now was all they needed.

Flora parked the car and Cal followed her into the house. On each post by the garden gate, sitting as if they were statues, were the cats Teddy and Morgana. Usually shy with strangers, they had both taken to Cal probably due to his calm presence, Flora thought. Even the more temperamental of the two goats Dolly, seemed to like him, accepting snacks without nipping at his fingers. She had always known that if animals instinctively liked a human being, that person could be trusted. This was something that she needed to know, considering the attraction she felt for him on so many levels and after the last debacle with Dan.

Cal's voice brought her back to the moment, 'Are you alright Flo,' he said, 'you look a little sad.'

'Oh no, I'm fine Cal. I guess I vagued out for a moment. I was just thinking that it's unusual, particularly for Morgana, to be so friendly. It's nice to see though, I feel comfortable around you because of it.'

'Comfortable!' he exclaimed with a smile, 'that's not exactly a compliment to a man you know. We want to be seen as in intriguing, mysterious and of course drop dead sexy,' he quirked striking a pose. Flora laughed aloud. 'Oh no,' he chuckled, 'that's how women want to be seen,' he finished.

'You're mad Cal,' Flora chuckled delightedly, 'why don't you show the rest of the group this side of you? You have many hidden talents but you always seem to stay in the background. Don't get me wrong, I admire the fact that you don't push yourself forward all the time and that you think before you speak.'

'Well Flo, I'm actually quite shy in groups and have been all my life. I feel comfortable with you too. I feel I can just be myself. One of the things I particularly like about you is that you don't expect people to be anything but simply who they are, that's a great gift.'

He turned again from patting Teddy as she jumped down from the fence to wind in and out of their legs, reaching out he simply touched Flora's cheek, spontaneously.

'Don't change for anyone either Flo. If anyone ever needed you to be different they didn't really ever know you at all, did they?'

His intuitive words were a balsam to her and looking at him directly she said, 'Thank you Cal, that's possibly the nicest thing you could have said to me.'

Their energies attuned and peaceful, they went inside, Flora to change into some old jeans before going out the back to the shed for containers, cutters and gloves.

They worked their way around the ancient elder, systematically taking the ripe fruit but leaving a little on each branch for the wee folk. Flora had always known intuitively what to take and when, it appeared that Cal knew too. His love of nature evident as he occasionally paused to take in the scent of the musky-sweet berries and to whisper to the tree and her inhabitants.

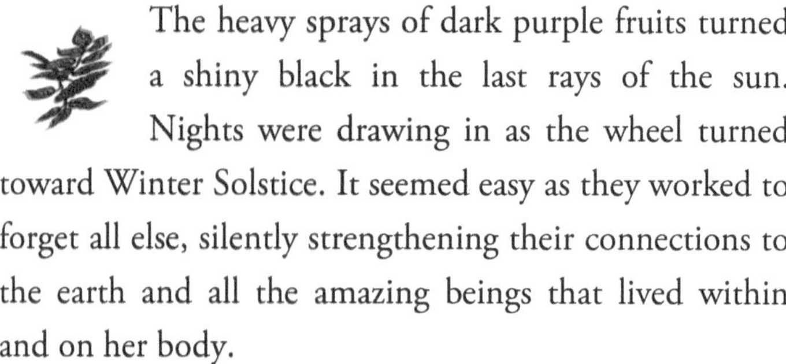 The heavy sprays of dark purple fruits turned a shiny black in the last rays of the sun.

Nights were drawing in as the wheel turned toward Winter Solstice. It seemed easy as they worked to forget all else, silently strengthening their connections to the earth and all the amazing beings that lived within and on her body.

When they had finished, taking only what they needed for a couple of batches of elderberry wine, tinctures and cough syrup they ceremoniously gathered anything that had fallen to the ground in their picking and placed it at the base of the tree.

They joined hands in honour of the act of harvest and gratitude for the yield. To Flora's surprise, Cal took one of her hands in his and placed the other on the trunk of the old tree.

'The elder is the tree of the Lady and must never be burned. When we need to prune or harvest flowers or berries we must announce our intention to the Spirit of Place,' he paused and with a deep breath chanted…

Yule is approaching, hear the horns sound; watch Jack Frost breathing ice on the ground, coating the world in a silence of white, sparkling like diamonds on bright moonlit nights.

Lady and Lord come a gathering in, so make cauldron-brewed wassail to share with your kin; made from ripe elder fruit, picked before frost so that their sweetness and light is not lost.

Honey and nut cakes for cold winter fare to give the wee birds to show them you care. Light up your candles of red, green and white they will act as a beacon of radiant light.

'Why that's beautiful Cal, where did you learn it?' Flora asked.

'It's one I picked up somewhere along the way in my travels,' he replied with a grin.

'We should use it at the Yule Rite,' said Flora.

'I agree,' said Claire as she came through the garden, 'it really is lovely Cal. Who would have thought my best intern would have such a repertoire of pagan verse,' she laughed. 'Hi love,' she greeted her daughter, 'Nice to see you here Cal. Are you staying for dinner? I already started a pasta sauce if that's okay with you Flo, I needed some kitchen therapy.'

'Oh go for your life Mum and yes Cal's staying. You're in for a treat Cal; Mum cooks a phenomenal pasta sauce.'

'Well in that case I'm doubly honoured to spend the evening with two beautiful women,' he said, 'and be fed too.

'...and get to do the dishes as an added bonus,' chuckled Claire as she walked back to the house.

'Ah yes,' was all Cal could say.

The two stood in a silent moment as the last rays of the sun hit the tops of the trees in the forest beyond. Birds called from the garden and the hens made gentle clucking sounds as they prepared to roost for the night.

A chill could be felt in the air and they could see the elementals dancing as the mists began to rise and float from the pond across the ground.

'Frost tonight then,' said Cal.

'Yes it'll be a ripper,' replied Flora, then, 'Look Cal, over there,' they held their breath as a huge Owl skimmed the treetops to land on the fence a stone's throw away. It had glossy brown and white feathers and huge orb eyes that held a look of knowing. A male that clicked its beak at them, nodding up and down as if in acknowledgement as the Lady Airmhid stepped from within the old elder.

She approached with a smile for Flora and a nod of the head to Cal. A cloud of nature spirits accompanied her, glowing like little flying gemstones.

'You must continue to work with the herbs,' she said, 'it is not enough that Samhain is behind you. Read my story and it will give you aid. Work with the Lady Arianwen and Morgan, Bard of the Lady Morrigan.' With another nod, Airmhid was gone.

'Was that Her?' said Cal astounded. 'I can't believe how relaxed you are around the fact that a known Goddess just drops by, as if it were the most natural thing in the world!' he exclaimed.

'Oh yes, that was Her,' smiled Flora, 'It's extraordinary, I was just thinking about her and the use for all of those herbs.'

'I can do the research part for you if you like Flo. I know a little of Her story.'

'That would really help Cal and then I can focus on the analysis results of those herbs that came back from the Uni. They still appear to be greening, so I need to know what part of the plant I can use and, where some are concerned, what their herbal uses are.'

'I know Sam's been helping you with that and Max is a great researcher, but he's busy with the next deadline for his book. I also think something's happened between him and Sam today too,' he trailed off.

'You're right Cal, there was an incident but I think it's one of those misunderstandings that can happen early on in relationships. Max has been very hurt and by Morgan's sister Lily too, so who knows what agendas are still there. They probably don't know themselves,' she paused, 'Anyway let's go in. I'm cold, the temperature must have dropped by ten degrees in the last half-hour and I'm getting hungry too.'

After carrying their harvest of elderberries back to the still room for the night Cal, for no known reason, simply reached out and took her hand in his with the excuse of warming hers and, walking back toward the house, just held on to it. Flora didn't complain one bit.

Over dinner, they spoke about the Owl they'd seen accompanying Airmhid, Claire was more than a little interested.

'That's actually very unusual,' said Claire, 'Owls are usually associated with Blodeuwedd and Arianrhod and a male bird you think Cal?'

'Certainly if size is anything to go by,' he replied, 'It's possibly the largest I've ever seen.'

'Hmm, I wonder,' said Claire mysteriously, 'I do know ...or rather did know, quite a few male shapeshifters, although the Owl is usually a familiar of Goddess energy as it is a nocturnal bird and symbolic of the Moon,' ...she trailed off, 'sorry guys you would know this,' she chuckled.

'Yes but you make a good point Claire,' said Cal thoughtfully, 'What God is associated with the Owl in Celtic Traditions I wonder. The Gods are mostly Sun Deities.'

'Perhaps a Deity that is a way shower through the' Between," said Flora.

'That's a thought,' replied Claire, 'I'll have to take a look on the ethers tonight I think.'

'Speaking of which I'd better be off Flo, if you're ready to run me home before it gets too late for you,' said Cal.

'Well I've got to duck into town for a couple of things,' said Claire, 'and I want to check on Sam, she seemed a little despondent this afternoon so I can take you Cal.'

'Done, I'll see you tomorrow then Flo,' said Cal.

'Goodnight Cal, I'll see you for breakfast here, everyone's coming so I'm sure Sam or Morgan can bring you in.'

'Actually Morgan has started sleeping out at Bethan's recently,' said Flora, 'They're really good for each other as they have their music in common. They've been working on the forthcoming Sabbats for the next few months so that they can get ahead a little. It'll be Yule before we know it and we have the whole Wheel to work with by the look of it.'

'What do you mean Flora?' said Cal.

'I'll speak with you about it tomorrow Cal. It's just something I've been mulling over where the herbs are concerned and their association with the lunar cycles.'

'Well all right then but that's making sense. Goodnight Flo,' he said, brushing a hand over her hair, snagging his ring in the tumbled curls.'

'Ouch, OW,' yelped Flora laughing, 'you can't take me with you, you know.'

'That's a pity,' he said, a serious expression on his face. I think I'd rather like to do that …here let me untangle that,' as he gently worked the ring from her hair and then smoothed it. Flora simply gawked at him, mouth open as he turned and strolled away, with a low chuckle at her reaction.

Claire giggled at her daughter's unusual loss for words.

Chapter 25
Callum Macintyre

Dare to wonder dare to dream
...when moonlight pools and things unseen
...move and fly on gossamer wing
...as hidden Fae their anthems sing,
...to Lord and Lady fair and bright
...gathering souls to aid their flight
...to places green where magicks reign
...where all may heal their fear and pain...
Ode to Airmhid ...by Callum Macintyre

 Claire dropped Cal off at the little rental house that he had been sharing with Morgan until recently, when he had defected to Bethan's cottage and had settled in. To give Morgan his due, he was still paying his half of the rent although Cal had said it really didn't matter.

'No a deals a deal,' he had said, his voice falling naturally into his Welsh-Cornish accent.

Now Cal had the space to his self, but would have liked the company tonight. He thought of Flora and the feel of her silky hair under his fingers; he hadn't really touched her like that before he realised.

Heading for the room he had set up as his research space, it looked as if a mini tornado had been through it as usual. For such an otherwise tidy man, his study notes never seemed to stay so and yet he always knew intuitively where everything was. Settling into the comfortable old leather chair he had found at a market, he pulled towards him a number of books, marked with sticky notes.

They all contained information about the various Celtic Deities and one in particular held some information about the Goddess Airmhid. No references to male association with Owls though. He paused, booting up his laptop before pulling a notepad towards him. Wow, he thought a real life Goddess had just casually dropped by. He wrote in his fine hand...

Airmhid

One of the Tuatha De Danaan, Airmhid is the sacred healer and herbalist of the Fae folk. She is the daughter of Dian Cecht the divine physician of the Tuatha De Danaan. They are the keepers of a magickal healing well, (surely that must be the Lady's Well in Glastonbury he made note), where wounded warriors are brought after a battle. When washed in the well, they immerge healed in mind, body, emotions and spirit.

Airmhid and her brother Miach healed the chief of the Tuatha De, Nuada of the Silverhand and so proved their miraculous abilities, causing their father Dian Cecht, to lose his superiority as the divine physician. He then challenged Miach to a competition, which resulted in Miach's death.

Three hundred and sixty five healing plants grew from Miach's grave and so Airmhid picked and dried them, pinning them on her cloak and apron so that they would always be nearby to heal all.

Dian Cecht snatched the cloak from Airmhid and some of the herbs were scattered. It is believed that, had this not occurred, we would have the knowledge of every herb that could heal all illness and disease.

Now the plants that are missing are part of the study of remedies that are arcane, secret knowledge that only Airmhid knows. The patron Lady of herbalists and healers, she is petitioned as a healer for people who have illnesses where there are no known cures.

Healers call on her in healing Magicks, learning herbalism and about family loyalties. Together with her brother Miach, she fashioned the Silver hand of Nuada when he lost it in battle. No damaged leader could rule and so the healing of Nuada was an important event in the history of the Tuatha De. She is, because of the hand, a patron of craftspeople too. The symbols of her wisdom are the Caduceus, the hazel wand, silver, chamomile and rosemary...

...he paused, considering the last months. He had been working on his thesis as an excuse not to go back to working in digs for the time being. They were still not sure what needed implementing next to bring Sybille home and now Maeve too so he felt an obligation to stay to do whatever was possible to help. It was a pleasant change to be able to help others with his skills but his finances weren't going to last forever. He needed to find a way to continue the studies without risking his reputation with the Uni as a sound archaeologist. This was after all his main source of income.

His study into anthropology and his thesis on the strange mutations between birds, animals and humans was suddenly more real than he could actually share with his peers or professors. His findings had totally changed what he had hoped to present as his thesis. He smiled to himself as he imagined Tara or Claire coming forward as volunteers for scientific experiments.

Cal often wondered what Tara Saark had done with the 'bird woman's' body he'd found on the Plains of Holderness in Yorkshire. She had never made mention of the occurrence and he thought perhaps he should ask Claire in the morning.

He wondered too what had happened to the silver bangle that she'd taken from his fingers that day. He noticed that she wore one, as did Claire and even Morgan, none as battered and tarnished as the one he'd found, though Tara's had a patina of incredible age which made him wonder just how old she truly was.

He was fascinated by all their shifting abilities and wondered, if it was something learnable and if so how? He knew that Morgan still called himself a learner.

Why he'd been drawn to the topic in the first place and why the one to find the remains on the Wold, who knew?

'That way lays madness,' he said aloud, 'and talking to your self's the first sign,' he laughed. His father's old clock that he loved struck eleven, 'Okay Callum,' he muttered to himself, 'time for bed.'

Chapter 26
Morgan Trethaway

Darkening skies and windblown trees,
Still the Lady walks with light-footed ease.
Calling to all ...hear Her voice on the breeze
Come to Her ...She will bring you home.

Morgan lightly strummed his Lute as he practiced a new piece that would not let go of him. He had composed it once again for Bethan as she seemed to inspire his music when she told of her journeys to the 'Between.' They simply unfolded from there ...magickally ...then putting aside his lute, he picked up the little lap harp Beth had loaned to him and played...

The Seer's Isle, the isle of dreams, hidden within the Mysts of Tyme ...far beyond the lands of human schemes ... lays a land of great design.

For deep within the Magicks return, if you feel your heart race it's for this that it yearns ...so wake up human child and before the year turns ...feel the fire in your belly ...let it burn.

A coracle drifts 'cross waters deep ...to the Seer's Isle the lands within sleep ...where the Otter swims free; on the shore stands the Deer ...and the Raven flies beyond all mortal fear.

Avalon of the Heart in the swirling Myst ...moist drops on your skin feel as soft as a kiss ...where the song of all Tyme are heard in the deep ...and the Mother calls to you in your sleep.

> *Wake up human child come dance with the wind ...wake up and see where new life can begin ...feel the sun on your face and the breeze in your hair ...wake up human child and let go mortal care.*

> *For the world is renewing ...if you wait it will cease ...you will miss the Quickening ...of the Green Ways of peace ...She has waited so long for you all to awake ...so wake up human child for your own sweet sake.*

...self-correcting and writing the score as he went until it was as he desired.

He often felt as if a trance state came on him when he played, discovering new depths that his own music brought to him. He paused, thinking of the woman for whom he had written the piece.

On the other hand, was it for her he pondered? Well it was a gentle piece that certainly suited her voice, too gentle for Maeve or even for Sam, Flora would be the only other that had such a strong yet gentle way about her.

As he mused, he played, letting the notes take him away so that he could stop thinking for a while. Respite he thought, I need respite. Should I go home for a while he thought? I could fly through the Veil and be back long before Yule. I could even fly so that I arrive almost before I've left. I'll speak with Tara and... At that moment, there came a knock at the door. He hadn't heard a car arrive and Beth must be somewhere close, probably with Max in the stable conversion.

Carefully placing the beautiful lap harp down on the bed, he went to answer the door. His surprise could not have been greater as he saw the little yellow hire car parked in the drive and on the doorstep, bag in hand, stood his sister Lily. As dark as he, with the same glossy black hair, she stood almost as tall as he did.

With a completely girlish scream, she launched herself into his arms straddling his waste with her long legs and covering his face with kisses, 'I have missed you so much brother mine,' she squealed.

'Where did you come from,' he laughed, 'I haven't heard a word from you in ages and suddenly here you are.'

'Well our mutual friend Tara brought me through the Veil. She said she thought you might be in need of some sisterly bonding. Tara filled me in on the way about what's been going on here, so I got as far as Springsmeet and wandered around until I found Sybille's shop. A girl by the name of Samantha told me where I could find you, so I hired a car. Now are you going to invite me in?'

Laughing aloud he said, 'Of course come on, but this isn't my home so I have to speak with my host.'

'Hmm host eh?' she quipped and at that moment Bethan appeared on the path from the stables.

She smiled at Lily, reaching out her hand to say

hello, 'I couldn't have missed your being Mor's sister,' she said with a friendly squeeze of Lily's hand. 'My goodness you two are so alike.'

'...except he's much hairier than me,' quipped Lily, reaching up to ruffle her brother's hair fondly.

Bethan liked Lily immediately and knew that it was mutual.

'Erm, Lily,' said Morgan, 'you know Max is here don't you, he's Beth's brother?'

Lily paled in the light of the hallway, 'Oh shit, she said, then 'sorry Bethan I didn't know and I wouldn't want to put you out so I'll just go back into town and find a room there.'

'Cal has a spare room or there's room at 'Earthly Rites' with Maeve away,' said Morgan.

'No, anything that needs to be dealt with can be in the morning' said Beth seriously, 'No more avoidance. I don't know what happened between you and my brother Lily, but you can deal with it in a civilised manner, surely. You wouldn't be here unless the Lady had wanted it to be,' she trailed of, 'sorry Lily, it's really none of my business but I know how injured Max has been and now he appears to be recovering ...' again, she drew breath seeing Morgan's expression of warning.

'Come on in, we can't talk like this on the doorstep and I would really like to get to know you a little. I've heard a lot about you from Max and from your brother here, so would you like a cup of tea or a glass of wine perhaps?'

'Oh a glass of wine would be lovely thanks.'

'I'll make you an omelette or something, will I?' said Morgan.

'Well you seem to have settled in well,' said Lily with a grin.

'It's nothing like that,' said Beth and Morgan together, Beth finishing with a laugh, 'we're genuinely great friends and I love him like a brother.'

'Yeah,' said Morgan, 'and we play together. Wait 'til you hear this woman sing Lily!'

'Great, perhaps we can try something together Mor. I have a song flowing through me that's really getting to me. I wake up with it on my mind and it's not going away. I think it was the final prompting to get me over here and then Tara just appeared.'

'Ha-ha Tara never *just appears*,' smirked Morgan. '
So you know about Mor then Lily?' said Bethan.

'Know what?' she grinned, 'Oh you mean this …' she changed into the prettiest Blue Jay Bethan had ever seen and back again.

'Did Max know of your gift Lily?' queried Beth, 'he's only just come to terms with the whole thing now really.'

'No of course not,' back then he would have totally freaked out. He found me difficult enough to understand without seeing me make the change,' she laughed hilariously, 'I'm not here to rekindle anything with him unless he wants it. I never really got over him I guess but Tara's visits have kept me in the loop so I have no expectation,' she paused for breath, considering her next words,

'No I'm here for different reasons,' she continued, 'firstly, to help in any way I can to find Sybille who I never met but adored and secondly, to talk to all of you about the shop I'm opening in Glastonbury.

I feel we might be able to work in synchronicity. I can get things through the veil that you can't otherwise bring in; nothing illegal of course and you can perhaps send me some of your beautiful work Bethan,' she paused opening her bag. On top of the pile of disorderly arranged clothes was an exquisite piece; a woven shawl in greens and blues that Morgan had sent through for Lily's birthday on Samhain. 'I thought together we might be able to really do some wonderful things for the Wytchwise and for the Pagan community on both sides of the planet. Oh and we share a birthday Beth; it's okay to call you that I hope?'

'Of course it is,' said Beth and it's wonderful that you're here and yes, we can talk tomorrow. We actually have a breakfast planned with everyone present so you're very welcome to join us.'

Seeing Morgan's face Lily, head on one side said, 'Okay Mor I can see there's something else you're not telling me.'

'Sis,' he said carefully, 'Max has met someone, one of our group. In fact, its Sybille's niece Samantha,' he paused, 'they've just had their first tiff too, so things are sensitive.'

'Well,' said Lily, 'this isn't the time for fun and games, is it? Sam's the girl who directed me here so she must have known when I said I'm Lily. They'll both have to get over themselves, 'cos I personally believe that there are far more important things going on, on our fair planet right now!' she exclaimed emphatically.

'Wow,' said Morgan, 'that's telling us. You've really grown up Lily!'

'Yes, well I really fell in love for the first time and so I guess I'm ready to follow through wherever the Lady takes me now.'

In that moment, a strange howl split the night. Beth heard the sound of the horn and ran to open the door. A veritable stream of hounds were coursing down the hill from out of the forest, Hercurin not far behind, his stag horns erect on his brow.

Lily blinked at the apparition and said, 'SHIT!' before running full tilt out the door toward the little car, that appeared covered in white hounds.

Baulking at the sheer number but refusing to be intimidated, she dived into the pack. Another howl split the night as she opened the door and the biggest hound of all leapt from the car and arrowed herself at Bethan. Hercurin simply raised a hand and the hound swerved, heading instead for Morgan. Man and dog reunited, as Honey knocked him to the ground in her sheer doggy enthusiasm.

'Honey Bear!' Morgan yelled with delight, becoming like a boy in the reunion.

Once again, man and dog wrestled like two children in the dirt. Hercurin watched horns retracting as he laughed aloud and then grinned at Bethan before sprinting once again for the forest, hounds in tow. At that moment Honey looked between Morgan and Hercurin and whined, she couldn't choose, not yet. The Master of all hounds …or the earthly friend she adored. Looking at her, Morgan knew one day, what her choice must be.

Lily stood watching the retreating Greenlord simply grinning from ear to ear, 'Oh wow, holy cow,' she said, 'and he's yours?' she stuttered turning to Beth.

'No,' said Beth, 'he's his own as I am my own …together however we make a whole; complete and undiminished by our gender or difference,' and she simply walked back inside.

'Well, that's telling me! Alright brother mine,' Lily, said a little breathlessly,' what were you saying about an omelette?'

Inside Bethan had already started preparing a meal for them all and Morgan opened a bottle of the fine sparkling Elderflower wine brewed at Covenstead.

It seemed like hours later that Morgan and Lily stood at the kitchen sink to wash the dishes. Bethan, pleading extreme tiredness had gone to bed; although they could hear the gentle strains of a harp, it didn't appear to be her playing.

'That will be Aithlin Farandir, Lily,' when she queried the sound, 'Bethan's Elven father. He comes to play to her every night without fail.'

'Wow, it must be extraordinary to know that you're not really human,' she said, 'Agh but then, who really is,' she finished wisely.

'I repeat, Lily, when did you become so cluey?' Lily simply grinned at him enigmatically.

She yawned and stretched, 'I'd better get going then Mor,' she said.

'No, you can have my bed, I'll take the couch and then we can work something out on a more permanent basis. I take it you're going to be here with us on and off to help solve this mystery of Sybille's disappearance love?' he finished, one eyebrow raised questioningly.

'Yes, that's really why I'm here, other than to bring you Honey who's been as miserable as anything the last couple of weeks in particular. She's been pining for you,' she walked to where Honey had sprawled on the rug in front of the kitchen stove. Squatting she ruffled the thick honey coloured fur and the wolfhound rolled over in her sleep to receive a belly rub.

Drying his hands, Morgan came to squat beside his sister, fondly scratching behind Honey's ear. They didn't see the face at the window as he looked with longing in on the scene.

Instead of coming in to borrow some coffee that he'd forgotten to buy, Max turned and silently walked back to his own space, his heart heavy.

He considered simply packing his bag and leaving Wells, Covenstead and Springsmeet behind him, to head back to Melbourne. The thought of his little flat was suddenly appealing but that too would be gone after a friend had offered to rent it and he'd said yes.

He hadn't thought his attraction for Sam and his enticing her to sleep with him would have left him suddenly so empty. Jealousy was not something he felt often, yet he'd been jealous seeing her with Morgan, even though he knew, it would not have been anything but a brotherly embrace of comfort. He also knew that where jealousy lay, love was not present and so he had withdrawn today to sort out his confused emotions.

Not meaning to hurt Sam, he sensed she would actually be quite pragmatic about it. They had enjoyed each other physically and the attraction was strong but each knew something had not been quite right. Max had actually held himself back rather than Sam, who had been ready to share so much more of herself with him. Her eyes had told him she knew and that she would wait; he sensed not that long though. She was ready for a full and committed relationship and would not settle for anything less.

He had actually found the twisting leaves and vines on her arms and shoulders discomforting. The little leaf sprites had joined them and he knew they were not tolerant of his discomfort either, often they attempted to make leaf patterns on his body but each time he felt as if he were being tattooed with hot needles and so again would draw back from her.

He knew that the man who eventually would share his life with Sam would also share his life with the leaf sprites and Max normally unselfish, could not imagine this sharing.

He poured himself a glass of Flora's herbal wine instead of the coffee he'd wanted to keep his mind sharp and took it back to his desk. He was still surrounded with unpacked boxes but hadn't gotten round to the task of opening them yet. He grabbed a small one at random; it contained photos of his time in England and right on top as if by design, was one of him and Lily laughing together at Morgan, who had taken it. Max remembered exactly the place and when; it had been his birthday a few years ago; his 29th, he and Lily had been inseparable then.

He looked into the beautiful piercing blue eyes; so much like Mor's and felt like crying. He had had the same frustration then as he felt now about Sam. Except with Lily he hadn't know what 'IT' was, he had only known that there was something else he was sharing her with, something important to her. Not someone, something and he had let her go, devastating himself and her in the process, he had thought for a while he would lose his friend Morgan too. Thankfully, his friend had been there for him, a wise and trusted soul.

He placed the photo on his desk, putting his face in his hands, he could finally let go... 'Agh Lily,' he sobbed.

Chapter 27
Covenstead

On days that seem they are like no other
...go deep within ...reach out to the Mother.
She hears every word that your soul ever cries,
...she whispers, 'Fear not, for you can truly fly.
Come with me; together we'll fly o'er the land
Come with me take full flight
...don't be scared, take my hand.
You will see that life's more than just day-to-day plans
...as you soar on the wings of your soul.

As Flora stirred from sleep, she heard the mourning cry of the Ravens and knew that Tara had arrived with her kin.

She had slept deeply and dreamlessly for the first time in months. She felt very happy about her slow blossoming relationship with Cal and her mother's plans to move into the dairy. Everyone was coming for an early breakfast and then to help with the harvest of early winter crops and with painting the old dairy too.

So much was happening in and around her, but she felt she was ready to face what the Mother had to offer today. With a lighter heart than of late, she went to the window with the intention of calling in the Lord and Lady's strength and presence as she did every day but a Raven head looked back at her as if it had been waiting for the moment. Ruark the Raven accompanied Morgan; like Tara, she had a slightly silvery flash on her black feathers and the same pure, intelligence that always made Flora think that she was not just a Raven; she wondered why she never showed her human self.

The nodding head of the great bird told her she was right and then the whole mob was there at the window, swooping and diving, making their usual raucous noise.

A head stuck out from the window next door and Claire yelled, 'shut up you rowdy lot!' emptying a bowl of water over one of them before breaking up in gales of laughter. Flora joined in with the laughter at the antics of both her mother and the birds.

Tara changed shape mid-flight, landing on the rooftop on delicate human feet before sliding down the roof on her backside and changing back as she fell past the gutter. Laughter turned to a loud 'caaaaw,' as she took flight to do it all over again.

Calling out and laughing to each other as they showered and dressed, Flora and Claire met at the top of the stairs to go prepare breakfast for the human mob they knew would descend promptly.

Flora collected eggs, while Claire let the goats out. They picked fresh herbs and the last of the late tomatoes from the greenhouse, together with pungent basil herb.

Chatting comfortably together more like friends

than mother and daughter, they were surprised at a knock on the back door; the friends never knocked, this being their agreed Covenstead in more than name only.

'I'll get it,' said Claire; Flora was busy removing a batch of fresh croissants from the oven, 'someone's either very keen or very hungry; the sun's only really just fully risen,' she laughed.

To her surprise, Harry stood on the doorstep a bunch of late wind roses in his hand. Politeness gone to the four winds at his unannounced appearance, Claire simply said, 'What are you doing here Harry.'

'Well I'm trying to work out what's happening Claire. You don't return my calls. I haven't seen you at home in days and you seem very angry about something,' he almost whined.

At that moment, Flora came from the kitchen to the door. Narrowing her eyes at her father, she said, echoing her mother's first words, 'What are you doing here,' adding hastily, 'at this time of day?'

'I came to see your mother Flora,' almost dismissing her presence as irrelevant. Flora bristled visibly, 'Well this just happens to be my home so I'll just repeat the question will I?'

'Okay girls,' Harry said a little more passively, 'what's going on?'

'I think that's something you might like to ask yourself Harry,' said Claire coldly and I suggest you get your lawyer to pull his finger out too. I assume you've been served with the divorce papers by now?'

'Yes I have Claire but I'm still not sure why. What did I do?'

At that Claire and Flora, exchanged glances and two unusually large Ravens appeared at the gate.
'Oh no,' he whispered hoarsely, 'you're not up to that again are you.' and that was it for Claire as she slowly and carefully changed in front of him, taking care that he saw every detail of how the changes manifested.

'You're sick,' he screamed at her and the two Ravens, who were shifting into human form, thereby effectively blocking his way, confronted him as he turned to bolt.

Morgan stepped forward and as if it were the most normal thing said, 'Good morning, you must be Harry. I've heard so much about you,' offering his hand for Harry to shake. At this, Harry pushed passed him and Tara where she stood and ran to his car.

'Well!' exclaimed Morgan and Tara in one voice, HOW RUDE!' before laughter overcame them. They stopped, seeing Claire and Flora's serious faces, looked sheepishly at them. Claire and Flora couldn't contain their soberness in the face of such natural joy and the four of them laughed 'til they cried. Noisily moving into the kitchen, each took a task as if pre-agreed, to prepare breakfast for the group.

Bethan arrived first, a reluctant Lily in tow with a more enthusiastic Honey, 'Why didn't you fly with us

Lily?' asked Tara, still giggling from the morning's activities.

'What?' said Claire.

'Yep,' said Tara, 'she's one of us.'

'I feel more and more like a minority, laughed Flora. Is there anything you need to tell me Mum?. Am I going to turn into a bat or something?' to which Tara and Claire burst out laughing again at the inference; the self-same expression Cal had used when he had first seen Claire make the change in the middle of the Yorkshire Wolds.

'Well anything's possible,' gasped Tara when she was in control again, 'Stick with us kid and we'll find out exactly what's hidden inside you.'

'Yeah, thanks Tara,' grinned Flora, 'Now are you going to introduce us?' she said indicating Lily.

'Sorry,' said Lily, 'I can do that myself. Hi Flora, I'm Mor's sister Lily.'

Flora and Morgan exchanged glances, 'It's okay, I'm not here to cause any problems,' Lily said, 'I'm here to help in some way. I just have to find out how?'

'Well let's go inside. It's lovely to finally meet you Lily,' said Flora letting the others go ahead, she whispered to Bethan, 'Can you see what I see?'

'Oh yes,' replied Beth, 'She looks like a slightly curvier version of Sam.

'I wonder how Sam and Max will cope with her appearance,' Flora questioned.'

'Lily and Sam met last night by chance,' said Bethan, 'and it appears it was more than civilised.'

They followed the others in and busied themselves finishing the breakfast prep, laying the table. Lily fitted in as if she had always belonged in the team and no one mentioned the elephant in the corner, Maeve. At least they knew she was safe.

Sam then arrived with Cal, sharing the journey to save on fuel for the sake of the planet, followed closely by Susan and Alex, surprising them all with their appearance. Sam was particularly glad to see Susan; she was in need of a de-briefing with her older friend and was excited to show her some of her drawings that she had given Sam tips on.

Cal and Alex immediately went into a huddle on their favourite topic The Celts, Morgan staying in the kitchen with Lily and the other women in case Max should suddenly arrive. He wanted to be there for his sister who was fitting in nicely but he didn't want her coming face to face with Max unexpectedly.

Already Lily had had no problem winning Sam over as a friend, no matter what had gone down with Max they were in silent agreement not to speak of him.

Susan greeted Lily a little coolly when she realised who she was, while Alex was his usual gung-ho self, the implications going straight over his otherwise intelligent head.

With no sign of Max, they decided to begin

breakfast. While sharing and enjoying the morning, they spoke of the work yet to do in the coming weeks. Sam paused mid-sentence; she could see a cloud of leaf sprites moving fast through the forest. She stood to see exactly what was happening with her little friends. To her horror, she saw that they were once again attacking Max as he ran full tilt. He broke cover and into the paddocks and eventually the garden, the others now watched, open mouthed as they saw what Sam was looking at

Lily's infectious laugh broke their attention as she watched Max's unfortunate arrival, 'Well,' she giggled, 'they certainly don't like him do they. How did he upset the natural world so dramatically?'

Sam turned from the window, rolling up the sleeves of her sweater and showing the rhythmically pulsing and moving tattoos on her skin.

'Oh, how cool is that?' gasped Lily, 'You lucky lady! I only have one tattoo and it hurt like hell. Did they hurt?'

'Only when I fought it,' replied Sam quietly.

By that time, Max had made it panting to the door. He crashed in glasses askew on his nose, hair sticking up in every direction. Honey, dozing by the fire saw an opportunity to greet the newcomer in doggy fashion. She launched herself at poor vulnerable Max as he stood breathlessly, looking at Lily sitting calmly sipping her tea.

Morgan grabbed a very enthusiastic Honey and

went to stand beside his sister. He wasn't sure why he felt the need to protect her as she was the one who had broken Max's heart …and then there was Sam, still standing quietly in the window.

She recovered herself rapidly, moving to pull out a chair for him because she thought he might actually pass out. Flora with calm aplomb busied herself filling a plate of food for him. Alex, seeing Max's discomfort patted the seat that Sam had pulled out next to him. 'Come on Max that was some entry you made there. Eat while it's still hot,' before burying himself in his plate again.

Everyone started speaking at once; his mother rose to give his a kiss on the cheek and his sister gave him a hug. 'Come on Nerd,' she said reverting to her childhood nickname for him.

Recovering himself Max said, 'Right, okay blondie!' From where he was sitting, he could no longer see Lily.

Sam still stood where she had been watching the little leaf sprites swarming outside the window. They were obviously irate and so, excusing herself, she went to see what she could do to calm them. They launched themselves at her, much as Honey did everyone, with sheer joy, 'What are you doing little ones?' she asked, 'Why are you attacking Max again? Is this something you're trying to tell me about him and our relationship perhaps?'

The pitch of their music lifted, in what Sam had

come to understand as ascent. 'Well things have changed any way my friends, look whose here,' as she indicated Lily, sitting watching with quiet pleasure at her interactions with the sprites. Once again, Sam heard their assent and knowing what was required of her, simply let go. She sat on the bench outside, the leaf sprites gathered around her.

When she immerged some time later, she had a new and very beautiful, silvery green tattoo on the side of her cheekbone that sent tiny tendrils of curling vines up to the corner of her eye, down her neck and into the depths of her sweater. She squirmed and laughed as they invaded her, becoming quietly relaxed and even blissful as they finished their work. They settled all around her, making leaf motifs like appliqué on the fine alpaca wool of her sweater with their own living bodies. When they had completed their work, she stood and walked back inside.

'Oh my,' said Lily first, 'that's beautiful Sam, have you seen?'

'No, only a glimpse of my reflection in the window,' said Sam.

'Here, look,' Lily passed her a mirror. 'It's truly amazing.'

'How can you encourage this,' said Max in his first direct communication with Lily, 'their scarring her.'

'Is that the problem Max?' questioned Sam, 'Is this why you withdrew from me, using a hug from a friend as an excuse? You knew from the start that I had made this connection with the leaf sprites and look,' she paused, closing her eyes and the markings disappeared, then reappeared as she willed it. 'You saw these markings from the word go.'

'I'm sorry Sam; I've always been a little conservative I guess. Bethy doesn't call me Nerd for nothing you know. I find the etchings beautiful but not on someone's skin ...your skin ...he trailed off.'
Susan stepped in '...perhaps it might have been better to come to that conclusion earlier Max? You've been exposed to magick, rituals and Sabbats all your life and witnessed often enough how your sister falls into trance,'

'...yes,' Max cut in, 'but this,' pointing to Sam, 'Tara and you too Claire and you Morgan, all such unbelievable gifts but not this close to me. The next thing I'll find out is that you can change too Mum!'

Cal, always the quietest in the group said, 'Get a grip Max, your own sister has a Greenlord for a lover but you can't take it when your new lover has tattoos that are alive!' There came an audible chuckle in the room and Morgan distinctly saw the little Merrow's childlike form, standing behind Max.

'Ah, it's you,' he said stepping forward.

'Excuse me?' said a bewildered Max.

'I'm not speaking to you Max,' he said quietly not shifting his eyes from the apparition grinning at him, 'I'm talking to the little monster who's trying to cause dissent between everyone.'

Before anyone could respond silence fell as music filtered in from outside. Immediately Tara and Bethan responded, moving toward the door.

'Come on everyone,' said Flora following, 'we're being summoned.'

They walked up the hill to the Grove; the tall Fae arrived silently as always, their faces betrayed no emotion except a small nod from Aithlin to Bethan, a quizzical smile at Lily.

Tara and Claire whispered to her to follow them, their roles as shapechangers being slightly different to the others; she followed without question.

Other entities gathered along with the Fae of all kinds and again they could only stare at the incongruity of some. Small with gossamer-fine wings like dragonfly, short and chunky, long snouts, bird like eyes or furry feet and hands, some with beaks and bat wings; so many and constantly changing their appearance, shifting and shimmering in and out of solidity.

Sam was given a particularly warm smile from the little Fae, as she calmly gathered with her swarming entourage of sprites; Bethan received a bow from the tall Elven Fae, some of the smaller winged beings moved closer to her whispering, *'Re naa' sinome'* 'She's here,' excitedly.

A hush fell suddenly in complete accord as Arianrhod stepped from the trees and out into the open, gliding directly to Bethan.

'You are making great progress Arwen Isil'Lindir. I sense you know of the urgency and yet all is 'now' in our world; only here in this realm are things truly out of alignment and disharmonious. That said it remains for you to be aware that a continuing disharmony here, leads to eventual imbalance everywhere in the known universe.

Lady Silver is ailing fast and her demise will result in a chain reaction through all the events of her Littleshape Sybille's aspects.

'Lady Arianrhod, with respect,' said Samantha, taking a step forward, 'I have a question please.'

'Yes, blood of Sybille whom my little ones love?'

'Well,' Sam began haltingly, her little cluster of leaf sprites stirring and humming, changing the patterns on her sweater as the Lady smiled at them, 'Why is it that if Silver has had many lives and many Littleshapes, that it is only the particular lives linked to Sybille that have created the challenge we face?'

'Ah, a worthy question. To give you the whole picture would perhaps overwhelm, due to the way the human brain functions. It sees only little pieces of the weave at a time. If you would consider perhaps that, the particular aspects of Silver affecting you now, are the ones who wandered too far from the Crooked Path. The aspects affected have unfinished tapestries and with those individual patterns incomplete, others cannot be entire

either. As your teacher told you, nothing happens in isolation.

Each of you, individually and as a group, holds a
thread of the tapestry that is now entangled and in part
unravelling. The Skeins of Tyme tore as a Maker fell
causing a human, a Littleshape to fall through the weaving. Sybille was that Littleshape.'

Arianrhod paused, looking at them with great
compassion, while the stark reality of their task hit home
yet again. Allowing them a moment, she continued,

'We know that the human form of Sybille is safe
where Silver placed her, to be tended by the Makers.
Her Littleshape's etheric body is the one that strayed,
wandering away in confusion to find sleep. Your task as
you know is to find where.

None of this however, would have created the
current turmoil in the individual lives, if it were not for
the greater number of Littleshapes that take this blue
planet for granted. Thus, it falls to those who care to
help heal the ailing Makers, for they are all the original
Littleshapes that helped to create this place where you
live. They cannot tolerate the level of pollution and dev-
astation that has occurred as humans rely more and
more on chemicals and electrical grid systems. We will
not even speak of nuclear fusion here. They will destroy
what they have built in their pain. Already you have seen
the blight, at present it is etheric. With the ethers affected so too, eventually, will matter also, for that is cause

and effect. What is wrought here will manifest there and vice versa.

There are among you,' Arianrhod indicated to their group, her eyes drifting from one to the other, 'in this very space, original Littleshapes whose first dream was this planet and who made the plunge into the deep sleep of humanity to be here now, to awaken and to assist others in doing so. That day is here. An original co-creator has fallen, dragging others along with its demise. Their intention was to help it heal but the darker aspects of others would keep it dark, as it is their way they believe, to power.

Sybille in her, in your terms, 'current life,' was blameless. She worked tirelessly to educate others, you included. It is other aspects, other Littleshape forms, which have made great errors of judgement and at times, have broken the vow 'with harm to none.' Every moment that one of the Wytchwise, the original dreamers of this plane, step even fractionally from the Crooked Path, they injure another and, most importantly, forget that they would in turn injure themselves,' she paused looking around the faces turned to her in something between awe and fear at her words.

'Now,' the Lady continued, 'you were each given a small clue from Sybille.' She turned to Bethan, 'these must be worked on. You have Sybille's Book of Shadows and much more, if you only look,' this to Sam and Flora.

'You have your fine minds to help solve the rhymes,' to Cal, Max and Alex.

'You have the abilities to find out what your adversaries are up to,' she said to Claire and Lily, 'and happy I am to see you here little Jaylily,' she smiled at Lily gently.

'Susan, do you remember the worlds you created as a child through your paintings and do you remember what Sarah used to say to you?' Susan frowned in concentration trying to recall what Bethan's birth mother, her dearest friend had said.

'Your fiery friend Maeve has been taken to a place where she must learn in a different way about herself and her difficulties in this aspect. Her stubbornness is unfortunate, but this was the only way we could act directly to assist her.

You Mirdhaucha,' she turned to the tiny figure obscured by Max '...you are one of Lady Mabh's own, but you once had a human mother and must remember that for your own sake, or bound you shall be in the web of your own intrigue.'

All eyes turned to the child like figure, all felt her pain in that moment but the Merrow merely made a rude gesture and sticking out her tongue at Sam, who would have approached her, vanished.

Arianrhod continued, looking this time at Flora she said, 'You had a visitation from your own patron, one of the Tuatha De Danaan. She gave you a bag of precious herbs that hide ancient wisdom. I know you feel the responsibility more deeply than most and your thoughts on the way forward have become highly intuitive. There was a question you had for me?'

'Yes Mother,' said Flora respectfully, 'I do understand the task but not how we'll accomplish it. My question is that we each have a riddle to solve and I know there's another rhyme that we haven't translated. We believe the elements and the elemental spirits themselves are involved, the plants, the crystal shard that broke for Maeve …' She broke off as a loud hiss came from the direction the Merrow had disappeared in …then continued. 'That little creature has a role to play, as does, Morgan and Beth's music, Cal and Max's research skills that you mentioned. Then of course, there are the shapechangers and Maeve no longer here to work out her part with us. So, do we work by the seasonal Sabbats, which means we have almost a whole turn on the wheel to work? There is also the role of the individual to consider and most importantly, how do we work out the link…the thread, to Sybille and thus to Silver that we each have in another space and time?' Flora trailed off.

'Well that is multiple questions wise one,' said Arianrhod, 'and I can see you have given much thought to the task at hand but in each of those facets is indeed an answer. You each have truly individual roles to play and if I could answer any of those questions for you then we would not be standing here at all. Therefore, Flora, work with the herbs but focus on the trees; Sam, listen to your friends they will show you everything you need. If you each take a component Flora and Sam have mentioned you will indeed see that one or the other better describes your individual skills.'

Arianrhod came closer still to the group and each could see her a little differently, as she became for them what they most needed in the moment.

For Bethan and Morgan she became the sister, for Sam the mother, for Max the stern teacher that he missed in Sybille and for Flora the midwife who gave all creatures life.

She spoke quietly to each of them, encouraging them to see the coming time as a lesson they would otherwise never experience in such intensity, best embraced as a test yes, but also as a great gift.
Arianrhod leaned in closer still so only they could hear what she shared with each of them, Max visibly blushing when it came to his turn.

At that, accompanied by the Fae she gracefully withdrew, Aithlin paused a moment to take Bethan's hands in his. He whispered to her of his love and respect before returning to the forest with his kinfolk.

Arianrhod's voice came to them on the wind, 'Stay strong, we may not interfere further but know that we will be here at the end, no matter what.'

A collective release of their combined held breath was audible as they went back inside. In silence, they cleared away the dishes and each chose a task for the day of harvesting, gardening or painting.

The air became clear and sharp, a tang of wood smoke lingering as the wind stilled with a last sigh.

Flora went with Cal to the Still Room where they had left the elderberries the night before. Without a word, they began to rinse them, discarding any bruised ones and carefully pulling the tiny berries from the claret red umbels. They separated the yield of luscious berries into large vats, one for wine making and another for soaking to make cough syrup or tincture and one each for jelly, jams and sauces.

The voices of the others drifted to them as they moved together through the garden and greenhouse, weeding, collecting seeds, or harvesting blackberries and late raspberries heard; words indistinguishable but a comforting presence, as Flora and Cal worked side by side.

Occasionally one or the other of the group would come in to ask Flora specific questions before going about their self-appointed tasks.

Max however had moved outside rapidly with Morgan, Susan, Alex and Bethan in order to avoid any confrontation with Lily and Sam although, did he but know it, he was actually the last thing on their minds in the moment.

Flora had decided to replant some of the raspberries that were encroaching into other parts of the garden. She enjoyed order in the areas she cultivated and these particularly hardy raspberries had become a pest, so vigorously had they grown, suffocating calendula and violets growing along the fence that was her demarcation line. She had warned them that if they wandered under the fence and into the herb garden, she would cut them back. Flora, as Sybille always had, left many corners of the property wild for the Little Folk.

As the day passed, peace and harmony reigned. Claire and Lily brought everyone a mug of steaming soup as each found a place to sit and simply be, preoccupied with their own thoughts after the morning's events.

Later that afternoon with murmured goodbyes and parting hugs, they wearily and happily dispersed to their own endeavours.

Claire disappeared with Tara for several hours leaving Flora alone with her thoughts. She was ready to explore the bags of herbs again and to put a plan that was forming into action in the morning, so she took herself off to bed for an early night. A favourite book, Moonheart by Charles de Lint, soon fell open on her chest as she wandered into dreaming.

Chapter 28
Annie Savage

Where do you go in your dreams?
Are you sure, you're awake?
Do you follow your heart or
...react for reacting's sake?
Where are you when you are dreaming
...is it a peaceful place?
Do you go to the lands of beauty?
...a sacred greening space
...how do you feel in the morning?
Are you truly her?
...or are you really still dreaming until
...small whispers of truth appear...

Annie Savage was plagued with dreams and when she awoke, she didn't feel like herself any more. She dreamed of gazing into a small body of water and saw only terrors there; of searching for something that shone in the depths, constantly snatched from her searching fingers. Eerie childlike laughter haunted her. Once she was looking in a mirror and she was someone else, someone with darker skin, eyes almost black in a wrinkled, wise face. Although it was, a face haunted with fear and dread, causing her to awake disturbed and edgy, a feeling that lasted all day.

She had tried to contact the illusive Lady Aelish

but had drawn a blank. She couldn't find any references to a Goddess of that name from any pantheon she researched, only a mention of Ailith meaning battle or strife, the dark Fae male also not seen again since the unfortunate rite of Mabon.

Bethan and the other girls she knew had held a Samhain Rite and had not included her or the Coven, in fact had made no mention of it. Therefore, she had gone to the Mount to a public rite, but not made welcome.

As much as she delved and ferreted through things, listening to their conversations when she could, she had no idea anymore what was happening, excluded from anything but the day-to-day business duties. One thing she did know was that Maeve had left and, according to Morgan would be back when she was ready; hmm the big beautiful Welsh Morgan she dreamed. No excuse given for all Maeve's things still being in her room, just one of the places she had fossicked in her need to know.

Entering Maeve's studio however she had truly been scared when the water tank started to vibrate and shake as if it were boiling and bone-chilling laughter had resounded through the quiet room. She had literally bolted, cannoning into Sam as she came up the stairs and ignoring Sam's query of, 'What are you doing up here,' merely gabbling, 'oh I was looking for Maeve, her mother called again,' even though she had just been told Maeve was away for an indeterminate time.

In truth, Annie didn't even know what drove

her, other than the huge ego she would certainly never admit to. Her encounter with the Lady and her consort had left her craving more of the power she had felt when she had witnessed their rite. The Lady had taken the poison from the sting in her neck into her blade and had given her the gift of returning youth, for which she would be forever grateful.

Since Claire had returned, her one time friend and fellow student from years ago, Harry had not been as attentive. He came and went from her cottage and she knew that his house in the city was for sale. She wondered where he would live when that happened and for that matter Claire too …then there was the other secret that she had never told a soul about …what would happen if that were discovered she fretted.

Claire hadn't confronted her, but she had a strong sense that she knew of the affair between herself and Harry and that it might well have been the pivotal point of no return for their marriage. Annie felt no remorse for this, she believed that Harry could provide her with the things she craved and thought Claire a fool for being away so often and for such extended periods; no matter that he was in fact a boring lover and obviously afraid of anything to do with the Wytchways.

Time for work Annie sighed, as she took a last look at her now slender self in the mirror; she certainly looked much younger than her years. She had noticed that Claire had let the colour rinse grow out of her thick chestnut hair, rendering her strangely even more like her daughter than before. Often together, the two of them would look at her long and strangely, whenever she passed them in the corridors or retail rooms; she wondered what they were thinking …did they know?

Shaking herself she decided she would brave the cold but sunny day and walk to work. As she was leaving, a large flock of Ravens landed in a tidy row along her garden fence, silent other than for a rustling of feathers. A flock of Ravens, a smaller blue bird that she couldn't identify and, stranger than that in broad daylight an Owl, silver white feathers streaked with chestnut brown markings.

'Shoo,' she called out to them irritably, 'Shoo, go away!' They simply sat and observed her intently but she could have sworn the Oland one of the Ravens tittered to each other, as she fled down the street.

Chapter 29
Just life

...the witch wheel turns ever round
...the winds blow strong over sacred ground
...go with the tides and love abounds
...fight and life's fire is no longer found

The wheel of the year spun on, each member of the group finding a measure of peace in their working day, gardening at Bethan's and Flora's, or helping Claire, Susan and Alex, make the moves into their new homes.

They gathered often to once more decide on the best tactics so that 'earthly rites' ran optimally, keeping a wary eye on Annie by putting Lily at the desk with her as often as possible, in the guise of learning about the running of a business.

Bethan made Morgan and Lily welcome at her cottage in Wells, on a more permanent basis and in spite of Max's proximity in the stable conversion, Lily was happy to be with her brother for a while. Bethan cleared out a small room where she had stored her spinning implements and extra tools, happily making it into a small loft bedroom for her.

Lily loved the outlook toward the wild forest from upstairs under the eaves, even though Morgan had offered her the larger space. She knew she would enjoy climbing out onto the roof to sit in her Jay form, to listen to the birds or to watch the wee folk play in the treetops.

Cal finally made the obvious move to Covenstead with Flora, as the spare room was free, now that Claire's dairy project was completed. He spent most of his time with Flora in the garden anyway when he wasn't writing or studying, the room was large enough to double as bedroom and study combined.

Sam invited Lily to come and go from the apartments upstairs as well. No one had a clue when Maeve would return, so it was only practical that her space be used, aired and that Lily could also do some of her own fine jewellery work from the studio that was Maeve's pride and joy, the rumblings from the water tank notwithstanding.

Susan and Alex moved into the lovely rental cottage in Springsmeet that Cal and Max had found when they first arrived. It would, the real estate agent told them, be coming on the buyers' market shortly and they knew it would be ideal for them for their future. Nestled on a the edge of a gully above the Springs it had a huge, well established garden and the studio Morgan had used for his music room, would make an ideal place for Susan's artistry.

Bethan was excited at the prospect of having them closer and out of the bustling city. Alex could work anywhere with his writing and a journey every so often, to teach in his professorship at a University in Melbourne, was no hardship.

Life continued as they felt the push once more to the next sacred turn of the wheel toward Yule. The days were shortening and the weather becoming colder still, rain beat a tattoo on the roof of the shop as they met to talk, laugh as friends and to share meals at their various homes. If it weren't for the internal tides that they each felt as part of their being, it was almost believable they lived normal lives. Almost that is but for the dreams and visions that were becoming more the norm than not. The inner tides that were pulling them apart and together, influenced by the patterns forming of where they had been in other aspects that linked them in the moment.

Chapter 30
Magdalena

Searing heat of passions burn
...cooling waters ...emotions churn
Airy breezes ...dreams aspire
...earthly rites ...manifest desire

 Each day Magdalena tended Nina and each day they became more like sisters. They told each other of their dreams and Nina shared with Magdalena all the visions she had. She spoke of the moments she spent listening to a woman who shared her consciousness, whispering to her of amazing things, showing her lifetimes in many places around the earth's globe that brought her understanding of the continuing life upon life, which every soul can experience.

Magdalena listened and knew that what Nina shared was no illusion; she truly had an amazing gift that not many would understand. Rather they would mark her as touched in the head, unstable or worse, mad.

She spent hours showing Nina the work she did with La Stregga, the rituals and the methods of making herbal and simple spells. She was eventually to be La Stregga's acolyte, when age and tiredness overcame her teacher. Magdalena had in fact noticed a strain around her beloved teacher's eyes and a slight tremor to her hands when she worked at delicate tasks. She was afraid, her friend and mentor was becoming unwell.

As much as Nina had extraordinary dreams of being elsewhere, someone else, so too did her own abilities begin to shift and change between dimensions. She had experiences of two other young women, one dark like herself but with paler skin and unbecomingly short choppy hair, she could only imagine was some sort of punishment for an offense. Yet, she thought, how freeing would it be not to have the weight of all her hair knotted at the back or on top of her head and hid under a cap, especially in the heat of summer.

The other had thick chestnut curls cut to the shoulder, warmer in her colouring. She too wore strange breeches and was as toned and as strong as a small man was.

Both girls were free from all constraint; no ties to bind them although she suspected that there had been someone who had put the sadness in both pairs of eyes, just as she felt the sadness of being in love with an unfulfillable dream. She knew from the moment Eduard Giraldi looked at her, she was lost.

She often wondered what drove the world of man; women bound, not free, as men were? Why did men think they knew anything about the business of birth and death? The Dottore thought they knew everything about the human body and mind and yet how could they know what it was like as a girl to grow, for the female lunar courses to begin, to become a woman and bear children?

When she looked at the girls in her dreams, so

different to herself, her life, should she envy the freedom they appeared to have or should she be shouting heretics along with the others who believed women were mere chattels. Then again who was she to cry heretic, she, one of the Stregga?

The dreams continued to intensify and she witnessed the dark haired girl writing and drawing, using strange implements she could not fathom, colours brighter than any imaginable.

The other, she connected with immediately, when she saw the beautiful herb and vegetable gardens she lovingly tended, the hens running free through the day and the goats that gave milk to gentle hands. A girl she envied because she had the life she most desired, although the other did have the lovely writing implements. She dreamed that both young women worked together creating the inks and herbal dyes. Yet another, a very beautiful young woman used the dyes for her threads to weave fine cloth. It made her think of the conversation she had had with Nina whilst sorting and untangling the skeins of silk.

Then the strangest thing happened. She was walking in the plaza heading home from the market after buying a few small items for Nina. The huge trees shading the cobblestoned square were sighing in the wind; a storm was coming and the seedpods rattled a hollow sounding song. She was suddenly aware that they were more than just the beautiful chestnuts, so much a part of her everyday landscape. Incredibly alive, appearing to move in a complex rhythm each leaf a sigh, each branch a song.

Magdalena blinked, thinking there must be something affixed to her eyelashes; she rubbed them, but no, she could see …she could see small winged beings in the shape of leaves and twigs. They were singing and one came close enough for her to see its eyes, bright as beads. It beckoned to her to come closer to the tree and from beyond the great trunk stepped a figure, a small being made entirely of leaves and leathery bark that rustled as she moved. Female in form, she reached no higher than Magdalena's thigh. Her face, wizened and wise was brown-skinned, her lips full and pomegranate red, revealed small white teeth as she smiled at Magdalena.

Furtively looking around for fear someone else might see her …see what she could see in broad daylight, she moved closer, fascinated. The small Fae stepped toward her taking her hand and walked with her as if it were the most normal thing to be walking the streets of Florence in the morning sunlight.

'Come,' the small Fae said, 'I show you things,' and with that took Magdalena's hands and led her into the gardens surrounding the plaza.

Magdalena resisted, 'no, I have to get back to my work,' she insisted and with that the small being scowled at her and vanished.

She hurried home, unable to believe the event as real.

She felt like pinching herself in case caught in one of her dreams. Looking around her and starting at every movement she knew something followed, she could hear their laughter and the trees rustled with their pranks as they pelted her with ripe chestnuts for good measure. Somehow, she thought, I must get to see La Stregga soon to tell her of this.

As she ran in the door, head down, mind seething with thoughts of her prior experience, she ran headlong into the figure heading toward her. Eduard was also lost in his own thoughts about the very person he now found in his arms, her parcels flying as Magdalena hurtled into him.

'I am so sorry Signor, so careless of me I was not looking where I was going,' she said flustered by his closeness.

'It's alright Magdalena, no damage done to me but are you okay? He stepped back still maintaining a light grip on her shoulders.

'Yes, yes Signor, thank you. I was …I must' …she trailed off unable to gather her wits at his proximity. Although a mature man, in his forties, he was fit and healthy, the wrinkles around his eyes, the silver-grey beard and thick hair, lent him an air of distinguished wisdom rather than age. She could not deny the attraction and to her surprise knew the mutuality of this.

Eduard withdrew his hands from her shoulders gently; he felt as if he held a frightened Doe and did not want to be the reason for her fear. He simply turned and walked away, leaving her to rush away into the kitchen so that he could deal with his own inner turmoil.

Chapter 31
Samantha

Talking with trees is a lovely affair
...they tell you such stories of sunshine and air
...of happier times when the forests were there
...and then...with a chuckle
...throw leaves in your hair
Listen, speak with them ...they have so much to share

Sam sat at the reception desk in 'earthly rites,' it being Annie's day off. The days were passing slowly and Yule would be upon them before they knew it and yet the personal issues of the group seemed to be taking priority, which was stupid considering what was at stake. She personally didn't really know what she was feeling right now.

The original, lightning bolt surge of attraction she and felt with Max on meeting, had fizzled out it would seem. She knew intuitively that his withdrawal was not simply due to the little leaf sprite's tattoos on her skin, as she could make those disappear at will if she so desired. No, there was more to it than that, more even than Lily's sudden appearance.

Thing is she thought, I really like her, we look a lot alike which is perhaps why Max was attracted to me in the first place, but what about my attraction to him? I'm not one to jump into bed with a man because of a chemical charge. 'There's definitely more to it than that,' she said aloud just as Morgan walked in the door.

'…more to what than what? Morgan asked with a grin, at finding Sam talking to herself.

'Sometimes it's the only way to get answers,' she grinned in return then, 'What brings you in today Mor? I thought you and Bethy were working on a piece together; which reminds me I think I finally got the hang of that more complicated piece you gave me to practice on the flute.'

'Clever Sam, but you didn't answer my question,' said Morgan noticing her rather flustered air.

'What? …oh yes well I was thinking about Max and Lily and sensing there's more to his withdrawal than my tattoos or Lily's arrival.'

'Yes I would agree Sam,' he replied carefully, 'It's a bit like Maeve and I, something was there but it's not from this time or these aspects of our Littleshapes. It's more ancient than that. For you and Max, I can't answer that but I'm willing to help you in any way I can. For myself, I'm coming to terms with the fact that Maeve is possibly dangerous and Tara taking her elsewhere on the web, is for a very good reason. Her past in this aspect as Maeve, must tie in with another that is truly off the wall as far as I can see,' he trailed off as he saw Sam's face.

'That's it Mor, thank you. My relationship with Max isn't about now, it's about a very different time and place and I think it might have something to do with the girl I've been dreaming about.'

Morgan paused to think before asking, 'So do you know what aspect she is and where she sits between you and Sybille for instance?'

'I'm not sure. Sybille used to speak of a life she occasionally true dreamed in Italy somewhere and a link with both Flora and I, but that might be a bit of a long shot. She used to talk about astrology and some odd conjunctions in a chart. I'm afraid I didn't pay much attention at the time but Flora probably would have.'

'Don't dismiss it Sam, everything's relevant in trying to sort the threads that might lead us to Sybille, we could well untangle, or entangle of course, our own,' said Morgan emphatically.

'Yes, you're right Mor but it's doing my head in trying to fit all the pieces of the jigsaw together. Things keep coming back to me, things my parents said and Sybille. They were always conflicting so I guess I have issue with that. Why couldn't they live and let live. Still that has nothing to do with the original thought strand, which was about Max,' she laughed gently at herself and her meanderings.

'Gees! I understand Sam,' said Morgan, 'the life aspects with Maeve are possibly more than one and also between all of us as a group and individuals as Arianrhod herself explained. Anyway, I suppose we can try guessing 'til we're blue in the face but what did you want me for

Morgan…?' but he had turned abruptly and hurried away like a man on a mission, muttering, 'That's it blue!' Sam's surprised laughter followed him. She supposed he had thought of a line in a song.

Shaking her head she reapplied herself to the stock control sheets she was working on, falling into a rhythm, her mind focused on the everyday task.

She could hear voices as people wandered the rooms and the sounds of Bethan playing her harp for a group who had arrived for readings and as they awaited their turn they could relax, browse and be entertained. Parts of the group were friends of Annie's but almost seemed relieved that Annie was not there. Sam had thought it curious and often plagued by doubts she couldn't fathom about their receptionist. She knew that once Sybille had been close with this woman and wondered what had happened to make Annie the way she had become.

Sam's thoughts drifted from her work to the thoughts of her Aunt, to Max then to Lily and back to Annie Savage again. There was something niggling at her …'Agh yes!' she exclaimed, freaking a couple of people out as they walked through the door, 'Sorry, good morning, just thinking aloud,' she grinned. Waiting for them to leave she dashed across the hall and up the stairs to Flora who was waiting for her client to arrive.

Sam, not waiting to draw breath gasped, 'The Book of Shadows, Flora where is it? We have a couple of simple older ones that Sybille used for training, we have the one with blank pages she said she'd left for us, but where is that really old one she had. I can't remember where she said it came from, only that it was hereditary and had come to her through her lineage as High Priestess, after she was the only one in direct line as a practising teacher of the Old Ways.'

Flora taken by surprise by Sam's abrupt entry, thought long and hard for a moment before replying, 'That Sam my clever friend is a very good question and as soon as we're free later, we're going to have a really good look for it,' she exclaimed, 'even if we have to pull the farm apart to do so. Meanwhile perhaps if you get time today Sam, although I know it's a busy day, you might like to search Sybille's office. Nothing much has been touched in there as the keys went mysteriously missing and Annie claims she never had them …but I wonder,' she trailed off as she heard footsteps on the stairs.

'That's exactly where my train of thought started Flora …as usual, we seem to be on the same track. Okay, I'll let you get on. I shouldn't have left reception but I just needed to tell you, there could be all sorts of clues in there about the herbs and some hints on formal rituals for seeking, too.'

Flora grinned, 'Now why didn't I think of that, you must have absorbed more than you realised being around Sybille so much Sam,' giving her friend a quick hug, before plastering a big smile of greeting on her face to meet her client.

Sam grinned and did a high five, practically dancing down the stairs. As she crossed back to reception, she saw Beth looking at her with a bemused expression, 'Later,' mouthed Sam to her, 'I'll call a meeting,' before continuing her way to the desk where a group of excited young women were waiting.

The obvious spokesperson for the group was a young and overtly witchy looking girl, long black hair, black garb and dripping with symbolic jewellery. Sam felt the tattoo tracery on her arms start to come alive and knew by that, that someone around was the genuine article, if not the assigned leader of the little group. Sure enough a tall girl stepped forward, 'We all want to see Tara,' she said quietly, her eyes riveted on Sam's hands all the while, I'm a friend,' she finished.

'Did you book ahead?' queried Sam, 'she's booked out,' all the while thinking, she's real she could see my markings.

'Oh no,' said the group as one, 'We've come all the way from the other side of Melbourne.'

'I thought you'd booked ahead Vanessa?' the original girl said to Vanessa angrily.

'Well my mother was supposed to have done it,' Vanessa said petulantly.

'Wait 'til she hears then,' said the first girl, 'she owns the place after all.'

'Erm, sorry,' said Sam, 'If you mean Annie Savage she works here but she's not one of the owners.'

All eyes turned to the girl called Vanessa again, the first girl who had spoken raised an eyebrow questioningly. Sam could see she was genuinely embarrassed, '…but I thought? Well never mind; what can we do to make it all happen?' she said a little less hostilely. 'We can't shoot the messenger girls can we?' with a grin that transformed her face to a younger version of her mother.

At that moment, Tara came out of her room to accompany her client to the door and to meet the next. She paused as she saw the faces of the expectant girls, focussing directly on the first girl who had spoken and then letting her eyes wander over all their faces; she ended up locking eyes with the one called Vanessa.

'Well here's a surprise,' she said, her face unreadable, 'little Nessa Savage all grown up.'

'Hi Tara,' said Vanessa, 'I haven't been called that in forever and how come you don't look a day older than when I was a kid?' she said all in one breath.

'Ah just the luck of the gene pool,' she grinned at Sam cheekily, 'So what are you all doing here Vanessa? If its readings you're after I won't be able to do it today, but we could have an informal gathering tonight if you like although it will be as a group, not individually.' Tara looked at Sam to confirm; she nodded assent saying,

'The small seminar room is free. Tara you're a life saver,' said Vanessa, 'the girls have been looking forward to this for ages and we have to get back tonight.'

'Alright them we're set,' said Tara. 'Sam will take your details and a deposit, the birthday girl …let me see, ah Lottie's on me though Sam,' which drew a gasp of thanks from one of the girls,' and you can buy her that wand she wanted, Nessa,' said Tara, before Vanessa could say anything in rejoinder and wisely, at the look on Tara's face, acquiesced gracefully.

Tara looked around the group again before saying, 'Hmm are you all over 18?' she questioned, 'if you lie, I'll know.'

'Well it's my 18th tomorrow,' said the same girl shyly 'and this was supposed to be my present from Nessa …er, Vanessa,' she stuttered as she saw the look on Vanessa's face, 'but how did you know?' she broke off in amazement, 'and the wand too …I,' but was unable to complete the sentence.

'Well, I guess a few hours won't make any difference will it Sam?' said Tara with a sweet smile at the shy girl to alleviate her embarrassment. 'See you tonight at 6.00 then girls,' and with that whisked her waiting client away, her musky perfume leaving a scented cloud behind her.

Even the outspoken girl who had approached Sam first was at a loss for words. Recovering herself a little she said, 'I'm Jo,' handing her a wad of money, 'this is for everyone, we took a collection for today so that no one missed out but especially not Lottie …so how did Tara know?' …she trailed off.

'Well,' said Sam gently, 'Tara is especially gifted but if any of the team were to read for you, our business is to give you the best we can. We don't tolerate frauds here,' Sam finished with a small sidelong glance at Vanessa. Curious she thought to herself, that girl really thought her mother owned this place. Where did that come from I wonder, before turning to the task in hand, settling their account and giving them the details for their evening's little adventure with Tara.

'Don't worry about dinner girls, unless you're particularly hungry that is. We'll add a little something to the evening in the way of a light supper while you're with Tara,' seeing their relieved, fresh young faces she said, 'Hey I was a student once too and not that long ago either when I think about it,' she laughed and even Jo and Vanessa joined in this time.

'Thank you,' they all chorused before leaving in an excited, chattering group.

Cal came through the door at the same moment, laughing at the veritable wave of pretty girls that flowed past him. 'They seem like a happy group,' he said conversationally to Sam.

'Ha-ha, yes,' she said, 'and one of them is Annie Savage's youngest daughter!'

'Oh do tell,' said Cal with interest, 'can you see she's Annie's girl?'

'Only when she smiles and her colouring, otherwise she looks like …' she trailed off in shock at her own thoughts, paling so that Cal stepped forward as she looked as if she might keel over.
'WHAT!' Cal exclaimed, 'What's wrong Sam?' and at that moment, Claire walked in, rushing over to Sam when she saw her sickly pallor as she groped for the stool behind her to sit down.

'Alright what's happened Sam? Can I help?'

Sam didn't quite know how to reply but she knew Claire and Flora would have to know soon enough. 'It's the girl who came in before Claire, Vanessa, Annie's daughter.'

'Oh yes I haven't seen her since she was just a toddler,' said Claire, 'Annie, Sybille and I were good friends once but what about her?'

'She was here with a group Claire and had been led to believe that Annie owned 'earthly rites,' for one thing but …' she paused to find the words, 'I guess that's just Annie being Annie but there's something else.'

'…and?' questioned Claire.

'Cal asked me if she looked like Annie, she does when she smiles and she has a similar colouring, being black haired like Annie …or was anyway before …'

'Spit it out Sam!' said Cal.

'No give her a moment Cal,' said Claire taking Sam's hands in hers, '...now what has you in a spin love?'

'Vanessa looks like Harry, Claire!' she blurted, unable to contain herself any longer.

Claire blanched visibly and then turning, simply walked out the door, rattling it on its hinges. They heard her car rev and she drove off, her anger evident in the sound of the tyres on the gravel.

'Well that went well,' said Sam ironically, 'SHIT, I hate being the bearer of bad news but seriously it's that obvious. Flora and Claire have been very secretive about Claire and Harry's separation, but this rather sheds another light on it, which apparently even Claire didn't know about.'

'All I know is I wouldn't want to be Harry right now.'

'Why what's my father done now?' said Flora as she came downstairs.

'I...I think your mum had better talk to you first Flo,' said Cal taking her hand, 'this is between the two of you I think.'

Flora sighed, 'Oh do you mean about Annie and Harry being an item. I know about that. Mum and I just haven't gotten round to telling you all. We were waiting until the whole, sorry thing is settled between them. Mum filed for divorce and Harry's still playing the innocent victim but Mum actually saw them together and

surprised Harry by coming home early from the UK
....the same time you got here Cal apparently. I'm also
sure I've seen him around a lot too; at the Mount at
Mabon and I saw his car outside Annie's recently too.
Does he think we're stupid?'

'I notice you call him Harry, rather than Dad,'
Cal asked.

'It's my way of seeing him as an individual rather
than what I would like him to be, the stereo typical father figure,' said Flora. 'Since his stance about my career,
there's not been much love lost between us and Sybille
taught us that if we call our parents by their given
names, instead of their title, we could actually see them
as individuals, aside from our relationship with them. I
find it helps,' she paused, 'but I've digressed, there's
more isn't there Sam?'
'Yes Flo there is but I still think your Mum needs to sort
it first and then talk to you.'

'No, look you obviously, inadvertently discovered about Annie and Harry, so what else have you
found out Sam? Come on I have a right to know, it's
about my family after all,' said Flora firmly.
Samantha took a deep breath in, steeling herself for what
could only hurt her friend, 'Flora, a girl came in with a
group today, firstly she was under the illusion that her
mother Annie owned the business but that's not it. She
looked like Harry, Flora, which makes her your...'

'...half-sister,' finished Flora for her. 'I have a sister and no one knew except Annie? I don't think so. No my father has a lot to answer for I think,' and with that she turned on her heels, much as Claire had, but instead of heading out the door she walked slowly and deliberately, upstairs to her rooms.

Sam sat down hard on the stool behind her, 'Sometimes I just despise human behaviour,' she said. Cal just shook his head in reply at a loss for once. 'Just as I think I could be getting a handle on things something else comes out of left field,' Sam moaned.

'Well,' said Cal wisely, regaining his voice, 'we have to remember that we must put all personal stuff aside for the next months until we find Sybille. We can only see this as another test on the journey I guess?'
More customers came in at that moment Claire trailing in, no less irate, behind. Sam tried to get her attention before dealing with the new arrivals but Cal mouthed to her, 'I'll do it,' as he followed Claire to the kitchen where he found her putting the kettle on.

'Flora knows Claire,' said Cal bluntly, 'she pushed Sam to tell her.'

Claire only smiled wanly, 'Yep that sounds like my Flo,' she said, 'Want a cuppa Cal,' she finished conversationally as if nothing was amiss.

He made a hasty exit as Flora came in and the two women simply held each other.

'I wouldn't want to be in Harry's shoes,' he muttered to himself again as he left them to their dry-eyed grief.

Chapter 32

Morgan

Blue the colour of the ancient tribes...
Ink for the tattoo the warrior inscribes...
Circles and swirls from the ancient isle...
Woad the plant that none may defile...
Spirals, curling vines and flowers
Drawn deep on the skin in ancient hours
When rituals danced, as seasons passed
To write messages in the skin of all casts

Morgan had flown to the library to check the symbols and colours he'd seen in dreams, suddenly remembering his aspect Bran's, forearm and cheekbone tattoos. They did not seem to be random, obviously a part of the symbolism of his race and standing in his community. Deep blue moons and stars, spirals, birds' feet, an eye and various leaf patterns, he realised were similar to the ones that constantly appeared on Sam's arms, like twisted vines. It was Sam's use of the term, 'blue in the face,' that had triggered a memory of Bran.

So many times, this life aspect as Bran had haunted his dreams, remaining a part of unfinished business. Beth's experiences in the 'Between,' had triggered further memories, when she had spoken of the young Cunning Man who had been a little girls' escort. It would be so much easier if Sybille were here he thought not for the first time recently. It was up to them to decipher things now, he wondered if Sam's tattooing might actually be some sort of language. They seemed to shift and change constantly as he looked at them. Perhaps Alex would know he thought. The unusual crescent moon shaped birthmark on his forehead, hidden under his hair was a puzzle, as it was the symbol reserved for priestesses in his understanding due to its lunar aspect. Just another twist and turn on the Crooked Path. He wondered if Bran had also had that particular mark.

He settled to read the text on the dyes that the Picts had used…

A blue dyestuff obtained, typically from the Woad plant, one of several herbs of the genus Isatis. The Picts, an ancient people that once inhabited parts of the British Isles, used them to decorate and ritually adorn their skin for battle and for Rites of Passage…

There came a tap on the door, Sam stuck her head round, 'Morgan there's a number of things we need to talk about. Claire and Flora called a meeting about something that happened today and Flora and I had another relevant thought too. Are you free to come in ten?' Morgan, scrubbing hands over his weary eyes said, 'Sure, I'll be right there Sam,' seeing her face he was tempted to ask if she was alright, but it seemed to be irrelevant to ask when he could already see the answer in her eyes.

Sam went, leaving Morgan to clear away the papers and books strewn across the desk after his search for information. He sat for a moment thinking about the last few days, Maeve's leaving, Max's behaviour, Lily's sudden arrival and, 'Now what?' he thought aloud before making his way to the larger seminar room.

Tara too was heading in the same direction, her usual chipper self, 'Hey Mor,' she grinned, 'How's your practice going? Are you able to arrive back and still have your clothes on,' she giggled, referring to the episode before he had officially met the group. He had shapechanged but had not been in complete control, arriving stark naked at Maeve and Flora's feet. Tara was never going to let him forget it he thought but grinned at her in return.

Morgan and Sam walked in together to find a somewhat serious group waiting for them. Claire stood up as soon as everyone had arrived, relating to them the entire incident, Sam had shared earlier that day. She would see for herself she said, later today when the girls arrived back for their evening session with Tara and that she would be discreet in her assessment. She wouldn't let anyone comment on what this meant to her and Flora, simply raising her hands for quiet and refusing to speak further on the subject.

Flora and Sam agreed to be there with her and they moved on to the next question Sam had raised earlier with Flora.

Where was the Book of Shadows that Sybille had always kept wrapped and hidden in the chest in her study at Covenstead? Sam knew her Aunt would not have gone away without first secreting it in a safe place but due to the nature of her more sudden departure than normal, it was anyone's guess, although she would not have left it lying around. It looked as if someone had actually swapped it with the blank paged book they'd found later in the chest.

Flora recalled it was in the chest when she found the document package and the leather binder from Sybille, when it had to her consternation, been left lying open in the chest. The lid of the chest was flung open too but at the time she had not checked whether it had been the original Book of Shadows in there, she'd been on her way out to meet the others.

It had been their first meeting and in her rush, she had assumed it had been the original. It was only now she remembered that this couldn't have been Sybille's doing because Sybille had already been gone nearly a year at that stage, unless it had been her wraith.

Bethan had also seen Sybille floating around the next morning, appearing to search the chest and obviously very distressed.

They agreed it was time to pull the place apart to find the missing Book and the place to start would be the library or Sybille's old storeroom perhaps.

They split up to look in every conceivable place but to no avail.

'Hmm,' said Flora reflectively, 'Who do we

know may have had a key for the farm?'

'Doesn't really matter,' said Claire, 'Sybille never locked the doors anyway. She always said if someone really wanted to get in they'd just smash a window or glass door!'

'True,' replied Flora, 'but who else would know that, who wouldn't have necessarily broken in but who might just have come snooping?'

'Any number of the old Coven would have been fascinated to know more about Sybille and what she knew,' interjected Bethan.

Cal stood reflectively, listening to the conversation, 'There's one obvious person who springs to mind,' he said.'

He found himself pinned by multiple pairs of eyes.

'Who' said as one?

'Annie Savage,' Cal replied quietly.

'Annie!' exclaimed Claire together, 'why didn't I consider that? But do you think she would stoop to theft?' she spoke to the room in general.

'With the strange behaviour she's exhibited recently anything's possible,' said Tara, 'I'm going to do a bit of snooping around her cottage when she's in at work in the morning,' she finished grinning mischievously.

'We can't do that,' exclaimed Flora.

'Well they can't arrest a Corvid can they?' chuckled Lily enjoying the moment.

'Or a Jay,' Tara laughed.

Everyone saw the funny side, their quirky humour as always helping to break the tension and frustration everyone was feeling.

Chapter 33
Sybille's Book of Shadows
Huath, the Hawthorn

…a crown of Huath next must you wear

…entangled deep in your silvery hair

…her thorns will not harm for …she knows that you care

…be at peace …listen …she will share

Hawthorn is another of the Fae triad of trees, along with Ash, Oak, Duir and Nuin. It is the tree of enchantment, whose flowers, worn at the Beltane rite as garlands or wreaths, also known as Whitethorn or May. Blackthorn is another of the species, bearing a larger, pinkish blossom in place of the delicate, honey-scented white of Huath, used for the traditional 'virgins' wreath. Young women would gather the flowers for their hair and to make May wine, (or November wine here in Southern Hemisphere.) They tossed wreaths over the shoulder towards the man of their desire. Today this is re-enacted with the bridal bouquet thrown to another woman, the 'Maid of Honour, instead of to a possible spouse or lover, as was the tradition. Hawthorn berries are blood red, the blossoms white; these two colours are associated with the Fae and the Celtic Underworld. Just as Hawthorn hedgerows, were grown to keep livestock in and predators out, so is the Hawthorn said to be a barrier of protection from otherworldly entities, psychic attacks and curses, particularly at Beltane and Samhain, when the veil between is at its thinnest.

Chapter 34
Atara en' lle atara
Daughter of My Daughter

Exhausted, Bethan returned home alone; the others still gathered, going over some of the work they were collating ...herbs, ritual, the threads that bound them, the associated Goddess' for the various skills they were strong in ...on the list went and tonight she was absolutely spent.

Perhaps tonight, the light fading He would come; it seemed like forever since the last time she had shared warmth and laughter with Him.

Honey, Morgan's huge hound kept her company often; he adored her and sensed she was edgy, nudging her constantly with her cold, wet nose as she stood, gazing dreamily out the window in the fading light.

Bethan fondled Honey's ears absentmindedly; listening to the distant lure of the pipe and harp; could see little lights that played on the last amber leaves and across the ground in a dance as the sun sank below the rim of the earth. Frogs sang, calling the rain and birds warbled their last farewells to the day, feathers rustling like desiccated leaves in the wind. It appeared as if something not yet visible, was moving across the forest floor and out into the open.

A stream of Fae moved through the trees heading toward Bethan's cottage, silently and purposefully; she knew they were coming for her. Led by an unknown female who appeared wise yet classically youthful as all Fae were, they appeared to be carrying something carefully and with reverence.

Beth didn't wait for them to call but ran to the door, followed closely by Honey, knowing they had something to share with her, to show her. Sure enough the group paused a respectful distance from her Hearth and the female approached alone.

'*Vedui, cormamin lindua ele lle Arianwen Isil'Lindir. Amin na'a Circaea, atara en' lle atara …lle 'ra'atara.*'

Beth understood, 'Greetings, my heart sings to see you Arianwen. I am Circaea, mother of your mother, your grandmother'

'My grandmother?' said Bethan, incapable of more.

'Yes daughter,' said Aithlin stepping closer, 'we have been waiting for the opportunity for you to meet. Circaea has something for you,' he bowed to Circaea.

'Here Arianwen is something that belonged to your mother, a shaper. Her shape was one you are familiar with, Otter.' She indicated the package that the Fae had been carrying but Bethan could only stutter,

'Oonah the Otter, who is my friend in the aspect Leah?' she smiled in sheer delight.

'Yes, the very same. You have travelled many aspects together, but as Sarah or in truth Minhiriath, which means in the elven tongue, 'Between the Rivers;' she struggled to be all that she was and could not maintain her Littleshape when it was most needed. She passed from this realm and none could prevent this. Your father came too late to help her make her shapechange after your birth and was unable to bring you to me. He did what he could instead, taking you to your mother's human friends Susan and Alex, who became your family.'

'When you say too late, Circaea, grandmother,' she hesitated on the unfamiliar word, 'ra'atara, why did my mother drown if she was an Otter shapechanger?'

'You must remember 'ra'tinu, granddaughter, she was a shapechanger yes, but only in her Littleshape could she survive in the water for long. Minhiriath, Sarah as you know her, in Fae form needed air to breathe. Someone held her under child, killed her after she gave birth to you. Your father could not save her, it was too late and you had not made a shapeshift, therefore he could only hope you would find your way to your own shape eventually.'

'Am I also Otter then and Fae? If my mother was Fae too, why was she in this realm as a young woman and how did she become friends with Susan?' asked Bethan.

'No your shape is different, due to the nature of your Fae blood from your mother and father who are of different tribes and she was in this realm by choice to discover what vestiges of Fae, humankin might have in their cells.'

'So you're saying it was by sheer chance that she was here in this realm when she was birthing me?'

'Yes 'ra'atara Arianwen, this is so. Your birth was not expected quite so soon, when she shifted between realms and was caught and murdered,' Circaea paused; her emotions were clear even for an inscrutable Fae.

Bethan sighed and Circaea reached out to her with her song; it sounded so much like her own that she simply went into the waiting arms of her grandmother. They stood for a while in mutual grief before Circaea beckoned the Fae forward with the package; bowing they presented it to Bethan, laying it on a table under the trees outside Bethan's cottage before melting again into the forest.

Circaea stroked her granddaughter's hair saying softly, *Tenna' ento lye omenta 'ra'atara.'* 'Until next we meet, granddaughter,' then turning, simply became a host of golden sparks winking; out like a breath of light.

Aithlin kissed Bethan on her forehead and smiling, ran his fingers over the delicately wrapped package and said,

'Enjoy Arianwen it was hers. It was my Minhiriath Farandirim's special treasure and then he too was gone, leaving a fragile trail of notes behind him that echoed from the depths of the parcel as if there were a live creature within.

Bethan stood for a long while, her hands trailing over the delicately woven wrapping before gently unfolding it from around, what appeared to be, a strange musical instrument. Holding up the delicate wrap it appeared to shimmer with phosphorescence in aqua blue and the palest sea green threads as intricate as a web. It was almost as if it spoke to her in a new way, a new song unfurled, hauntingly sweet and the smell of water and ozone floated to her on the melody from deep within the folds of a cloak; her mother Minhiriath's ritual robe.

She brought it to her face, breathing in her mother's essence and knew that her mother was of the Alu'Quessir, a Sea Fae and her father must be Arda'Quessir an Earth or Forest Fae, which gave her both aspects …what did this mean to who she was she wondered, before turning her attention to the strange instrument revealed.

At that moment, Morgan arrived home with Lily and Honey took the opportunity to bounce from the spot that Bethan had sternly told her to sit at, barrelling into Morgan as he got out of the little car, eagerly licking any bit of skin she could reach. Telling her sternly to sit, Morgan approached Bethan where she stood, looking as if she were in a trance.

'Bethy…' about to ask her if she were okay, he drew in his breath sharply, the sound bringing her back to herself, 'Where did those come from?' he said in astonishment, 'That looks like a set of shepherds pipes but nothing quite like I've ever seen before! It's ancient!' he exclaimed.

'Whaaa?' Oh sorry hello Mor, yes my grandmother visited to give it to me. It was my mother's, her name was Minhiriath and…' she trailed off exhausted, tears welling.

Seeing Beth struggling, Lily ran over, 'Whoa Bethy, take a breath,' she said, as Bethan started to sob.

Morgan stepped forward and just held her before helping her to a chair. He waited for her to recover herself; Lily ran in to fetch a glass of water for her.

'Wow,' Morgan said as he looked at the beautiful instrument, 'Oh wow, Bethy its exquisite.'

Pulling herself together she stood, 'Yes I've never seen anything quite like it either. Goodness knows how you play it but seriously, I would love to try.'

'I'm sure I've got info on the French and Irish

versions of the shepherds pipe or 'Uilleann' pipe,' he said, as Beth sat again to take some hasty sips of water.

'They're truly amazing Bethy; never seen the like either,' said Lily, giving Beth's shoulder a comforting rub, 'can you tell us what happened?'

'Yes, sure,' said Beth with a smile, 'My father turned up with a whole entourage of Fae including my maternal grandmother, Circaea.' She continued to tell them what had transpired as the sun set below the tree line and an icy chill crept into the evening air. Shivering with something more than the cold of the night, they wandered in to find warmth, a glass of wine and some dinner.

Honey stopped a moment on her way in as the music of the forests swelled to a crescendo; the Lord of the Greenwood ran with the hounds; she longed to follow but it was not yet her time.

Chapter 35

Max

Each season round the Silver Wheel
…as humans struggle not to feel
…and yet in feeling all shall heal
…no more their wounded thoughts conceal…

Max had spent an hour or more staring at the computer screen. His mind seethed with everything but the task he should be applying himself to for the group and for his writing deadline, although the latter he had almost given up on at present.

Lily's face filled his vision everywhere he looked and he didn't have the first idea what he was going to do with the feelings scorching his brain. He still loved her, it was as simple as that but how could he have felt what he felt for Sam, only for it to diminish at the first sight of Lily. He felt like a fool and he knew he had hurt Sam even if she seemed to be her normal beautiful self, albeit probably more than a little angry with him, at his reaction to her leaf sprite tattoos.

He removed his specs to rub his eyes and there came a knock at the door. 'Yeah?' he called out.

'It's only me Nerd,' as Tara stuck her head around the door.

'Oh hi Tara, sorry about earlier I'm not myself right now. What can I do for you though?' he asked.

'It's not what you can do for me Max, it's what

you can possibly do for yourself and the situation you are in.'

'What's that Tara?' he asked one eyebrow raised

'Well for a start you can stop feeling sorry for yourself I would suggest,' she grinned but seeing his scowl deepen she softened, 'Lily is here for you Max. She may think and say differently but she is.'

'Now how do you know that?' he scoffed.

'Well as you know, I have access to many realms Max, not just this one and although I am not supposed to meddle, there are times when a little prompt goes a long way to help mend broken hearts in particular.'

'What are you saying Tara, are you adding cupid to your resume now?' Max quipped his humour returning.

'That's more like it,' Tara grinned in response, 'There are a couple of things that may help you. Firstly, there is an aspect that you share in the same realm as Sam.'

'What do you mean,' Said Max, rubbing his eyes again, 'that sounds really obtuse to me?'

'I'm not meaning to, but all I can say is that Sam has been having dreams of a life spent in the same time frame as yourself and that life was not necessarily completed between you. Now is the time for you both to complete the unfinished business perhaps. Talk to her, she may well recognise who you are in that time, it's worth a try don't you think? Then you can get on with your life with Lily, although she has a surprise or two up her sleeve that may not sit well with you either.'

'Okay, I guess I can do that. I'm not sure what you think we can do from now, about then though?'

'Yes you do Nerd!' exclaimed Tara, 'You know that everything is now!'

Max couldn't help but laugh at the familiar name Beth used, when she was frustrated with him.

'I guess I'm afraid to stuff things up again with my inability to commit,' he said soberly.

'If you do nothing you'll never know,' said Tara, as she changed in front of him slowly and deliberately, 'and this you have to start getting used to as something normal rather than weird, my friend,' before she shifted completely and was gone Between the Veil leaving him sitting in stunned silence.

He shook himself almost physically, 'Will I ever get used to that though?' he questioned to the room.

Chapter 36
Skeins Entangled

Deep within the fragile strands
…altered by Unsidhe hands
…halflings, mixed-bloods, contrabands
…their blight then spreads across all lands…

The group of giggling teenagers arrived back at Earthly Rites promptly where Flora had magicked a spread of finger foods for them. Tara took them in to the seminar room with a roll of her eyes toward Flora and Sam at the desk, receiving a grin and thumbs up in return. Claire stood stock still, searching the faces of all the girls until they came to rest on Vanessa's …ah yes, no doubts there then, she thought but what now? She exchanged a look with Flora who, closing her eyes a moment, nodded in agreement …no doubt.

Flora felt as if she would bleed for her mother's pain, the last nail in the coffin of her relationship with her father. How did she feel? Strangely numb she thought.

It wasn't the fault of her little sister; she hadn't known she existed until today. Now they must make the best of things, there was too much else at stake to really worry about Harry or even Annie Savage. How would Vanessa feel she wondered, the innocent one in all of the, so-called, adult doings. Whether mum likes it or not she thought, her face giving nothing away of what she was feeling, I'm going to have a word with my father …in fact more than a few!

When the girls went in with Tara, the giggling muted behind the closed door, the three turned to each other.

Wordlessly Flora and Claire hugged again and then hugged Sam for good measure, there was nothing to do and it was what it was. 'Did Sybille know?' Claire said aloud.

Chapter 37
Sybille

Deep within the fragile strands
…altered by Unsidhe hands
…halflings, mixed-bloods, contrabands
…their blight then spreads across all lands

Sybille stirred within the old tree, dreaming of other times and places, struggling to wake to finish something, but what was it? Little creatures moved around her, spiders had made webs across the entrance to the hollow where she lay. Small winged beings, Makers she recalled, were working to keep her safe and comfortable in her reduced state.

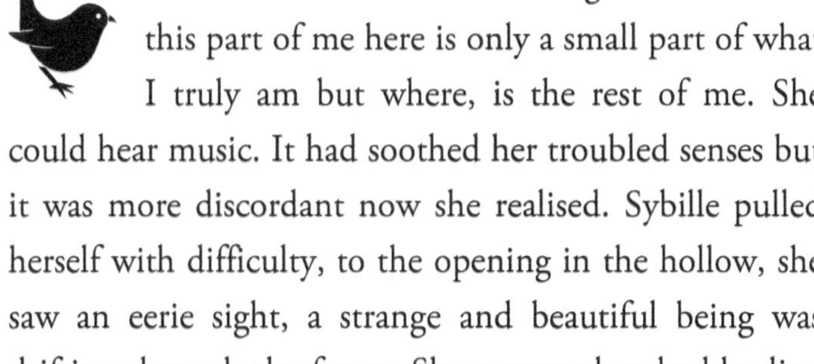

I know I'm not dead she thought. I know that this part of me here is only a small part of what I truly am but where, is the rest of me. She could hear music. It had soothed her troubled senses but it was more discordant now she realised. Sybille pulled herself with difficulty, to the opening in the hollow, she saw an eerie sight, a strange and beautiful being was drifting through the forest. She appeared to be bleeding dark ichor from her belly. The same small, split-winged beings, were encouraging her to go somewhere with them and little dark ones with pointed stingers were battling to take her with them.

Sybille stayed still observing, with a knowing that she was safe if she remained hidden. What would happen if they found her, she couldn't imagine but eve-rything screamed, *'be still!'*

Placing translucent hands over her ears didn't halt the cacophonous sound the little dark beings made and so she withdrew inside herself, deep within the hollow of the tree, finding peace once again in sleep.

Chapter 38
Nina

From earth to sea and sea to sky
...on air's bright wings like gossamer fly,
Across the realms where none shall die
...to within the web, where all truths lie

 Nina's energy seemed to wax and wane with the moon-tides. At full moon, she was bursting with energy but as it waned in size and in vital potency, so too did her will. Magdalena would spend hours sitting with her as her energy diminished, reading to her of the Ways of La Stregga, the Wytchways of old. Eduard too would come to join them, sitting quietly and listening to their quiet voices.

He would blatantly observe Magdalena, the set of her head on her long neck; the eyes that blinked only occasionally like an Owl. He was fascinated and would on occasion; invite her to dine with him when Nina slept. They would light candles and sit in the window of Nina's little room that she loved, speaking quietly of the things Magdalena learned with La Stregga, of the broken crystal bowl, of herbs and potions to help Nina stay strong and finally, after a while of their own lives and selves.

Eduard shared with Magdalena the death of his

wife, the pain of raising a child alone after her mother's death of a fever, when Nina was only a few days old. Society said she should have a mother and that he should marry again after a suitable period of mourning. No one it seemed understood the ways of his mind and heart. He was no ordinary man it would seem and he raised Nina with the help of a wet nurse, a Nonna and a firm and steady hand. Nina had thrived until just over a year ago when a strange illness had overcome her. He thought he would surely lose her but she had recovered. He felt no guilt about the deal he had made with La Stregga to help her recovery. Eduard believed that the Lady had indeed willed it so for whatever purpose, only She knew, therefore, their friendship bloomed and they became closer as each moon cycle passed.

Nina would watch them covertly through her long lashes when she feigned sleep. She observed her father take a stray curl of Magdalena's hair when it fell in her eyes as she read, tucking it behind her ear gently. A subtle touch of hands would bring an audible gasp from Magdalena, causing Nina to smother a giggle with a snore.

Slowly but surely as time passed, Nina knew her Papa would not be alone after she was gone from this world.

Every now and then, she would have extraordinary dreams, quite lucid and profound, when once again she lay, curled in a hollow tree or floating, tired and broken through dark forests, harried by small dark beings that would poke and prod her into submission. Then little Maker spirits, as she had come to know them, would rally round chasing off the dark and bringing her to a safe, secluded cocoon of silken threads, where she could rest until the next restless search for something, someone, began again.

Nina now knew that the being, hiding in the tree was the etheric form of Sybille, a future aspect of herself; that the other diminishing soul was their mutual True-shape Silver and as Silver diminished, so did they. It was a vicious cycle of hide and seek; win or lose.

Physical survival was her part in all of this for at least one more turn on the Wheel, so that Sybille would wake up and remember, Silver would find her and renew on the Web. Sometimes she wondered if she could make the effort, but then there would come a surge of energy from somewhere and a small being would enter her room. A female, wizened and dark skinned, brought her strange potions to drink and unknown roots to chew on, berries of such sweetness she thought she would never be able to swallow them. Each time she came, Nina would rally and astound the people who cared for her, yet again.

One blissfully cool day, after Beltane and before Litha, Magdalena and Nina wandered the garden. Magdalena stopped to look more closely at a strange kind of lichen growing on the side of a tree.

'Why,' said Nina, 'that looks just like the bitter stuff I'm given to chew on by...' she trailed off realising she had said too much as Magdalena looked at her searchingly, '...in dreams,' she finished hurriedly.

'What are you not telling me Nina?' Magdalena asked her seriously. 'Who visits to give you this?'

'I have a visitor who brings me all sorts of strange and interesting things to help me stay strong, Magdalena. She is of the other realms and what she gives me works on my etheric body, so that it can remain strongly attached, not become fragmented.'

'Why did you not tell me of this, little Signorina' Magdalena reverted to the formal title for her charge, softened only by the diminutive. 'It is important I know these things, so that the herbs I give you as a tonic, may not clash with anything else. Does your Papa know of these visitations?'

'No, this is the first time I have let slip about my occasional visitor. She is female, small and wrinkled like a dried apple. She is stern and knowledgeable and is of the nature realms,' said Nina quietly but firmly as if to end the topic there.

'I think I have met this entity,' said Magdalena, 'when I was coming home from the market a while ago. I had completely forgotten her and I'm afraid, may have dismissed her quite rudely at the time. She frightened me and I was in a hurry to get back to you, when really there was no reason for my rudeness, other than fear of her unknown qualities. It was wrong of me,' she finished. After a pause Magdalena asked, 'Do you know who she is?'

'I know that she is the Deva of all healing plants and that she tries to show me things that I have no knowledge of. She is fascinating and her name is Nangini, an unusual name but who knows what the other realms hide eh?' she finished, with a giggle.

With her name spoken quietly, as if in invitation, Nangini manifested, before their startled eyes. Smiling sweetly she approached, an entourage of tiny winged beings accompanying her and they could see that she was actually made up in entirety of these little folk.

Pale leafy-green in colour, they could be mistaken for insects clustering, their wings, delicate and translucent, made rustling sounds as they flew in tight formation so that Nangini's face was constantly flitting and changing as they moved. The sight made Nina a little queasy.

They heard in the susurrus sounds, her voice, whispering to them, '*Rin i' apsa kol hini! Rin, lle cael i' onsint a' naa' nat'. Rin Arwen Airmhid! N'yar Nina a' n'yar Flora, re sinta en' i' nosta'a,*' and as fast as she appeared she was gone, the tiny creatures dispersing in all directions as Eduard walked out into the garden.

'What was that?' he asked sternly, 'I'm open to many things but that sort of Magick? Surely the Old Ones cannot visit us here in broad daylight.'

'Why Papa,' said Nina, 'I never took you for a sceptic,' she grinned at him but for some reason he was not amused by the visitation.

Magdalena gave Eduard a quick, shy smile before leading Nina inside. She didn't know how, but she had understood what Nangini had said.

'Remember the bag of herbs. Remember. They hold the secrets to all. Remember Lady Airmhid. Tell Nina to tell Flora, she knows of the birthing.'

With all his knowledge and in spite of the fact that he had called on Magick to save his daughter, Eduard had not imagined it was as real as his own eyes had seen. He began to see that Magdalena would indeed be the next Stregga. What would this mean to their relationship and to Nina? How selfish of me, he thought, I am only thinking of myself.

Nina dreamed that the little Fae visited again. She was unable to communicate with Magdalena as if they were blocked and so Nangini would speak with her instead. She whispered that the journey begun would be longer than expected, to stay strong, take the herbs daily and to hide them if necessary from prying, sceptical eyes.

She began to sleep better from that day forward; Litha approached and the weather became hot and stormy. She seemed to be thriving on the herbs she took secretly, that Nangini brought her and those Magdalena mixed. She reminded Magdalena constantly that she must ask Nangini to forgive her rudeness and start to learn all she could about the herbs. Magdalena tried but the little being would not respond; only speaking to her through Nina's dreams.

Chapter 39
Maeve

Darkening skies and windblown trees
...the Lady walks with light-footed ease.
Calling to all ...hear Her voice on the breeze
...come to Her She will bring you home.

Maeve woke stiff and sore as if she had received a thorough beating, which in many ways she had. It was as if she had been in Scathach Hearth forever but she continually felt ineffectual against the strong, wiry, warriors in training with her.

She thought often of her life in Springsmeet, of her friends, of Morgan, Sybille and even her mother. She knew that the flow of time, between and in the other realms, was different. She realised that her friends could have been gone forever, or an hour and that she may never see them again. She had regrets but away from the harrowing influence of the Merrow; Mirdhaucha, as the Tuatha de called her, she also realised that she had not been strong enough to fight the cunning and vindictive energy of the little Dark Fae.

Now she had a focus that truly suited her physically, mentally and emotionally. She was becoming used to the early morning and evening rituals, of the training and the divided tasks that all shared. She had shown promise as a fletcher and a smith, the latter due to her Athame making skills, which now translated into creating daggers and other cutting implements, such as skinning knives. Mostly the Tuatha used bow and arrow or staves, the energetic pain of the metal blade, being very weakening to those of Tuatha de Danaan blood.

In what was probably a short space of time, as humans know it, she was fitter than she'd ever been, lean and flexible. She was beginning to find peace, when the Cunning Man Bran showed up again, his eyes scrutinised her as they had the first time but were at least somewhat friendlier.

He came to check the tribe for wounds and disease, to teach the children basic skills with harp and voice. Although they were a healthy bunch, wounds left to fester could kill even a healthy warrior and the oral tradition of learning through story telling was a coveted skill. He was also there to see which of the people had other skills that were passed down to their children, music, seership, herbal lore, smithing, everything was respected, encouraged so that each may find their own niche in their society.

Bit by bit Bran had mastered more than many in a short space of time, following the instructions the shapechanger Tara had given him a little over three years ago. He had brought a small child to the Isle of Seers, he had been but a boy in truth when he thought of that day, but he would never forget the meeting with Leah and the child Alma who had proven to be more than anyone, even The Cybil of that time, could have ever imagined.

Alma had been sent to Scathach Hearth to hone and train her physical skills as much as The Cybil had trained her seer's gifts. Neither Scathach, nor The Cybil, knew what to do with the little wild thing and with approaching puberty, she was potentially a rock exploding in a hearth fire. Now he had been instructed to assess her skills and the link that had grown between the strange creature Maeve, who had been brought through the 'Between' from who knew where, and the child Alma.

Chapter 40

Sybille ...several years ago

Falling leaves floating, green, red and gold
...a soft scent of wood smoke recalls times of old
Where will you be when the wind sets you free?
Safe in your bed or outside in the cold

Sybille at just over 60 was agile and active, her garden and work, teaching and writing about the Old Ways, were the sustaining forces of her life. She had always been aware of how different she was to girls of the same age, as a child and right through her life. Now, as a mature woman, that had not changed. Many women of the same generation had already given up work and their gardening activities for the gym, strength classes and the latest kitchen gadgets or fashions. Fund raising for a worthy cause was one thing but the, 'seen and be seen,' aspects of the bobbed hair set were just not her 'thing.'

For one thing her hair was wild and silver, still worn in long curling strands no fancy 'do' would tame. She preferred loose, natural fibers rather than hip hugging jeans or straight skirts, although she could dress up with the best of them if needs must. She just didn't and couldn't fit the mold.

Living a little out of town on a sprawl of land didn't help the equation either where her peers were concerned, particularly not when she had chosen to live simply, off the grid. Her converted barn was ample for her needs. A room to teach a more private group and for her research and writing, a spacious living area, big country style kitchen and a long sunny dining room with a huge old refractory table that sat sixteen comfortably, were her pride and joy. Loft bedrooms with skylights to watch the stars were another feature that she couldn't imagine being without.

Soft gas, oil lamps and candles lit the evenings and a huge wood-fueled stove took centre stage in her kitchen for warmth, hot water and cooking. She didn't need the gym when she had a huge garden of vegetables and herbs to tend, along with her hens and goats. Walking was a passion, carting firewood a strength class in itself.

Then there was her work, her shop and reading centre in town. People came from the city just to see the group of handpicked and versatile readers, who formed the team that was the hub of her work.
Books, candles, incense and crystals in gleaming bowls, enticed the eager and the wary alike.

Fragrant oils and herbal brews lined the shelves, rubbing shoulders with all the paraphernalia of the Wytch's craft.

Her ability to gauge people's needs was paramount to the success of the business she ran like a well-oiled machine, with the help of another small team of lovely souls.

Writing was taking up much more of her time now, together with monthly workshops on Tarot, Palmistry and Wytchways. In all, she was more than content with the life she had created for herself.

Now the rite of Yule was fast approaching and she had work to do in preparation. Her new intakes for her workshop on psychic and creative awareness were proving to be an intelligent and hungry to learn group. There were three very different young women in particular, who had been working with her for a while. She was sure they were going to keep her busy. Flora, Bethan and Maeve, the first two she knew would shine quietly and brilliantly and the latter would be unquantifiable.

Maeve, she thought to herself …something unusual there, 'I must speak to Silver about her,' she muttered to herself before reaching for her Book of Shadows to write out the ritual for Yule that she was going to surprise her three students with.

They had already grasped the basics of what she had to teach them and were ready to awaken to their true selves. She was very familiar with the process of understanding self and the courage it took for a person to be able to come right out and admit, 'I'm a Wytch!' but Wytches they were without a doubt.

Taking a deep breath, she settled to her task the

words spilling from her and onto the beautiful fragrant parchment sheets like liquid…

Yule 

21 June Southern Hemisphere
(22 December Northern Hemisphere)

Yule is approaching, hear the horns sound
…watch as Jack Frost breathes ice on the ground
Coating the world in a silence of white
…sparkling like diamonds on bright moonlit nights
Lady and Lord come a gathering in…
…so make cauldron-brewed wassail to share with your kin
Honey and nut cakes for cold winter fare
…feeds the wee birds to show them you care
Light up your candles of red, green and white
…to act as a beacon of radiant light

Day and night battle for supremacy as the wheel of the year turns on. At Yule, the cold is manifest and the earth held in winter's sway. Although the point of the shortest day and longest night has arrived, we know there are still all the cold and wet days ahead, even snow, here in the highlands, but we are also aware that the days will surreptitiously begin to lengthen from this moment on.

To our ancestors this time would have been one of joy as the light returned slowly to the world. Some of their more perishable, winter stores may already be becoming low, but they would know that the sun's rays would soon warm the earth again. They would share some of the late harvested foods in celebration of the Winter Solstice.

At Yule, the Oak and Holly King, battle once again for supremacy. The Holly King has held sway until this hour and now, aged, will be defeated for the waxing year by the birth of the Oak King, bringing the returning light and the Holly Kings thanked, for everything learned in the introspective dark days.

It is the time of rebirth for the Lord of the Greenwood the Great Horned One, also known at times as the Sun King. He is born from the womb of the Great Goddess and we can see with this, why the Christian folk then took this time of year to be the birth time of their own new, young 'God.'

The rite of Yule, (which comes from the Scandinavian word Jul meaning wheel), is one of joy ...even today, when we have so much and do not necessarily rely on our own hard work to produce our food, as the ancients did ...we celebrate as the sun returns, His warmth and light.

We decorate with Holly, Evergreen and Ivy, creating wreaths and table centrepieces. The Yule log, made from Holly, decorated with a red candle, a symbol of light returning and the blood shed at birth, a white candle for the innocence of new life and a green, for the growth process of a greening, burgeoning spring to come and the renewal of hope it brings.

We celebrate the change from Holly to Oak King, symbolic of fire and the warmth of the sun's return as He is born anew from the Mothers cauldron of rebirth. Feasting is a great part of the rites with good seasonal foods and of course, Wassail, the mulled spiced wine traditional for the season.

For the Wytch it is a season of giving, not in the way of the commercial Christian traditions of Christmas, rather the giving of time and energy to a good cause in the community, is our way, just as the Yule Log is not a gooey, bought chocolate cake, in the shape of a log.

In most tradition, the partially burned Yule log is kept for the year to light the fires at Samhain, Celtic New Year. All fires extinguished, a tall dark haired young man would knock on the door, bringing a smouldering coal to kindle the first fire of the New Year, to represent light and warmth during the approaching darkness; he would also bring a coin for prosperity. This coin is the origin of the gold; foil wrapped chocolate coins, which many of my generation will remember in their Yule stockings that traditionally have New Year/Samhain origins rather than Yule.

Even the orange, which our northern ancestors would not have had readily, it being a tropical fruit and which I can remember was quite an expensive item, was a symbol of the orange sun in the sky. The nuts, traditionally hazel and chestnut, were also for the children as gifts in their stocking, symbolising the last harvest of Samhain rather than Yule. Nuts, highly nutritious of course, would be one of the foods stored and brought out to share for the Yule Feast, which is why the celebration of Yule in December is somewhat incongruous, going against the natural turn of the wheel here in southern hemisphere!

Somehow, our Samhain symbols have become skewed, interwoven with the all-encompassing Christmas and New Year of the Christian beliefs, taken anyway from the Old Ways, to bring people to their new God and to worship indoors rather than in the temples of nature.

Yule gifts exchanged by the Wytchwise are small tokens, a giving of something that we personally love, that we have made or been given. It is then like the giving of a little piece of ourselves, as the object is imbued with our very essence by the making and our love of it.

We can see today the horrendous expenditure of bigger and better, impersonal and often, hastily bought gifts that have nothing to do with the true joy of giving. A gift without meaning is empty. When we give of ourselves that is true giving, albeit somewhat bittersweet.

Primarily we take the time to contemplate the coming season, enjoy introspection, dreaming and planning for spring, to mend or make things needed, plan ritual working sand project healthy images out into a cold and in places, violent world.

We can feel a little stir crazy; cabin fever is the worst feeling for normally active people. It is important to take some time in a ray of wintery sunshine even if it holds little warmth. What it does hold is Vitamin D, the deficiency of which, in the human system, is creating the disease of our age...

...Sybille paused as she considered all the Solstice celebrations through the years and all the gatherings she had hosted right here at the farm in Covenstead. Sixty she may be in human reckoning but ancient she truly was. This year would be a shared one with the three young women she mentored and the Coven that had grown from her teachings. She was to lead a public celebration on the Mount and had convinced her niece Sam to join them for the day.

Her thoughts returned to Maeve, the wild card in the deck …she did not know how to draw her out of herself, to help her recover from a childhood of unspeakable events. Just recently, she had been observing a strange little being with her. No one else appeared to notice, even the super sensitive Bethan …why is that I wonder, she pondered? Bethan was usually the first to see or sense otherworldly beings. Sybille knew that Bethan had gifts she herself was not aware of and that they shared a history somewhere in the Akasha …the Skeins of Tyme.

She had researched several known periods in history that they shared and was still looking for a few missing links that were relevant to their immediate time together.

Sam too, Sybille knew had an underlying resistance to the Old Ways, partly fear and partly fascination perhaps, but eventually the call of her blood would be the victor, of this Sybille was sure. There would be no denying the Mother after all and many things would come to light soon enough she thought, before returning once more to her task.

Chapter 41

Winter Solstice Preparations

Moon tides turning...fires burning
...winds blow cold across the land
Inner dreams and visions glowing
...bringing warmth to cold, cold hands.
Winter's darkness now approaches
...creeping closer on tiptoe
Go within to seek the silence
...move in the cycles...ebb and flow...

As the wheel turned again, so the weeks had flown. So much had happened and lives changed as a result.

Maeve's forced removal, a sister discovered for Flora and the end of a marriage for Claire. A tentative new relationship developing and one with potential had fizzled out. Tension between grove members was not conducive to a successful Sabbat but still they struggled on, always hoping for the best and that their best would be anywhere near good enough.

They prepared as they did for all previous Midwinter fests when Sybille was there, Sam, Flo and Beth, very conscious of how much they missed her. Yule had always been a fun time and they would begin the three-day Sabbat by decorating the farm. This year was nostalgic rather than celebratory. They missed Maeve too and, in spite of her recent strange behaviour, her rather caustic wit.

After asking permission from the tree sprites, they brought in boughs of fresh holly, covered in blood red berries, evergreen fir, mistletoe and ivy, to hang and to create a centrepiece for the table they covered in a snow-white cloth.

Bethan wrapped the ivy vines around the stair rails and across the loft balustrades, interspersing it with the rich red holly berries, with their shiny green leaves and the subtle mistletoe's, white berries, like little deadly pearls.

Morgan made the Yule log from a piece of holly branch he found on the ground at the base of one of the four huge and ancient holly trees on the hill; he cut hollows for their green, white and red candles to grace the centre of the table.

This year they would step out of tradition, in order to apply the energy of returning light more strongly to illuminate their magickal working, rather than the simple honouring of the seasons.

Flora had dried cinnamon-spiced apple rings, wafer thin and fragrant, to hang in strands across the windows and over the mantle in every room. Nothing artificial used in any way; nature provided it all, including the harvest of shiny brown Hazel nuts, scattered down and around the centrepiece on the table.

They shared in preparing a feast for after the rite, with everything that was in season. Nutloaf replaced the muggles roast meat to serve with a rich onion and wild garlic sauce. They prepared home-grown, root vegetables, strewn with fresh rosemary, sage and thyme, to bake slowly. It would fragrance the whole house when each individual showered and robed before the rite took place.

Winter Solstice, shortest day and longest night and then, after the coldest time to come, once more spring would tentatively emerge …ah the longing that always arose when the cold and wet hemmed them in, a wonderful time for research however.

The weather had become increasingly wild and each had bought and dedicated to their ritual purpose, new thermals to wear under their robes; traditionally, nothing was worn, but it would be silly to have their focus skewed by the simple fact that they were freezing.

Sam recalled a Beltane rite when it had been so cold it had been more like Samhain, dressed in their summer robes they had frozen, but it had only leant to the hilarity of the day; today was different, as every rite around the wheel would be, until they brought both their friends home.

When all was prepared for the feast and before they bathed, they walked together to the sycamore grove carrying everything they needed for the altar and circle casting. Flora swept away some of the dead leaves to give them a clean clear space of loamy grass to work on, that released its damp fragrance to the

air as they worked.

Wind lanterns were set at each quarter and behind the altar, together with small yew trees in pots; candles being, easily extinguished, by the blustery Solstice winds, not to mention the mischievous behaviour of air sprites, perfectly capable of blowing out candles as fast as they were lit, the Yew for protection at the elemental gateways.

A cauldron was set in the south, filled with earth and set for a small fire with sacred wood, to illustrate the darkest and shortest day of the solar year, in the place where the sun does not transit.

The Altar was set as always, with a small bowl of salt, a chalice with water, smudge bowl with charcoal on a bed of black sand and a small bowl of herbs as incense; Flora and Sam had chosen, hand ground and blended, cinnamon, sage, rosemary, ginger and chamomile.
The Altar Candle, Pentacle, Athame, Wand, Boline and the Chalice for wine were in their traditional positions on the Altar.

A besom lay in readiness on the ground in front of the Altar. Its bristles facing sunwise to indicate the direction the circle would be cast,

Once again, they were hesitant to use a blade in their rite, but had decided to have a bowl of earth that they would cover the blade with after the casting. It was important for the metal to be neutralised so as not to harm the little Fae who flocked at the merest whiff of a magickal working, although the leaf sprites seemed to be with Sam almost permanently now, making patterns on her skin and on her clothing where they clung, singing quietly.

The Athame would be used to cast and the Wand to release afterwards. The Athame for the fire element, the light returning and the wand to release their magicks to the air and ethers, rather than grounding the energy as would usually be done for physical manifestations.

They had spent hours combing all their notes and Sybille's, to find just the right way of going about the rite. It would be strange to cast the circle in a non-traditional way and even more strange, to call the quarters in an unfamiliar fashion, but there was a different need now.

As they were preparing they spoke quietly to each other, Flora recalled, 'Bethy do you remember what Sybille always used to say to us …?' she laughed as they spoke as one,

'Throw out the clocks and look to the sun or your circle will end where it should have begun.'

Morgan said, 'It still does my head in a little doing everything in reverse to what she taught me for northern hemisphere, but it makes sense. Why do Wytches here follow the North when they live in the South I wonder?'

'Yes,' interjected Sam if you do that you'd be releasing when you thought you were casting and vice, versa. That would have to be somewhat counterproductive wouldn't it?'

'Of course,' said a voice from the tree above, 'You would be unprotected when you most needed it!' Tara slipped from the tree changing as she landed. Max gave an audible groan as she did, Claire followed her and Cal just laughed with delight.

'Oh wow Claire! That's extraordinary.' It wasn't the first time he'd seen her change but not quite that close up. He thought for a moment, noticing the silver bangle Claire wore, before turning to Tara, 'What happened to the shapechanger from the Wold's bracelet Tara. Do you still have it? I've been meaning to ask you but things just kept getting in the way,' he grinned.

'No,' she said ruefully, 'I dropped it as I flew. I went looking for it straight away. I even called a whole Corvidae crew in to help, but it had simply disappeared. We might have to enlist the aid of some mud dwellers come to think of it, 'cos it was very wet underfoot if I remember rightly,' she finished.

'Hmm,' said Cal, it's been on my mind the last few days, I noticed you wear one and Claire, Morgan and Lily too …how come you do Lily?' he asked her directly.

'Oh this old thing,' she said, glancing at Morgan for help. 'I gave her that,' said Morgan hurriedly, 'it's very old. We found it on a junk stall at the market in Glastonbury,' he lied, fingers crossed behind his back.

Max stepped forward from where he'd been listening, 'Your lying,' he said simply, 'you're a changer aren't you Lily? That explains so much about the times you got back from places in record time, when it would have taken us mere mortals twice the amount,' he sneered. 'All the while you were lying to me!' The hurt was evident in his voice.

'Now's not the time,' said Tara stepping between. 'We have a ritual to perform, if you remember. Control those fear based agenda of yours Max. It would seem that Maeve was not the only one to be influenced by the Mirdhaucha,' she scowled, 'Get a grip Max,' she finished sternly. 'Now,' she said, turning to Lily, 'there's no more reason for hiding yourself from anyone is there? Get it over with please. Change!' she commanded.

'Hang on,' said Max, 'when did you become the group head kicker then?' He broke off, stepping back quickly as Tara grew in stature...

She shifted shape, appearing to have multiple heads with sharp cruel beaks, huge talons on outthrusting, part bird, part human feet ...black wings unfurled to become arms and wings combined, before the wings settled around her to become a seething cloak of glossy blue-black Ravens.

Tara's face reappeared, her tawny arms outstretched, swathed in the huge feathered garment. Her eyes flashed in anger, 'Since I lost patience with human attitudes to anything even remotely different to the 'norm' they expect,' she roared, causing Max to take several steps back in fear, raw power emanated from the entity towering over him.

Silence reigned in the group as they witnessed the manifestation of The Morrigan, of which Tara was an aspect.

Morgan was the only one who found his voice, being himself a Raven changer. He remembered a time when he had stood on the edge of a forest and a beautiful, raven-dark being had manifested, accompanied by a flock of unusually silent Ravenkin. Morgan remembered suddenly what had happened after the Raven changer Rowan, had been pierced by an arrow of the Dark Fae.

Taking a deep breath he stepped forward, bowing to the stately being, he said, 'Lady you honour us here, forgive our human fears. This one,' indicating Max with a nod, 'is unused to your ways and has been corrupted by one of the small folk.'

'Of this I am aware, Bran-Morgan,' she said with what was almost a gentle smile on her full red lips, 'He must learn to be strong again or much will be tainted. He adds to the blight that has in truth been created through human fear.' She looked sternly at poor Max, who was by now almost quaking in his boots, 'Come forward,' The Morrigan demanded; like a sleepwalker, he obeyed. Placing her hands on his heart, she drew a small Sigel on his chest. With an audible sigh, he almost fell to his knees, not in pain but in what appeared to the others to be utter relief.

There was a tearing sound and a scream, as The Morrigan drew a small, dark being from his energy field and to everyone's horror, simply gave it a little shake and a slap. 'Be gone from here,' she said to the little Dark Maker and with another movement of her hands, it changed before their eyes. Small split wings appeared; the stinging tail vanished. It started to glow with a light so bright they almost had to shade their eyes and the Maker began to sing in rich thrilling notes of pure joy. One flew straight at Max, burying itself in his energy, cleansing his being to the core, before, with a dip of wings to the Lady; it flew gurgling with laughter to join its gathering siblings. A cloud of leaf sprites lifted from Sam to sing and dance in rapturous abandon at the Maker's release.

Bethan's eyes filled with tears, Flora grasped Cal's hand and squeezed, receiving a warm smile in return. Each of the group hugged Max as if he'd been away on a long journey. Lily changed fluidly into the most beautiful English Blue Jay and flew summersaults with glee.

'So this is what has happened to Maeve,' Max said when he could speak.

'Indeed,' said The Morrigan.

'Then, if the Makers can be healed by the Gods, why is it up to us to do this work when we're so inept at handling even the human realms,' he faltered as her eyes became stern again.

'The human condition is of its own making,' she said, quite gently. 'It is time to be self-responsible for the plight of your planet and your selves.'

'Yeah,' said Max, 'of course …I knew that,' grinning at The Morrigan sheepishly.

At that she shape shifted, shrinking back to the diminutive form of Tara again, rapidly '…SHIT, yelped Tara, 'I hate it when you do that Lady!' …the answer was a husky laugh from the ethers as The Morrigan withdrew, 'Get to work,' they heard through the laughter.

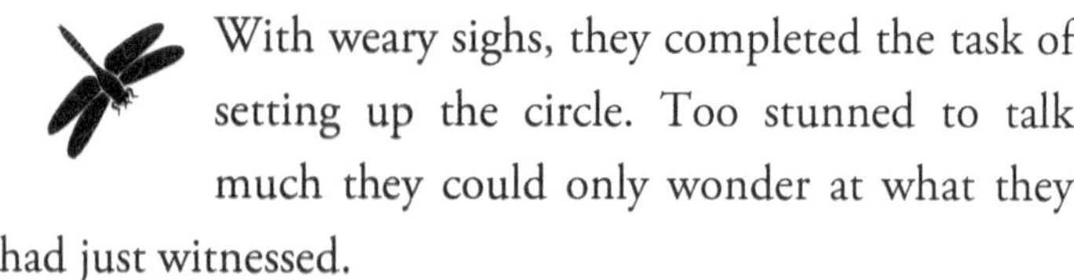 With weary sighs, they completed the task of setting up the circle. Too stunned to talk much they could only wonder at what they had just witnessed.

'How could any of us doubt even for a second ever again,' whispered Cal, regaining his voice, to Flora. She simply smiled happily up at him in agreement.

Lily changed back to her human form grinning with joy. She was free, her secret out.

Claire smiled in understanding.

Max ginned at Lily tentatively, mouthing quietly, 'Sorry!' to her as the others finished the work and they all walked quietly back to the house.

Morgan walked with Sam, giving her hand a quick squeeze as Lily and Max stood looking into each other's eyes.

'It's all good Mor,' she said candidly, 'He's not for me. There was a time I believe but even then, I think things were too hard for him to understand. I can live with that, look what I have as a reward,' she finished as the little sprites returned to her, still singing.

One by one, they found a quiet seat or a couch to sprawl on, there being plenty of time for meditation and introspection before the rite would not happen much before midnight. Occasionally one or the other would drift outside and return, restless with the need to move, as the energy started to settle on them in preparation for the ritual.

Cal and Max played a game of chess, Lily sat watching quietly, her gaze drifting often to Max's face, watching his concentration waver, each time he caught her glance.

Beth had gone out to the garden in quiet solitude and Flora had decided to go on another hunt for the missing Book of Shadows, accompanied by Sam and Morgan. Tara and Claire had once more disappeared. All was peaceful yet charged with energy waiting, silent and unknown.

Chapter 42

Sybille's  Book of Shadows
Shapeshifting-Familiar Spirits

The softness of feather s...the strength of her claws
The power of her flight...her beak...strong as jaws
Yet she will fly ...the moon on her wings
...and gently glides down to the Lady who sings

Shapechanger

Shifting, changing, morphing, rearranging
...bones creaking, skin sliding ...stretching, wings widening
...soaring, song outpouring ...drifting, weight shifting
...light gleaming, feathers streaming
...eyes glistening, deepest listening
...body tightened, senses heightened
...turns spinning, dives ...winning
...beak snatching, talons catching
...load bearing, flesh tearing
...hunger sated, warm, elated
...strength fed ...soon feathers shed
...reshaping ...almost breaking ...freedom waning
...shifting, changing, morphing, rearranging

The ability to shape shift is an ancient art but this of course does not necessarily mean one may shift in the literal sense, into the familiar shape. It is more likely that one would mind meld with a creature that has chosen us to work with to mutual benefit.

Raven is notorious for their ability to wait. They will wait for a creature to die or for the meat of that creature to be just right to eat. They will wait, watching the daily rounds of human gauging, for instance, when eggs are laid and when collected. No margin of error is available to the collector who wants fresh eggs for breakfast; Raven will have been there first. These characteristics give one an idea of what the Raven brings as a familiar spirit.

For most of the year, Ravens fly in mobs known as a, Conference of Raven, (as opposed to a Murder of Crows), due to their often being seen in a circle, all facing inward as if conversing and debating a cause, each taking a turn to lead. During the mating season, they will pair off and are dedicated only to each other and the raising of their young. They will chase off others of their Conference if they enter their territory. They are known to abandon their young to care for themselves quite early, as they will otherwise not bother to pick up food, even when it is literally right under their nose. They will allow a human to hand feed them if they are given the opportunity.

They are the bird of The Morrigan and of all battle Goddesses and to be one of their kin is an honour. Owl shapeshifting, like any raptor, holds its own dangers; particularly to vegetarians who find themselves in Owl form craving a morsel of Mouse or a snack of Moth. Owls mate for life and are in some cultures the harbinger of death. It is said in some tribes that the Owl will call your name when your time is due. Mostly, in Western culture it is the bird of wisdom and knowledge due to their ability to see in the darkest of nights, therefore they are claimed as the 'seer into the soul.'

Otter bears the symbol of freedom and playfulness, to take on their form, is to learn to find joy in simple things. They will play for hours with a small stick or stone and even their food. At times, they are quite cat-like until they enter the water and become more like seal with four legs rather than flippers and tail. Otter is the finder of buried treasures, not of the gold and silver kind, but of soul aspects that are childlike and innocent.

So many possibilities of interaction and shape change, as we meld our minds to become another creature, while retaining the consciousness of human. Could we get lost in the joy of less complex creatures and lose ourselves, or can we borrow some of these qualities to claim them as a part of ourselves?

If we consider that, all things return to universal energy to become cells in the greater source, would it not be possible that we already possess those cells from another space and time? What if the cells are already a part of our cell memory and enable us to relate more closely with the very creatures we are attracted to, who from time to time, make their presence felt so strongly in our lives we cannot ignore them.

The art of conscious shape change may well be the art of affiliation with those perceived missing cells, which we search for through millennia.

Chapter 43
Winter Solstice Rite

May your Yule be blessed
...may your heart be light
...may your belly be full
...may you share the joy of this blessed night

Quietly, one by one, they bathed and changed into their robes. Susan and Alex arrived, greeted soberly as Bethan told them of the events that afternoon.

Animals and children love the energy of magick and the two cats were already meandering up the hill to the grove, long before the human were ready. Honey too followed at a discreet distance; she had discovered that cats were more than able to look after themselves, as her sore nose was a testimony to.

Lighting torches to carry to the grove they walked in line, female then male alternately. Morgan and Alex lit the perimeter flares to shed light in the gathering gloom. It seemed as if the very air itself was dark and sombre, an energy more akin to Samhain than the returning light of Yule.

They shivered in their heavy robes, in spite of the warm under garments, a chill mist crept across the ground to circle the grove in white moisture that would no doubt, become frost before sunrise.

Without Maeve to share in the casting, they had decided to make it a dual rite. Cal and Alex would take the two masculine elements of fire and air, while Flora and Lily the two feminine, earth and water.

This time a male and a female would cast the circle and then make a doorway to bring everyone in, although there was still no sign of Claire and Tara.

Morgan and Sam would cast, although Sam had been nervous at the thought, then the other four would call the elemental quarters. Bethan had thought it important that all should be involved in some way in creating their Solstice rite.

Morgan and Sam cast the circle as if they were performing a graceful dance; Morgan lit the Altar candle on opening, Sam performed the salt and water blessing and cleansing of earth and water. Unerringly, the more experienced Morgan, in spite of casting against his usual directions in the UK, led her through, as he formed the walls of smoke and then of fire, lighting the quarter candles before the final cast.

Sam didn't falter, even at the end when she filled the circle with light and energy, above and below, forming a complete globe of blue-silver light; the leaf sprites almost lifted her from the ground as she spun, the words coming unbidden, as if they were whispering them to her in chorus,

'I cast thee oh circle, that thou be the boundaries between the realms of men and the realms of the mighty

ones; a guard and protection that will preserve and contain the energies we do raise within thee ...wherefore I do bless and consecrate thee.'

The others waiting beyond the sacred circle where astounded at the energy this slender young woman had built up in the last months. Her once short, choppy black hair had grown out almost to her shoulders; sparking static energy as she moved and her constant companions glowing, translucent leaf and twig shapes, their autumn colours now faded to winter's pale, silvery-greys. Sam glowed with health and light.

Morgan gave her a smile of acknowledgement and encouragement, before picking up the Athame and walking to the southeast to cut a doorway to invite in the others. Sam stood with blessed water, greeting each with, *'Merry Meet, Blessed Be,'* taking their hand, splashing them with water and kissing them in welcome, as she drew them into the sacred space.

Alex walked round the circle, moving smoothly into the east, Cal following to the north. Lily walked gracefully to the west and Flora finally to the South.

Sam sealed the entrance with a Sigel and walked with Max, Susan, Bethan and Morgan to the centre facing southeast, arms out at their sides' palms forward, to embrace the energy as each of the group called the elemental quarters with the words they had created especially for this rite.

Alex began, speaking the words while inscribing the pentacle of the east, of air in front of him with his Wand, to form a gateway for the elementals, that they may lend aid in the working.

'I call upon elemental air, as of your currents, I become aware. The force of wind my intellect brings, whilst your music, of inspiration sings, Blessed you are and Blessed be, I thank you for attending me'

He brought the tip of his Wand to his third eye to the matching psychic gateway on his brow, while each of the others brought their arms up and across their chests in a gesture of gathering-in and of reverence to the element.

Cal then followed in the north quarter, with the pentacle of fire,

'I call upon elemental fire you are the flames of all desire. All my natural powers invoke, from your flames and through your smoke. Blessed you are and Blessed Be I thank you for attending me'
Repeating the gesture of opening, he felt relief as the newest recruit that he had not faltered on the words in his nervousness.

Lily flawlessly repeated the ritual of greeting in the west,

'I call upon elemental water, I greet you here as your daughter. Your cooling flow becoming still and through your tides my emotions fill. Blessed you are and Blessed Be, I thank you for attending me,'

…and finally Flora with her usual quiet, earthy strength in the south,

'I call upon elemental earth the greater part that gave me birth. Solid, grounded, centred here, my reasons for being becoming clear. Blessed you are and Blessed Be, I thank you for attending me.'

Wing beats heard as if from afar indicated the Ravenkin's arrival in the trees above and the hoot of Owls, as Claire and a few other kin payed homage to the Lady of the Night.

Yule, the longest night, it is Oak Moon when the energy for their ritual turns to the light of the Oak King …the young Greenlord of the wilds, birthed.

They turned as one to the Altar; approaching to anoint oil in the shape of the seven-point star, calling on the Fae to guide their journeying and to guard their circle. Each placed a sprig of dried oak leaves and a few acorns on the Altar as offerings to the coming light. Morgan lit a taper from the Altar candle in reverence.

They watched in awe as Sam's little accomplices flew to the Oak leaves, transforming them with their essence to fresh new growth, urging them to plant their offerings around the circles perimeter.

That done the group sat in circle, Bethan in the centre; Morgan wedged the taper into the soil in the cauldron of earth. They held hands as Bethan settled into a comfortable position facing south, the cauldron of earth see before her. I held small pieces of woody herb and sacred trees, dried and ready to bring the light in, before her; Rosemary, to remember the way of her ancestors, Oak for strength and endurance, Forest Ash …the wild Rowan, to transform the rite through action and Hawthorn to guard her.

Morgan, facing Beth, leaned in to light the sacred flame transferred from Altar to taper, to sacred wood. Even though they were bringing light to the place where the sun never shone, the little fire-sprites leapt to life at his touch, sending sparks and small wing-like, coloured flames into the twigs. They ran along each little branch and leaf in apparent joy, transforming Beth's face, infusing it with their flame.

She gazed deep within the shimmering fire and from her brow, again the antlers grew; the smoke surrounded her like a cloak, ashes falling into her hair. Small ember like creatures created sparks of energy, lifting her hair from her head in silver skeins. She shifted…changing, her eyes becoming soft, those of a White Doe, then deep liquid brown, round as Otter's, her hair appearing to drip with water. On and on she changed, grew and shrank as if all life dwelt within and for her, each elemental present, in her and through her.

Sam could feel the shift as Morgan sent the charge around and through them all sunwise, to Flora, to Cal, to Susan, to Alex, to Lily, to Max and through her, back to him and so on. As they began to spin the energy she began to chant, the others following,

'Two in one and one in two the gift of life they bring to you. As above so below, your heart is light when their truths you know. As without so within, cast your circle ...let them in.'

As the energy they raised grew in the circle and within each of them, they rose as one stepping the traditional steps of the circle dance, moving, spinning faster and faster, until the only audible words were, **'LET THEM IN,'** repeatedly. This opened the elemental gateways so Bethan could scry in the fire in the darkest places; the salamanders fed the channels to let in the light.

They spun, until each lost all trace of self, becoming as one great blue-silver flame, filling space and all time; growing split wings like dragonflies hurtling through the Skeins of Thyme singing before scattering like sparks, to harvest knowledge from every seed-aspect they were throughout time.

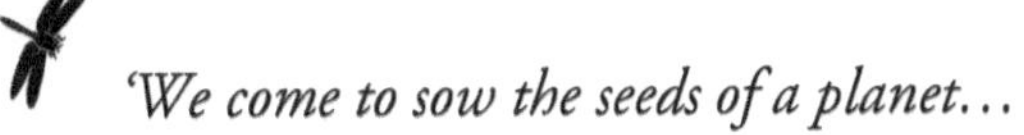

'We come to sow the seeds of a planet...'

Chapter 44
Sybille's Book of Shadows
Arianrhod

Moon dark draws near ...respect life, have no fear
Go deep within to the shrine of your soul
...drink of Her Cauldron ...sip from Her Bowl
Watch the wheel turn ...see the stars spin away
...that same turning wheel ...will bring a new day

Arianrhod, Lady of the Silver Wheel, which is a Celtic metaphor for the moon. One of her children was a sea spirit perhaps a Merrow. Beloved of today's pagan community particularly there are only snippets of information about the beautiful Arianrhod but these have been somewhat Christianized even though these Christian aspects were taken for much older Celtic oral traditions. Often depicted as a moon Goddess, She is birthed of the sea. The silvery tract created as moonlight flickers on deep oceans, is perhaps the pathway to her and from where she came. She is said to have birthed the sea as much as being birthed by it and to have given birth to the sun/son. Her Silver Wheel in the sky is the Lunar Wheel of the Year, that all women particularly relate to through their own menstrual cycles and thus, tribal women held the key to the paths of the moon and sun in the yearly, natural cycles, through which the Sabbats were created and celebrated.

Chapter 45

In the Dreaming ...Samantha

'Earth you are, from earth you came,
Your intellect from Air you gain,
Your Fire should burn, with flaming ire,
Yet Water has put out your fire.'

Spinning out of control Samantha found herself wrapped in a cloak of leaves that were the entirety of all her little sprites. They flew her through the skeins to her aspect of Magdalena, the one she dreamed of who stubbornly refused to acknowledge the little deva Nangini and who was falling hopelessly in love with a man who was not as she had thought.

'Max,' she said aloud, 'why it's Max, that's why he has issues with Magick. That's why he cannot commit.'

She was pulled to where Magdalena sat, holding the hands off an aging woman. After the rite of scrying La Stregga had performed and the breaking her of crystal bowl she had lost all energy, all will to live. Riddled with guilt at what she might have done, even though the Lady herself had said that the working had developed a positive twist to a negative situation, she struggled.

As her aspect Magdalena, Sam could feel the young woman's grief at the possible impending death of her teacher, empathising deeply when she thought of her own loss. She could see how their lives were paralleling and wondered what she had not learned in this aspect Magdalena that she may be learning in the concurrent one as Samantha.

She could see a small being at the foot of the bed that seemed to be attempting to draw Magdalena's attention but to no avail. Sam spoke quietly to the little Fae and was surprised when Magdalena started, looking round for the source of the distinct voice.

Acting as a go between Sam reached out with her mind to the wizened nature spirit, her own little tribe of leaf sprites cavorting with sheer glee as they dived at the Fae creature, covering them in their cloak and leaving Sam exposed to a brief deep scrutiny from both the Fae and Magdalena.

'I dream of you and your strange clothes, your hair all short and choppy and I dream that one day I may be as free,' said Magdalena.
The nature spirit smiled at Sam and stepped closer to her, 'Please tell her my name is Nangini and I am here to help her with her trials,' she said. 'She continues to ignore me, or simply cannot see; for some reason the veil has fallen and it is changing the nature of the tasks she has been set for this time. I fear for her safety,' Nangini concluded.

Sam repeated the words to Magdalena but she could not hear her. It was as if there was a barrier of energy in the way.

'It's because she denied me,' said Nangini, 'I am here to teach her about the herbs and trees, to help her remember their properties as once she did. La Stregga may not be long of this world and when Magdalena takes over her role, she will lose the ones that she most cares for. Her life may be in danger from her own naivety, that everyone she tells her secrets to, is trustworthy. Warn her if you can, make her listen or she will warp yet another strand in the Skeins of Tyme.'

With that, Sam felt herself whisked away, falling like a stone to earth, where her body waited to embrace her again.

Chapter 46

In the Dreaming ...Flora

'Earth you are, compassion grown
Fire and Water, becoming known,
Air will sing, when Fire alights
And Water washes all things bright.'

Flora was asleep in a huge old bed, she felt distinctly weak and ill. She knew this was not her, nor an aspect of herself. Somewhere deep within this being was something else, a sleeping secret that would cost her, her life if discovered.

'Why this is the girl I have dreamed of. She is sensitive and wise for her young years and oh Goddess, she's dying. What keeps her here is but a wispy thread; indeed, she should be gone,' Flora spoke aloud causing a woman, sitting unnoticed to stir from her concentration of the girl. She could not see or hear Flora but had felt a strange presence and had seen a small shadow pass across her little Signorina's face.

She tenderly drew the coverlet over her, tucking it in lovingly, but the girl only threw it off in her approaching fever.

A little spirit manifested by the bed, she held an ancient bag of herbs in her arms that Flora recognised immediately, Airmhid's bag. Nina Giraldi rallied yet again as Nangini, the wise Woodwife, wiped a small amount of fragrant salve over her lips. Flora could taste its heady sweetness on her tongue as she too was whirled away, back to her own time continuum.

Chapter 47
Sybille's Book of Shadows
The Three Souls

Dare to wonder dare to dream
...when moonlight pools and things unseen
...move and fly on gossamer wing
...as hidden Fae their anthems sing,
...to Lord and Lady fair and bright
...gathering souls to aid their flight
...to places green where magicks reign
...where all are healed of fear and pain...

The first part of the human soul was what governed the physical manifestation, the body, housing the mental self that humankin call ego. In truth this was a composite in itself of many Littleshape memories, gathered into one coherent moment on the time continuum; tiny fragments of memory written in the cells of a frail, yet resilient human frame. Any memory of where it had been, what it truly was, watered down by the inability to maintain awareness as it descended, deeper and deeper into the earth realm's torpid energy.

In its constant search for truth, it has fallen into the illusion of time as a straight line, past to present and into a perceived future. This stretched the Skeins of Tyme so thinly, just one single thread remains to attach each human life to the web; just one, these are the Onceborn.

The second, Higher or Soul self, as the humankin call it, the Trueshaper, was the one who gathered the threads of life experience needed to weave the relevant memories into a tapestry, for the long journey back to full awareness of Oversoul; Goddess self, which forms the third part of the triad. When one is aware of this aspect, consciousness is heightened; we can then achieve a sense of the concept, 'everything is now.'

A myriad of tiny Makers, our human or non-human spark of consciousness together, make up the entirety of the Trueshaper and they in turn, make up a complete Goddess aspect, that is a spark of the Primordial One …that which was, is and will be, eternally and to which, all must return.

Chapter 48

In the Dreaming ... Morgan

Bright the soul that hidden here
...finds the truth in the turning year
Music sings within his soul
...and through his music makes things whole

Morgan followed the thread to his aspect Bran within the Skeins of Tyme, he was lean, brown and strong, music flowed from him like quicksilver.

'I can learn so much here,' said Morgan to himself, 'I want to remember, I want to know it all again, everything taught here, the music, the Magick and the shapeshifting. It's no wonder that changing comes easier to me than ever before, now that I am in contact with my aspect Bran.

He merged his mind with Bran as he sat under a tree plucking his journey harp, a sweet sounding instrument that was like running water over stones.

Bran's rich baritone echoed out across the grove, drawing children and adults alike to him. Morgan heard the stories of the Duir, Nuin and Huath and remembered the time when he had learned the language of the trees.

He paid rapt attention, saw Maeve, tall and proud leave her chores at the forge and walk across the grove toward the Bard who smiled at her with deep knowing eyes.

'Ah,' thought Morgan, 'so that's how we met.'

'Yes,' said Bran,' in Morgan's head, 'that is the link between time and space. Remember the music Bran-Morgan …my own one-day self.'

Then Morgan, like the others was flying back to his waiting body, shapechanging in and out of the 'Between,' fully conscious of his journey.

Chapter 49

In the Dreaming ...Lily

Song of the bird that's blue as the seas
...smart and sassy, flying with ease
Who would notice a little blue Jay?
...until small precious things are vanished away

Lightest of all, Lily flew in her other shape fully aware of being both Jaylily and Lily. She was free. Her consciousness soared as she sped through the Skeins of Tyme and out the other side in the long ago.

The Yorkshire Wolds opened beneath her wrapped in the mists, etheric layers revealed as silken threads, dripping with fine droplets that settled on her blue and buff feathers causing her to land, shaking the weight from her wings.

It was heavier here she realised, somewhere between the realm of perceived yesterday and today. 'Why am I here?' she thought, as she sat looking down at the wet, spongy ground, from a gnarled dead tree.
From her vantage point, she could see water trickling from out of the root system and across the ground. Small mushrooms, moss and lichen, were fed by the underground spring that would find its way to the Gipsy Race, as the coming moon-tide pulled it up to the surface and then onwards, plunging deep again below

ground, on the ever-moving, rush to the sea; to the Mother.

She could see a small being, the Merrow, she thought alarmed. She was fossicking in the rill of water and communicating with the nymphs, busy on their own journeys.

Ave yer seen'a silvry thingy? An'arm band, all a'twisted metal? It'd 'urt yer it touch yer,' she warned.

'Then why do **you** want it if it burns?' questioned a water sprite.

Dropping all innocent pretence, the Merrow said, ''cos some're in't Skeins I've acquired 'uman blood a'nso dunna feel pain as yer would,' in unusual honesty, so desperate was she to find the treasure to add to her collection.

As Jaylily sat, she heard a great flap of wings and ducked in case it was a larger predator than she was. With a loud 'ruaark,' her friend and brother's mentor, Tara landed on the branch next to her.

'I wondered where you'd disappeared to so suddenly. Have you seen anything?' Tara asked her.

'I've just arrived,' Jaylily, replied, 'I've been observing the busy little Merrow searching the Wolds and the running spring for something. I think she may be looking for the same thing I was,' she finished, ruffling her feathers to spray droplets of water in all directions.

'Thanks,' said Tara, grooming vigorously before making the change as she dropped to the sodden ground.

The nymphs vanished and the Merrow followed, blowing a raspberry at them with a scowl of annoyance.

'Well that got rid of the rabble,' said Tara with a laugh, 'Let's search.'

Jaylily launched herself from her perch, fluttering just above ground level as she searched the area. She could sense there had been something here that had caused the Fae to leave the place untouched for ages. A death, a sorrow for something that could not be at peace, its soul was undying.

Tara noticed her thoughts, returning to Jaylily where she fluttered.

'It's a sad story Jay;' she said, 'one of our kin was injured by an elf bolt and could not make the full change from woman to Corvidae. Cal found the body and I have it well hidden, but the secret key to her identity, hid within her silver bangle, which I lost, holds the text that will free her from where she is bound.'

'Then we must search, we need all our sisters,' said Jaylily, as she continued to search the area, pulling at grass with her beak until in frustration she made the change to her human form. Squelching and slipping through the rill as it ran singing. She had only a moment to change back to her Jay form before she had to return to the circle of friends waiting.

Chapter 50

In the Dreaming ... Max

All that knowledge hidden within
...yet none that will aid if it's hid 'neath the skin
Superstition and fear is not your good kin
...wake up ...turn around ...the veil thins

Max found himself flung unceremoniously from his orbit and into a strange, unknown consciousness. It was sharp and keen, it smelt different to who his own skin and fair bit older.

He felt the need to shake himself and found he was looking down at an Italian tiled floor in an old and beautiful bathroom. His hands were gripping the edge of a porcelain basin and his head was spinning as if he had drunk too much wine.

Eduard and Max merged briefly,

'What the ...' said Eduard Giraldi aloud.

'What the fff...' said Max Fenner.

Raising their eyes, yet sharing a body, they looked into strange depths, Eduard into Max's cool grey gaze and Max into Eduard's dark brown.

Just for a moment, the two were as one and Max received all the information this aspect held close; all the wisdom and ancient knowledge hidden away came streaming from Eduard and into Max. It was kept hidden, partially in fear of discovery, in a world too soon indoctrinated with the laws of a new God, the other part battled for a voice and belonged purely to the Goddess Aradia.

Eduard was such a knowledgeable man and yet his life would be a lie if he loved a Wytch and then denied her heritage… 'So that's why,' said Max before he was thrown unceremoniously back into his body.

Chapter 51

In the Dreaming ... Callum

Cal felt that he was drowning in energy; his very skin was turgid with the squalls that hit him like miniature tidal waves. Buffeted by the elemental winds and burned by the flames of his intent.

I must find the bracelet, his only conscious thought as he flew across a lake and saw the Dark Fae step from the trees. An arrow tipped with Wolf's Bane winged its way to its target. He heard a female voice scream shrilly, 'Flee, FLEE,' before she fell and he heard the thunder of hooves as a man fled, urged on by her screams and by his horse's fear...'MORGAN,' he cried.

Then he was flying over a great ring of standing stones where a young, red haired woman, lay on the ground, her face pressed into the moss and dirt by a half-naked warrior woman. 'MAEVE,' he called but swept on...

...he flew over spires and cupolas of ancient Italy where a young woman lay asleep and he felt the energy of one he loved. FLORA! He yelled her name in his head and she smiled, before focusing again on the young woman sleeping, her secret hidden deep within.

Through the same beautiful house he flew, through a stately bathroom, where a man was hunched as if in pain or fear over a basin ...'MAX,' he yelled in frustration.

On he flew to where a young woman wept as she sat by the bed of her dying mentor, La Stregga. 'What will I do?' she cried, 'How can I become La Stregga and still have Eduard's love?' Once again he felt the energy of a dear friend ...'SAM ...he called out.

Whirled faster yet, he flew over a grove of trees, aged and gnarled, where a young woman stood hesitantly at the gaping, dark mouth of a cave. He heard the hounds' bay and a horn rang out ...'BETHY,' he called, but he knew she was safe when he saw the Horned One step from among the trees; more he was not to see of her journey.

He was dizzy with energy, full of information with no time to collate it, as he flew across the wilds of Yorkshire. A small blue Jay and a larger, glossy black Raven sat in a dead tree. They flew down over the swampy ground in search of the very thing he had come to find ...then ripped away, he hurtled through the Skeins, until looking down he saw a circle of flames, where a group of extraordinary people were spinning energy.

The friends combined intent was causing a maelstrom that filled the sacred space, threatening to blast it open. He spiralled downward to his waiting body and collapsed with all of them. Spent, they lay flat on their faces, arms outstretched, palms on the ground to release the energy coursing through them; third eye pressed to the wet earth in an agony of fragmented images, colour and sound …they fell into silence.

Chapter 52
After the Dreaming

Water drips from ancient trees
...silent the birds ...still the bees
Rivulets of water ...currents run deep
...soon to wake earth from Her long winters sleep
Gone longest night and the shortest of days
...there's cold still to come but spring's on the way.
Not yet visible, not yet seen but below the cold ground
...the trees thoughts are of green.
Slowly roots stirring ...She stretches to wake
...drinking in water Her new buds to make.
Ice and snow form but in darkness below
...new life awakens in beauty and flow.

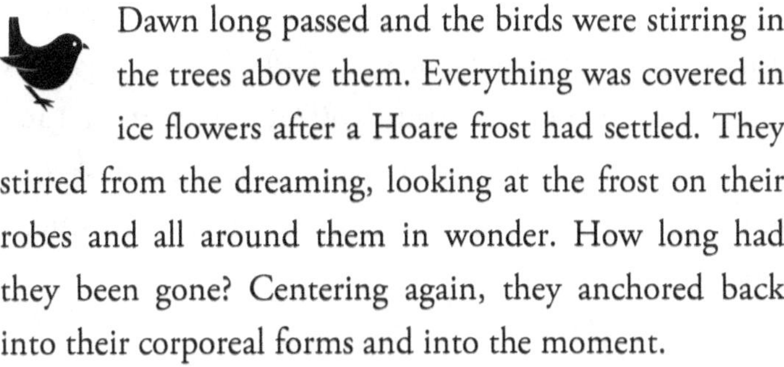 Dawn long passed and the birds were stirring in the trees above them. Everything was covered in ice flowers after a Hoare frost had settled. They stirred from the dreaming, looking at the frost on their robes and all around them in wonder. How long had they been gone? Centering again, they anchored back into their corporeal forms and into the moment.

They didn't ask where Bethan had been. They all shared but not she, not right away. She was changed, this time beyond recognition. She was Arianwen and would never really be Beth again. Her skin had a slight greenish tinge to it and little nubs, where her antlers

grew, were visible just on her hairline. Her hair was almost dreadlocked, small bells, bones and shells interwoven in the silvery mass. She was an amalgam of Green-
woman and Trueshaper, her features constantly
changed, depicting many different creatures that flitted
across her face and in her energy field, at times the constant shifting, disconcerting.

'It's alright,' she said to the group, 'it's a tempo-
rary thing, something I can change much as Sam can
make her tattoos disappear, but I wanted you all to see
what I truly am, of earth and water; Fae and Water-
changer; Shapeshifter and Trueshaper. I am free to be
anything I choose and I choose me. As long as Sybille
and Maeve are gone, I shall remain Bethan but there will
be times when I must go to be in the wildness of myself.'
She smiled her brilliant smile and hugged them all ec-
statically.   'Now,' she said, with a grin as cheeky as
Tara's, *food,*' she exclaimed, *Let the feasting begin!*' A
loud, 'caaaaw,' of agreement signified the return of Tara,
accompanied by Claire and a couple of other bird-tribe
kin; they had been continuing the search for their sister's
bracelet,
'Thought you'd never ask,' Tara giggled.'

Let the wine also be Blessed,' spoke out Morgan,
grinning, as they performed the ancient rite of cakes and
wine.

They decide not to open the circle, but instead
cut a doorway to fetch their feast of food, Wassail, to

ground their energy, blankets and cushions to warm their bodies. For the moment excitement won over approaching exhaustion.

This time they had all collected more data than they could hold thought to. It was important they write it all down so that it didn't slip away again, as can happen after an intense journey. It was Yule and from now on, the light would grow a little each day, as Arianrhod's Silver Wheel spun on. They took time to laugh, celebrate and greet the rising sun …the birth of a new day.
'The Circle is open, yet unbroken …Merry Meet, Merry Part and Merry Meet again.'

Chapter 53
A Little Clarity

Each season round the Silver Wheel
…as humans struggle not to feel
…and yet in feeling all shall heal
…no more their wounded thoughts conceal …as
From earth to sea and sea to sky
…on air's bright wings like gossamer, fly,
…across the realms where none shall die
…to within the web where all truths lie …where
Deep within the fragile strands
…altered by Unsidhe hands
…halflings, mixed-bloods, contrabands
…their blight then spreads across all lands

They left what little remained of the feast for the wee folk, the four-legged and winged ones, adding some honey and nut cakes and bowls of goats milk for them, before wearily trudging down to the house. The adrenaline was leaving them and soon they would feel spent.

In unspoken agreement, with a weary but fond smile to the group, Cal followed Flora to her room, closing the door gently behind them …the others just smiled, especially Claire, happy to see her daughter's quiet happiness.

They decided later would be soon enough for sleep as, in spite of their exhaustion, relief took the upper hand. Later they would look at it all with eyes less tired, head less overawed and try to fit the pieces together like a jigsaw puzzle; or threads of a tapestry, laughed Lily high on energy.

With hugs and tired goodbye's, leaving the car where it was, Max, Lily, Morgan and Bethan walked back through the forest toward the cottage at Wells, their footprints glistening in the frosty rime, their breath puffing little apostrophe's in the air as they spoke or laughed. Relief was palpable.

Tiny creatures followed Bethan now, her every footstep inspected and touched. Faces appeared in the trees and through the undergrowth and Beth became aware of the teeming, burgeoning life that went on around them, no matter the season or time of day or night. Life she thought, how much people miss in their fear of the unknown and of magicks.

She walked with Morgan in companionable quiet, her features slowly returning to their usual quiet beauty, yet there was an, other-worldliness with her now; it would probably never completely disappear. Honey glued herself to Bethan's side, nudging her for a scratch or a rub as they walked, basking in her song.

Time enough later for a complete gathering of all the information they'd gained that night, thought Morgan, sleep and then a fresh start to share. Work waited in only a few hours, the business that now sustained them all needed nurturing too, as they all fell naturally into a role of some sort, there as much as on the journey of discovery they had undertaken together. There was no time or space to waver; they were all committed for the duration whether they resisted or not.

He was personally happy to have received a few music gigs around town that he found balanced his energy and now Lily could be a part of that when she was around; he just had to persuade Bethan to find the confidence to come on the journey too. Her gifts were something else that developed daily, her talents for music matching her skills at spindle and loom. Later he thought to himself, just something else for later.

A truce, silently called between Lily and Max left them feeling a little less restrained, bantering together as they walked through the cold dawn. Max felt more at peace with himself again and the experience of the night had shown him the reasons for his reticence, now he had the opportunity to learn and grow from it and hopefully, make good with Sam and heal the breach with Lily.

On reaching the cottage Bethan kissed them all goodnight before disappearing into the forest to the waiting Fae. Morgan just had time to see her embraced by her father and a stately female figure, before Lily pulled him away.

'Not out business brother mine,' she grinned at him. Calling goodnight to Max they stumbled in and up the stairs to their waiting beds.

Sleep no longer seemed to be something Bethan needed much now. Well, perhaps Bethan did the remaining human aspect, Arianwen however, was a far more natural creature, not bound by the sun's rise and set but more by Lady Moon's tugs and pulls on her senses and psyche. She was a composite creature of many aspects, all her complex selves merging as one; the major difference being that she appeared to have more choices even than most Trueshapers had. She didn't quite have an understanding about that yet but, soon enough she thought, soon enough and all the answers will unfold. Then I can help the team in a different way perhaps establish a new way of discovering the missing or tangled threads.

After walking with her friends through the forest to home she felt rather than heard a calling, irresistible and warming; her family, her tribe called her to celebrate, to claim her home. Bethan however had other things she needed to do first, to help her humankin with the search for Sybille.

Walking to the forest edge, after saying goodnight to her brother and friends, she said as much to her father and grandmother who waited.

'Time enough for celebration when the work is done,' she said to them emphatically and with a brief hug she turned and ran back to the cottage and to her loom, perhaps even some sleep, she smiled to herself.

Aithlin and Circaea smiled too, at her strength and purpose and at her emergence from the human cocoon of entrapment.

Chapter 54
'Earthly Rites'

Lady moon shines ...feel Her light on your skin
Bow to Her beauty ...be at one with your kin
Her light in the darkness dispels all the gloom
...open your windows ...let Her into your room

The halls of the building creaked and groaned as Beth entered later that day, as if even the timbers had memory of life and thus through her were awakening from stasis.

Unable to sleep, she had finished several pieces of weaving for customer orders much quicker than usual. Somehow, even her weaving had picked up a speed and elegance that out shone her earlier work. The difference of before and after was manifest in that elegance.
Stretching luxuriously it felt as if she'd slept for hours instead of steadily working her way through the outstanding orders. Now she was ready to face a working day and to reorganise her thoughts about the search for Sybille. Perhaps she would be able to slip away more often to seek her out from wherever she hid to bring her home.

At that moment, the main doors rattled as someone inserted a key in the lock, with apparent difficulty. She ran to open the door, thinking it was Flora or Sam, to find Annie making a frustrated attempt to extract her key from the lock where it had obviously jammed. She almost fell in the door as Beth opened it.

'Have you changed the locks Bethan?' asked Annie in a brook no argument tone.

'No, of course not, why would I do that and not give you a new key …and good morning to you too,' said Beth quietly, with a pointed stare at Annie, as she threw her keys in her bag and with a 'tut,' flounces in, pushing past Beth rudely.

'Annie,' Beth repeated, 'I don't know what's got up your nose this morning but I simply said good morning and I actually happen to be one of the people who pays your wages.'

'What?' Oh sorry Beth,' said Annie grudgingly, 'I'm not sleeping well and the bloody Ravens won't leave me alone. I swear they're throwing chestnuts on my roof. You should hear the clatter and the l…,' she halted frowning, she was about to say laughter but thought better of it, fearing Beth would think her completely loony tunes.

Beth smothered a giggle at the image but said, 'Were you going to say laughter Annie? They do that you know Raven,' unable to stop smirking.

'Yes, well I'd better get on with it then,' said Annie at Beth's obvious change in attitude. She had always been the quiet polite one, she thought to herself. How people can change, she scoffed.

As if she had heard her thoughts, Beth simply burst out laughing. Annie turned to see Tara and Claire arrive together and what she saw caused her to blanch as Tara deliberately walked in past her with an obvious bird like face.

It was too much for Annie and she simply slumped to the hall floor. Between them, still unable to still their muffled laughter Tara and Beth half dragged, half carried her to the kitchen and sat her in a chair; Tara roughly pushed Annie's head down between her knees. Beth brought her a glass of water.

'Wwhat are you?' stammered Annie still reeling with shock from what she thought she'd seen.

'Why, what can you mean Annie?' giggled Tara unable to contain herself, 'You know me I'm Tara,' she gurgled and with a friendly pat of Annie's head went to check her roster for the day.

Claire had long fled the scene in stitches. She couldn't manage to stay in a room comfortably with Annie for long, but this had totally changed the dynamics of it all and she could only see the funny side. Tara had the ability to make people laugh at themselves and not care, what others thought either.

She was remembering the days when she had been as light and easy about life, remembering the freedom of her kind and revelled in the thought that it really didn't matter what someone like Annie Savage thought, she was just who she was and glad of it. In fact, Annie was welcome to Harry and all his hang-ups but she did feel sad for Vanessa. If she didn't already know about her parentage, she would soon undoubtedly; Claire wondered what she had been told on that score.

Sam had stayed at Flora's the night before, arriving together in obvious good spirits, Cal trailing behind with what could only be described as a silly grin on his face. Glances were exchanged but they didn't have the heart to tease him. He was such a lovely and caring man and they were all happy that he and Flora had found each other.

Morgan, Max and Lily weren't far behind and soon the team set about their day with an underlying air of excitement. They couldn't wait for the opportunity to go over everything, piecing all the bits together to find at least a small picture in the tapestry.

Flora had clients that day, Morgan, Lily and Bethan were going to practise for a gig the next night at The Harvest, Bethan having surprised everyone by spontaneously saying yes, to her joining them, the boost in her confidence evident as she smiled happily at their stunned faces. Even Sam had agreed to practice a couple of flute pieces and Tara had also offered to join in, her husky rich voice an amazing contrast, complimentary to Bethan's high sweet sound and Lily's warm tones. They had decided to call themselves, 'unearthly tones,' in honour of 'earthly rites' and the origins of some of their music that came to them in dreams or on the wind as it sighed through the now bare branches of the winter trees or beat a tattoo on the iron rooves.

They all missed Maeve; in that moment thinking fondly how she had not possessed an ounce of musical skill. Totally, tone deaf herself, she enjoyed listening but even Honey would moan when she attempted to sing. They realised that they were actually speaking of her in past tense and fell silent, Tara immediately coming to the rescue with, 'She's fine everyone, just fine. She's where she needs to be and is, I'm sure, thinking of you guys too. If Mor can get his head around a conscious shift to his Bran aspect, he'll soon be able to pass messages between you all anyway.'

They all looked at her in wonder.

'I can't quite get my head around that yet,' said Morgan with a wry grin, 'but I'm willing to give it a go, with your help Tara.'

'I don't think, after last night, that you're going to need much help at all Mor,' said Cal, 'From what I witnessed with all of you the momentum is really picking up now.'

'Okay,' said Sam, 'let's get to it and then the day will fly and we can sit and work out what we're going to do next.

On that note, they scattered to their various tasks for the day. They didn't notice the small being that stood in the shadow of the stairwell listening, a tarnished silver bangle in her hands and a look of absolute glee on her face.

'S'mine,' she grinned, 'Letum go a seek'n now. S'empty seek'n 'tis.'

It was here that Annie Savage found her and without thinking grabbed the strange child by her collar, believing it was a child from the village who had snuck in, as they did when opportunity allowed.

'Oi,' said the Merrow baring her sharp teeth at Annie, 'Oo d'ya fink y'are,' as with a wrench she pulled herself, with untoward strength for such a small creature, from Annie's grasp. About to vanish she halted however, taking a deep, soul piercing look at Annie.

'Ah,' she said, 'ya bin touch'd by t'Lady init!'

'Whaa …what, who are you,' Annie stammered realising the being was not of this earth.

'I'm of t'Lady,' she grinned and vanished, taking the opportunity as Annie stood, stunned by her second encounter of the day with The Lady's little magicks.

'I have to find Lady Aelish,' yelped Annie in panic.

'I'll take 'ya t'er then come Imbolc,' came a giggled reply before the door to Maeve's studio slammed and the resounding rumble of the water tank could be heard through the stair well.

Chapter 55
The Road to Imbolc

...and so the days passed on silvered wings, slowly once more the wheel turned on, ever on.

The days lengthened and the group of friends felt the energy begin to rise through their feet, up through the base of their spines, to match the slow rising sap in the trees, as life stirred from apparent dormancy.

Six weeks or more, they spent fruitfully, pulling threads together by sheer will and intent and with calm, knowledgeable help from Alex, Cal and a very changed and steady Max.

Morgan and Lily took trips through the 'Between,' readying everyone for the journeys they would have to make to follow the threads revealed to them at Yule. Their discoveries would lead them to the wilds of the Yorkshire Wolds, to Glastonbury and to the border countries of Wales and Cornwall, eventually to Italy in another space and time. Their journeys would be real and in part metaphorical. Not all of them could shapechange and so needed help to pass through the webs of Ungwe in their etheric form as they had at Solstice or they would have to take the lengthier route by plane.

The former was daunting enough, but when Tara announced they would have to make the journey in their physical skins, it was almost more than Flora could imagine,

'I'll help you love,' said Claire, 'do it just once and you won't know yourself I promise,'

 'That's what worries me Mum,' said Flora, tongue in cheek, but now they were all preparing themselves for the strange and disconcerting feelings this form of travel created. They had all made short forays, Tara helping too and she had instructed Sam further to find her way with the help of her little leaf sprites, Sam had christened 'leaf hoppers,' to their delight.

With the Imbolc Rite set in their minds already, it would be the pivotal moment of travelling again, as

they had at Yule, this time in the more literal sense, however.

Sam and Flora fluctuated between sheer excitement and raw fear, Cal was his usual calm stoic self and Alex and Susan would be back up if needs be but both of them were nervous at the thought of travelling in this manner. Tara reminded Susan of her journeys through the gateways she painted and said simply,

'You can do it Suzie, hop to it! We just have to make sure you don't get lost in your former landscapes, so keep it simple; chances are we won't need you but you still need to be prepared, just in case anything untoward were to happen.

They used a vision board to chart where some of the threads interchanged and why.

Sam as Magdalena had had an amazing opportunity for growth with La Stregga and Nangini but somehow things had gone awry. She had tended Nina, whom Flora had gained an insight into but they were not sure what that link was, only that a secret lay hidden, deep within Nina's sweet innocence.

Max in his aspect Eduard Giraldi, obviously had issue with something about Magdalena's Wytchway and had a secret too, yet to reveal itself. Max had felt it as a resistance to something, fear perhaps. He seemed to be battling the new ways of the time, when magick became science, when belief in the Goddess became a heresy, punishable by death and Eduard Giraldi loved a Wytch.

Morgan in his quite conscious, Bran aspect knew his journey to the Goddess was clear and strong, but he was yet to know the relationship with Maeve and the child that he had seen twice, once when he met the Priestess Leah and again at the Battle camp of Scathach. He knew that his skills with the harp came from that time but the mandolin; he had yet to discover where they came from. Tara said it might just be an instrument that triggered musical memory for him and that if they were to look at every aspect of their existence within the Skeins they'd go mad trying to find all the 'why's.'

Cal had a brief synopsis of each of the other's aspects as he had hurtled through all of them individually and briefly. He shared again each experience and remembered that he had seen Sam as a dark haired young woman, weeping over a dying friend and mentor and had drawn a possible conclusion that Sybille may have been that teacher, although he hadn't felt Sybille's energy there but rather, briefly, a familiar but as yet unidentifiable one. Sam had no memory of her teacher-friend, La Stregga, having a direct link with Sybille and that was the odd thing; she wondered if she was off track with this.

Flora thought no she wasn't because it linked her to Nangini, to the bag of herbs and for some reason, this young unidentified woman Nina. She also wondered why her dream link had been with someone not an aspect of herself.

Therefore, the days passed and they blossomed and grew in awareness. Each and every one of them watching Beth in awe as her changes manifested to such a degree, she was embarrassed at the number of men who almost fell at her feet as she passed in the street, such was her growing beauty and other-worldliness, that shone through her skin. If anyone looked too deeply into her eyes, they could be lost, drowning in their misty depths.

Finally, Beth was ready to share with the group the occurrences at the Winter Solstice Rite and how, as a result, she had come to understand her differentness. Her not being human was something she had thought long and hard about, wondering how many others like her there may be who did not know their ancestry.

Without a doubt she was unique, her modesty a rare and precious characteristic, her gentleness, tempered now in a very direct and forceful way, had led to her new confidence, she no longer tolerated fools lightly.

Everyone who knew Beth had always loved and respected her, now that respect had become almost a reverence at her skills and for her absolute fairness and understanding, indeed she had become the one all looked to.

Her keys to finding Sybille were of the other-world and ancient aspects, which linked her through Leah. More recently, she must trace the link through her birth mother Sarah, or Minhiriath, she reminded herself.

The facts of Minhiriath's death alone must now be her focus, as she acknowledged only having a little human blood.

Would she find these links through her rite of passage with Hercurin in the aspect of Leah, or Bethan? Where had Leah come from, what was her role? She hated to think of it only being Leah's body needed for the rite, when the consciousness of Arianwen had still been separate. Now she and Leah were one and her Trueshape was becoming apparent; it had few earthly links, except through Leah herself. The Cybil would know her origins, of that Bethan was sure. It gave her pause to think that Sybille too may well have known all of this already.

In the human sense, it did her head in as much as it did everyone else's. It was important that she didn't separate herself from her friends and that she share, when she found the words, all that was happening in her dream walking.

They sat one cold evening, it was snowing and the light from outside was eerily bright. The lamp light reflected on to the snow in glistening bands of white. The windows were faceted starbursts of snowflakes, caught in a moment as they froze to the glass. The wind howled and they were huddled around the fire in Sybille's favourite sitting room, the cats on the back of the sofas, Honey sprawled across several pairs of feet on the hearth. Ruark dozed, head under her wing, she refused to remain anywhere and had become attached to

Beth, Cal and Lily in particular. She would often disappear with Tara and Claire, Lily occasionally too, when
they shapechanged and flew the 'Between,' searching for
the bangle lost somewhere in the web, on the Wolds,
who knew?

They settled quietly, expectantly like children
waiting for a favourite tale, Beth began to
share her journey. As she started speaking, her
shadow, thrown across the floor, shapechanged, antlers
grew, hair lifting from her head in silver tendrils…

Chapter 56
In the Dreaming ... Bethan
Initiation ... long ago

The wild folk ride through forests green
...twice a year they're easily seen;
...they come from beyond the in-between
...breaking through the veil
Their horns sound bright; voices light;
...riding through the dark of night,
...with faces oh so pale
The Wild Hunt rides
...hounds at their sides, to chase the dark away,
...as the Green Lord comes a-gathering in
...those who were led astray
She waits for them in a lightened glen
...where the Fae folk play
He leads them through the forests fair
...to the Summerlands faraway.

As Bethan's friends had spun out into the cosmos on Winter Solstice, to find the threads of Silver and Sybille, Bethan went through the changing, within the dreaming she followed her song and was running. It felt as if it were through dark sticky treacle that impeded her progress forward. She struggled but a voice within said, 'don't fight it,' and the moment she relaxed, she found herself outside the cave of initiation once more but now it was Beltane in the Between.

Inside the cave was strangely warm after the chill of the day; it smelt of water and earth and of the sacred herbs prepared in readiness. A small fire in the centre produced a little light to the smooth rock walls but otherwise the perimeter was in total darkness. A sound from the cave opening caused her to start like a hunted doe and she realised that the priestesses had sealed the cave entrance for her rite of passage. In spite of being prepared for this, it still brought a chill to her soul at the thought she may not see the light of day again, for as her first initiation had been to part the mists, so must she now be able to open the cave entrance herself.

Schooling herself to be calm, she walked to the small fire, warming her hands and once more embraced being Leah and Bethan consciously, in one physical body; two aspects as one.

Next to the fire, were a thick mat of herbs and a small bowl of pungent smelling, amber liquid. Slipping out of her robe, she sat to sip from the bowl, screwing up her face at its acrid taste and odour. She could smell mugwort, aconite and something else that made her almost spit the liquid out …Mistletoe she thought, praying that the dose be right for her diminutive size as the brew rapidly took hold of her senses. She lay down stilling her mind and allowing the potent herbs to take

over, forcing herself to remain aware, the onslaught began on her consciousness.

She sat up in her etheric form, her physical body
laid eyes open and staring; she knew she could see herself.

Stepping completely from her physical form, she
saw the wee folk come out of hiding, watching as they
inspected her naked form, rubbing it with sacred oils
that smelt of honey and sweet cicely. Others ran a comb,
made from the fine ribs of an unknown creature,
through her long tangled hair, gently working through
the snarls and knots until it lay spread around her like a
silver cloak. She watched as a tall slender woman,
cloaked in midnight blue appeared, leaning over her and
whispering words she couldn't hear into her ear, kissing
her forehead before anointing it with oils.

Bethan felt herself sucked back into the physical
body as the beautiful Lady gently covered her breasts
and pubis with a cloud of white moonflowers and hawthorn, fragrant and heady; the Leah aspect cried, 'but
this isn't part of the rite, what's happening?' the wee folk
soothed her gently.

Bethan couldn't move and battled to remain
conscious as the other aspect fought for control. She
stilled herself again, willing Leah to be calm as she heard
the Bodhran start to drum and subtle sweet music filled
the darkened cave.

An Eldrytch Wytchlight, swelled as the music soared to tones almost beyond human ears and the Lady lay down in Leah's body as if donning a sacred robe, her essence merging with Bethan and Leah's both …Bethan heard…

'…*three in one and one in three …leaf, flower and berry of the sacred tree …the gift of all life is given thee …as we do will, so mote it be.*'

 …antlers reared from her brow, her skin became a smooth green, reflecting blossom, leaf and tiny pearlescent berry etchings, rising on the surface then burrowing deep tendrils, under and within every pore, deep into every organ, bone and cell. She was infused with the forest; one with the oceans as the Lady's essence mixed with her lymph and blood.

She was filled with the fire of the cool immortal blue-silver flame, caressed by subtle breezes that kissed her skin …as the Greenlord stepped from the shadows, matching antlers jutting from oak-brown forehead, limbs like smooth ash wood, phallus, erect and proud; she smiled and lifted graceful arms to call him into her…

… and the Makers sang the song of Arianwen… *'Spirit sings within your frame, on your loom and through your pain, Water washes all things clean Air brings truth to you again.* **Fire is needed, Earth to ground***, when the web you weave, all things abound.'*

'Am I dreaming?' thought Arianwen…

'We're dreaming,' said Bethan and Leah together...

'...but this means you're renewed in the Lady herself,' whispered The Cybil in their ear, 'Nobody else could make that connection with the Greenlord but Her and tonight is Beltane.'

'...agh, then Bethan is not one of my Little-shapes,' dreamed Silver as she felt Sybille's essence shrink away...she is her own Trueshape...one with the Lady ...I am too late.

Epilogue

Rowan

Danced at dawn as the earth was waking
...danced as the sun rose; a fiery ball
Danced as the earth slept ...danced as the winds rose
...danced until I found home ...in Oneness with All

As the arrow pierced her to the bone, Rowan knew she needed to warn the one named Brandubh and keep him safe ...he was crucial to the survival of many lives, including one day her own.

She screamed at him to, 'Flee, FLEE!' His horse took up the warning, bolting for home.

In her pain she changed, feeling the Wolf's Bane taking hold of her senses, eating into her skin, ...she flew through the 'Between,' then fell, plummeting through the veil and down toward misty wet moorlands that seemed to be coming up to meet her at an alarming rate.

Rowan tried to bank, but felt herself changing to her human form again. Unable to take control as her injured wing would not make the complete shift; instead, her human arm became a full size wing, the flight feathers remained imbedded to the bone. The Ashwood shaft broke off as she fell, pushing the arrow head deeper into her flesh for the Bane to do it's task, seeping into her blood, freezing the nerve channels to her brain.

Dropping …faster now, her Bangle of Naming fell from her wrist and rolled across the boggy earth, on an icy cold winter's day just past Solstice.

Her shapechange came too late, as the bangle fell; her familiar Raven-spirit tore free, alive but sorely damaged. In the final crashing dive, awareness fled. Rowan's blue gaze misted over, her sight gone. She tried to call her familiar back to her but 'Ruuuark…' was the last sound her Ravenkin heard as it echoed through the veil, vibrating the Skeins as she flew '…Ruuuark,' she replied mournfully, '…Ruuuark', hurtling blindly into the 'Between.'

…continued in Silver's Threads, Book 3
… Warp and Weft

Follow the road to the ends of Tyme
…seeking the paths that make sense of the rhyme
In dark and in light let your footsteps stray
…let the Crooked Path lead you to the Goddess' Way

Follow the road into the Green
…look to the Lord and the Faefolk unseen
…to guide you home, never more to stray
…as the Crooked Paths leads you to the …Goddess' Way

Bibliography

A book of this nature requires research, even when aware of the ins and outs of the Wytchways and so my thanks go to the following Authors of these amazing, 'must read' books, for their insights.

Illes, Judika, Encyclopaedia of Spirit,
Harper One

McCoy, Edain, Celtic Women's Spirituality,
Llewellyn Publications

Sheard, K.M., Llewellyn Complete Book of Names,
Llewellyn Publications
Evert-Hopman, Ellen, Scottish Herbs & Fairy Lore,
Pendraig Publications

Mueller, Michelle, Voice of the Trees,
Llewellyn Publications

Nazdar, Adele, Element Encyclopaedia of Signs & Symbols,
Harper Element

About the Author

Penny Reilly Author 2014

Renowned as a clairvoyant and a teacher of the Western Mysteries at Daylesford School of Arcane Knowledge, Penny Reilly is an initiated Bard in the Tradition of the Druid. Moving on this year to the Order of Ovate, Penny has a passion for the Old Ways of the British Isles; she will be returning there this year to carry out research for her nonfiction books and her second 'Cloak of Magick' series to come. She feels that the gentle path of the Druid, Pagan-Wytchway is the path to take for a sustainable future, connecting us to the land, no matter where we live on the planet. She describes herself as a 'nature writer'.

Her own visionary experiences are very much a part of her storyline, poetry and lyrics …this is her fourth published book. She has previously written articles for alternative magazines, blogs regularly about her ideas and way of life, writes for 'starts at sixty' lifestyle blog and has over 6,000 followers on her poetry page 'earthly rites', her school and her author pages on Facebook.

Penny moved to Sydney, Australia in 1980 and to the central highlands of Victoria with her husband David, 18 years ago. They share space with an 'all sorts' terrier, an old tabby cat, a small flock of hens and a fat wombat fondly known as 'Chocolat', who has adopted them. Keen gardeners, they are becoming self-sufficient on their beautiful rolling acres on the Great Divide; their blended mob of children are long 'grown and flown' the coop.

You can find out more about the author, her books, poetry, tours and workshops, through her website, amazon.com and social media pages

http://www.silversthreads.wordpress.com/
http://amazon.com/pennyreilly
http://facebook.com/pennyreillyauthorpage
http://facebook.com/earthlyrites
http://facebook.com/daylesfordschoolofarcaneknowledge
http://www.goodreads.com/pennyreilly
@PennyReilly.twitter